Just Out of Reach

Barbara Jeanne Fisher

Llumina Pres

Requests for permission to make copies of any part of this work should be
mailed to Permissions Department, Llumina Press, PO Box 772246, Coral
Springs, FL 33077-2246

ISBN: 978-1-59526-938-6 (PB)
         978-1-59526-939-3 (HC)
         978-1-59526-940-9 (Ebook)

Printed in the United States of America by Llumina Press

Library of Congress Control Number: 2007909245

Dedication

As with all my writing I would be amiss if I didn't thank all the people who have supported and encouraged my love for writing. A special thanks to the people who have *inspired* me to write *with my heart*. It is my goal in writing to always use the feelings in my heart to touch the hearts and lives of others in a positive way.

To the hundreds who asked me for a sequel to *Stolen Moments*, well finally, here it is! A special thanks to Sandy for always coming into my store and asking me when this book was going to be done! Your anticipation was always a reminder to me that this story had to be written.

Last and not least to my precious family and friends who have always been here for me, and understood me even when I didn't understand myself. To Jennifer who read and re-read the manuscript helping me to find little mistakes I overlooked. To Suzanne Lewis and Father Mark who in their own unique way have shown how important it was to finish this book.

Thanks everyone for always staying close to my heart and never being *Just Out of Reach*.

Chapter One

The air seemed to grow lighter as Dr. Don Lipton entered his cluttered office from the vacant hallway. Inwardly, he smiled, remembering that he had forgotten to close the small window that opened to the lushly green and well-manicured courtyard outside. The air in his office was as fresh and dewy as the moonlit sky.

He sighed deeply as he flicked the light switch, and was surprised at how relieving the sigh proved to be. A tangible weight rushed out from within him.

It had been a long time since he had last felt pleasure in retreating to his office. In truth, whatever joy he had known in this place had expired long before. Back at Whinburg Community College, he used to relish the opportunity to retreat to his stuffy collegiate haunts to grade a stack of student essays – a stack similar to the one he now clutched beneath his heavy right arm. But now, he dreaded the chore. Not even his move to a new state and university, not even his promotion to the head of the English department had brought him any reprieve.

He no longer welcomed the rich smell of his mahogany desk or the warm, inviting comforts of his brown, leather-backed armchair. He no longer thirsted for the familiar taste of stale coffee from the grimy thermos he would place on the corner of his desk each morning.

All he wanted was a good long walk under the stars, a good long walk with a dear friend.

Settling behind his desk, Don dropped the stack of essays onto the blotter. Oh, how tedious it had become, grading uninspired stories from his creative writing students. This being the summer semester, few of his students even demonstrated the desire to be in his classroom, let alone pour themselves into their work. Not one of them showed the passion and flare that he longed to read.

Regardless of his newfound mercy toward such tired efforts, he occasionally found himself wanting to tear the entire stack of essays into confetti and toss it all up over his head.

Despite the refreshing air in his office, the professor quickly returned to his glum mood. He grumbled, clearing his throat. Then, he slipped the top paper off the stack, slowly leaned back in his armchair, and began to read. Immediately, he found error in the piece, which of course caused him to ponder the usual urge: *go home, watch the news, and go to sleep. Get up and grade the papers in the morning.*

He immediately deferred to his better judgment and decided to stay and finish grading. After all, the usual distractions he would find at home would not bother him here. The smallish television and barren refrigerator would not beckon. The ever-quiet phone would not remind him of how much he yearned to hear it ring. If he stayed to finish these papers, well, that was just one less thing to worry about the next day.

He reached forward to the center drawer of his desk and rifled through it for a red pen. For a moment, he felt a bit of the old Don Lipton surge anew. He would be merciless on this day. No errant punctuation or common misspelling would go unpunished. No limp plot device or two-dimensional character would stand uncounted.

Just as he found the pen and readied himself to dissect the essay he held in his quivering left hand, he heard a low and quiet knock upon his door. Funny, he hadn't remembered closing it. He rarely closed his door these days, especially on such late nights as these. Closed doors had once meant security and comfort. But ever since he had met *her*, they seemed little more than barriers to a much more inviting outside world.

"Yes?" Don said. He absentmindedly placed the unmarked essay down on the desk, bumping and jostling the stack out of order with the meat of his hand. He darted his eyes down just as the stack toppled into a messy pile at the center of the desk. He grumbled at the sight.

"Hello," sounded a quiet soothing voice. "Excuse me."

Don turned his gaze to the doorway just as the comely outline of a strangely familiar young woman gently pushed open the door. Her slender, delicate forearm leaned against the harsh old pine of the doorframe. His eyes were drawn to the expressive freckles that flecked her cheeks and the bridge of her narrow nose. And those eyes! Those brown, doe-like eyes . . . *It* couldn't *be her!*

"Can I come in for a minute?" the woman asked softly.

Don was taken aback. He felt almost as though he had forgotten how to breathe. "Who the hell are you?" he finally barked. His heart raced in his chest. Hope- but a strangely empty kind of hope-flared within him.

The woman in the doorway laughed uncomfortably. He had heard this laugh so many times before. But something was different, maybe it was her voice.

"Well, that's certainly not the greeting I expected," the woman said.

Don said nothing. He simply gawked, unable to speak.

"Look, if this is a bad time . . ."

"No, no!" Don said, all too loudly. All at once, he had returned to reality and remembered his niceties. Nervously, he began to shuffle the essays on his desk back into a haphazard pile. His cheeks flushed red. "No, this is fine. I just . . . I just wasn't expecting anyone. And it's just that . . ."

The air in the office seemed to deaden as a long, pregnant pause followed Don's flailing words. The man who made his living talking could think of absolutely nothing to say.

As the young woman's awkward smile faded into an equally awkward frown, the professor noticed little differences in her. Her lips were not as wide or full. The color and texture of her hair were still that same wispy-brown and curly. But it was her eyes that finally tipped the scales. They were definitely different. There was less sparkle. No hopeful and playful light.

No, this was no ghost from Don Lipton's past. This was no apparition of the one person who had come to touch the center of his heart and soul. But she looked so much like her . . .

3

"Listen," she said, turning to go, "I'm sorry to bother you."

"No, no," Don repeated, in a much more reassuring tone this time. "I'm sorry for my outburst just now. It's, well . . . It's just that you remind me so much of a friend I once knew. I thought for a moment that I was seeing things."

The woman in the doorway smiled warmly. "Well, I hope that's a good thing, my looking like her." She laughed nervously. "You're Dr. Lipton?"

Don nodded and pressed his palms together around the uneven pile of papers on his desk, arranging them into a neat stack. He didn't know why he cared so much to hold the appearance of neatness in front of this woman – he only knew that the desire to save face was overwhelming.

"Oh, good," the woman said. "My name is Jill." She made an odd little wave with her clearly delicate hand. "Jilly Larkins."

Don suddenly stood, the pressure of his shuffling legs causing his armchair to slide loudly away from his desk. The noise startled him, and he looked back at his chair as he reached out to offer his hand to Jill. He felt ridiculous, and probably looked ridiculous, but what could he do?

Jill walked to the near side of Don's desk and meekly shook his hand.

"Ah, well, right, Ms. Larkins," Don said. "I'm Professor Lipton. But I guess you already knew that." The professor smiled warmly, finally feeling as though he was getting his bearings back. He ran his thick hand through his salt-and-pepper hair. "You can call me Don."

No, up close, in a better light, this Ms. Larkins definitely wasn't the mirror image he had originally thought. He motioned for her to sit down in one of the two wooden guest chairs in front of his desk before taking his own seat. He knew the chairs to be uncomfortable, and he felt somewhat angry with himself at that moment for not having something better to offer this unexpected guest. "So what brings you to my office this evening, Ms. Larkins?"

4

Jill folded both hands over one arm of the chair in which she now sat. As she did so, everything about her looked dainty and entirely endearing. Don found himself utterly captivated by the familiarity of it all.

"Well," Jill huffed with a proud smile, "I'm the new owner of a bookstore very near campus."

"Ah, are you talking about the Open Book?" Don asked. "I believe I passed by there just yesterday."

"That's the one!" Jill said excitedly.

Don began to fidget with the stack of essays once again. Catching himself, he quickly slid the stack to the side of the desk, where it wouldn't distract him further. At that moment, he encountered the unmistakable scent of Darjeeling tea. It had been a favorite of his in his youth, before he took to college and switched to bland, black coffee. "Do you have a teashop in your bookstore?"

"That's right!" Jill said, practically bouncing. "How did you know?"

"I believe the Darjeeling has left its mark on your clothes," Don said with a smile.

Jill clutched at her light woolen sweater. "Oh, I hope it's not too overpowering."

Don laughed. "Oh, no," he said. "I rather enjoy it. Darjeeling is my favorite."

"Mine, too!"

She's not the same, Don thought. *My love preferred rosehip.* A long, grinning silence followed as they both waited for the other to get to the point.

"So, anyway," Jill said finally. "Last week, the president of the university stopped in to the store. She just dropped in to get some tea. While we were talking, she suggested that I contact the head of each department to see what I can do for them."

Don leaned back in his chair and began to roll up the sleeves of his plaid shirt. He couldn't understand why he felt so warm, but he knew he had to do something about it. Otherwise, he would begin to sweat – and that was never a sight to behold. When he finished, he crossed his hairy forearms in front of his chest, feeling the coarse fabric of his shirt brush against his bare skin. To his credit, distracted though he was, the welcoming smile never faded from his bearded, ruggedly handsome face.

"So what *can* you do for the English department, Ms. Larkins?" The professor detected a slight and remarkably brief blush from his lovely guest.

Jill giggled. Then she began to ramble in a way the professor found charming: "Well, to begin with, I'm willing to give every professor a discount on books they'll need for their classes. So I was hoping to gather a list of titles that you and the other professors in your department might like me to carry, maybe a suggested reading list for the students taking English and literary courses. Earlier today, when I stopped in, your secretary downstairs told me you might be staying late, and here you are, so here I am." She blushed much more noticeably when she finally ran out of breath and stopped speaking.

Don Lipton laughed heartily. "That's quite a sales pitch, Ms. Larkins."

"You can call me Jill."

Don smiled and nodded. "Jill," he said softly.

The young woman stood and brushed her hands against the front of her thighs as though smoothing down a skirt. As she was wearing jeans, the action made Jill blanch and Don chuckle again.

"Right, well," she said. "I shouldn't take up any more of your time. Is there a cafeteria or canteen around here? I'm famished."

The professor, so taken with his guest's sudden befuddlement, simply stared dreamily at Jill.

"Okay, then," Jill said quickly. "I guess I'll find it on my own. Thanks for your time." She turned and walked straight for the door, her arms practically pinioned to her sides.

"Jill, wait," Don called, standing so quickly that he bumped his knee against one of the legs of his desk. He briefly reached down to rub his knee, then stood and frantically began gathering

up his papers and stuffing them into a tattered leather satchel he
kept next to his chair. He stopped momentarily and sighed, shining an exasperated grin at Jill.

Jill had stopped in the doorway at the professor's call. A
mildly coy expression alighted on her face as she looked back at
him now.

"I'm tired of working on these papers," Don said, still stuffing
the stack into his satchel. "And besides . . . it's too nice outside
for me to stay in here. Give me just a minute and I'll walk you to
the cafeteria."

"You really don't have to do that," Jill said, smiling and looking down at her feet. "If you just point the way, I can find it
myself."

"Not at all," Don said, finishing with his packing and slinging
the long strap of his satchel over his broad shoulder. "I'm headed
that way, anyway. The staff mailboxes are in the same building."

Don found himself reasoning about a change of scenery. Maybe
if he got out of the office, things about this Jill would make more
sense. She had just swooped in as though on the back of a dream.
How she reminded him of Julie. How he missed her . . .

The professor got up alongside the doorway in which Jill
stood. He paused as he reached up to turn off the light, smiling at
a pleasant memory. This light was never darkened until he and
Julie were ready to leave . . . and, well, they were never ready.

"Dr. Lipton," Jill said, "are you okay? I mean, you look like
you're on another planet."

When Don turned his attention to his companion, his eyes
warmed in a kindly way. "I'm afraid I *was* on another planet," he
said. "But not to worry. I'm back now." He flicked the light
switch and followed Jill out the door.

"To the left," Don added. "We can take the elevator down."

"I didn't know there *was* an elevator," Jill said with mock
frustration. "I had to take the stairs up."

"Yes, those stairs seem steeper all the time. Or maybe I'm just
getting older." Don found himself lost in memory once more as

he and Jill reached the end of the hall and stood staring at the elevator buttons. As he pushed the down button, his love's beautiful face came to light in his mind. All the times they had shared in this elevator, all those stolen moments.

"Dr. Lipton?" Jill said, waving her hand in front of the professor's eyes.

"Don."

"Don. You're doing it again."

Don shook his head playfully. "Oh, I'm sorry, Jill. I guess I'm a little preoccupied today."

A long silence followed. The elevator seemed to be taking its time this evening.

"I have to ask, Jill," the professor said suddenly, and a little conspiratorially. "Do you have any relatives living around here? Do you have a cousin or a sister about your age?"

Jill shrugged. "No," she said. "I'm an only child. And I don't have any relatives in Michigan. Why?"

"Oh, it's nothing really." At that moment, the bell sounded the arrival of the elevator. The cold metal doors parted to reveal a small carriage with tan, rubbery lining.

The couple stepped inside. Jill's hand hovered over the buttons for a moment, hesitating on which one to press. Just as she was about to push the button labeled *G*, Don beat her to the punch. For the briefest moment, his fingers brushed against hers. She blushed. His heart pounded. *Elevators . . .*

"So, Dr. Lipton," Jill started.

"Don," Don interrupted.

"Don. Sorry again." The young woman smiled politely. "You're the head of the English department."

"That's right. I just took the chair this year."

Jill rocked back and forth on her feet. "Must be a tough job."

"It is."

"Do you ever have time to do any writing for yourself?"

Don nodded modestly. He began to toy with the clasp on his satchel. *This elevator*, he thought. *It's taking forever.* He recalled fondly how he used to relish its slow pace – how there was a time when there was no place else he would rather be.

"Wait a minute!" Jill suddenly yelled. She clapped her hands on Don's shoulders, as if turning him toward her to size him up. "Don Lipton!" She then let go of her grasp and turned to face the shiny veneer of the elevator's doors. "Okay, brain, where are you?"

Don chuckled.

"I have your books at my store!" Jill burst out. "You're on the bestseller list! Oh my! I'm in an elevator with a *real* author!"

Don couldn't help but be pleased at his name recognition, but still, he did his best to remain humble. "I like to piddle with writing," he said. "I've always loved poetry, and that bestseller about which you speak came naturally. So many things were happening in my life at the time to inspire me."

Jill took what looked to be a deep, star-struck breath.

"How about you?" Don asked calmly.

"How about what?"

"Do you write?"

Jill shook her head slowly. "Oh gosh," she said. "I wish I had the time. I mean, I love to write, but I'm always reading, you know?"

Don nodded. "You have to stay on top of all those new books coming into the store, I suppose."

"Exactly!" Jill said with a wave of her hand. "Maybe I should take a writing class to keep me disciplined."

"Maybe you *should*." The professor meant what he said. A part of him would have loved nothing more than to have a woman who looked so like Julie sitting in that familiar position at the head of his class.

The elevator doors opened. The two exited to an empty and almost eerily dark lobby. The English department secretary had obviously gone home for the night. Outside the long rectangular windows that spanned nearly from floor to ceiling and parsed their way down the halls to the left and right, the moon projected a ghostly gray onto the beautiful, tree-lined campus of the university.

Jill placed her hand on Don's forearm, causing his skin to electrify with excited tension.

"But now that I have you talking about the store again," she said, "is there a time we might be able to get together to discuss the reading lists for the professors in your department?"

With a smile, Don nodded. "I'm sure we can work something out. I don't have the lists with me at the moment, though. If it's okay with you, I can bring them by your store tomorrow." He then motioned for her to follow him through the glass double-doors leading out to the main quad. From there, the two of them would head west under the starry sky to the adjacent red-brick building which housed the cafeteria.

"Just be sure you get there before Tuesday afternoon," Jill said quickly. "The orders will go out on Tuesday evening. The books will be there on Thursday, which should give you two weeks before the start of the semester."

For a moment, Don's tone changed. He became all business. "I don't know about that," he said. "I sent the syllabus out to my students last week. I know some of the eager beavers will want their books right away. Thursday might not be soon enough."

Jill's tone changed, too. Hers was slightly more pleading. "Well, you can email me the titles and I can put your order in before the others," she said. She rifled through her small, black handbag and pulled out a card. It read, *The Open Book; Jill Larkins, Proprietor*.

Don grinned as he read the card. Then he looked over at his companion, noticing for the first time that she was having a little trouble keeping up with him. He was walking at an uncharacteristically quick pace. As he glanced around, he noticed that they had already come up alongside the cafeteria.

"My email address is on there," Jill added quickly, pointing at the card in the professor's hand.

"Ah, so it is," Don said before stuffing the card in the breast pocket of his shirt. "I'll hold onto this, but I think I'd rather stop in to see your store first. I'll be there in the next day or two."

"Of course." Jill bobbed her head in a placating fashion.

"Besides," Don added, "it's been a long time since I've allowed myself the pleasure of reading a good book. Maybe you can help me find one."

The young woman beamed. "I would be glad to try!"

The professor turned to face the building next to which they stood. He pointed toward the glass doorway leading inside, indicating that the two of them should pass through. They did, the older man holding the door open for his younger companion.

"But now, Ms. Larkins, we must part," Don said. As he allowed the door to close behind them, he motioned down the brightly lit hallway to his right. "Your stop is down this hall, the first door on the left." Then he pointed down another, much longer hallway stretching directly in front of him. "Mine is all the way at the end of this hall. They make us professors work to get our mail."

Jill laughed. "So the food in this cafeteria . . . is it any good?"

Don looked up at the ceiling ponderously. "If you have a good imagination, I suppose. Or if you're hungry enough . . . you might find something reasonable in there to eat from time to time."

The young woman laughed again, this time more freely. "Thank you, Don," she said. "I look forward to seeing you at the store."

Don waved and watched as Jill strolled down the hall. She looked so like Julie. *What strange fate brought her knocking on my door?* He wondered. *And do I dare to tempt it again?*

Chapter Two

Don jerked awake, spilling a pile of papers from his lap as scant images from a dream slowly faded. Once again, he had fallen asleep in his favorite easy chair while grading his students' assignments and reviewing his own work. A shaft of early morning sunlight traced across his arm and lit up the computer screen on the desk next to him. He felt that familiar dull ache well up in his bones.

Memories of the previous night's hours of fruitless brainstorming came to him in bits and pieces as he herded the printed pages into a stack beside the computer on the desk and rose creakily to his feet.

Too often lately, whatever inspiration he had to write seemed muffled as if by a dark blanket. The problem had interrupted a new novel he had been working on. Indeed, it was a novel with which he was nearly finished. But no amount of rereading had been able to shed light on how to end this story.

And so, like many other recent evenings, he had fallen asleep unfulfilled. As he slowly returned to full consciousness, his frustration began to mount. He was so close to finishing this book, but . . . He remembered a quote he'd read somewhere: "It's easy to start writing, but finishing is another thing."

His eyes scanned around the room, and stopped as they usually did on the photographs resting on the antique walnut stained hutch. Though he knew it would bring him pain, he couldn't help himself. He walked groggily toward the hutch, wiping sleep from his eyes as he approached. As he stared at the pictures, his life seemed to pass slowly before him. One by one, they stirred the deepest memories to the surface, replaying themselves upon the beating of his heart.

There, on the top left, in a frame of simple blonde wood, was Emily, the first love of his life. He focused on the vision of her deep blue eyes, those delicate lips, her sharp, hypnotizing features. He recalled all their wedding plans, their first home, and their dreams that were supposed to last a lifetime. She had always been so strong, so unflinchingly dependable, and so desperately loving. He knew that if it were possible, she would be there with him, helping him navigate his way through all the roadblocks of writing. She had been such a joyful, inspiring, and selfless woman in life . . .

This had always been one of his favorite pictures of her, taken right after she had discovered that she was pregnant with Abby. He remembered the satisfaction he felt in his heart as he snapped the picture that day. Here was the most beautiful woman on earth, and hidden within her was the confirmation that he would soon be a father. He remembered trying to visualize holding a son, then a daughter, and thinking he would go crazy until he knew for sure which it would be. But he also knew, even then, that either would be perfect.

Beaming from the picture next to Emily's was little Abby. There she was in her tiny pink sun-suit, her long, blonde ringlets circling her face. She was so adorable, and had always possessed the kind of personality that reminded him of Shirley Temple in her early childhood movies. His little Abby even knew the words Shirley had sung in the song "Animal Crackers in my Soup!"

For Don, it took no more than a small dose of imagination to conjure what his life would have been like if Emily and Abby had lived.

The questions panned through his mind, as they had done thousands of times before. How could it have rained so hard that night? How could he have lost control of the car? Why did he have to be the one to go on living while they were taken away?

They were questions he had wrestled with for years, to the point where he had nearly given up on life – had truly thought there would never be a reason to live. That was, until he met Julie.

He glanced up at the picture in the center of the second shelf. Framed with a wreath of silver, the beautiful, feathery-brown-haired woman in the photograph seemed to be smiling directly at him. God, how he missed her. Julie had come into his life as one of his students. He had made most of her time in his class miserable. But no matter how hard his heart, he could never ignore her remarkable, luminous writing. It had opened his mind to the notion that he had been punishing others, including her, for his own painful past.

In him, this frail young woman had seeded great change. In the process he had fallen deeply in love with her; something he had never dreamed could happen again.

Tears began to cloud Don's eyes. Julie had been married when they met. Painfully, the two of them had honored that commitment. Yet through this torment, they managed to build a love far deeper than most. And tragically – like the way of all things for Don Lipton – even that unique bond would sever long before its time.

Don ran a hand down the side of his aging face, feeling the bristles of his beard grate against his palm. He closed his eyes and all at once felt washed over by a fresh wave of pain. Not for the first time, he wondered if he could ever get past these great losses in his life. He wondered if he would always live with this sorrow, this void.

He would never forget the days he had spent sitting beside Julie as she grew weaker and weaker, talking to her, helping her travel to places with him, if only in mind and in heart.

Despite the torment of her death, Don continued to draw on the inspiration that Julie had left in her wake, feeling and imagining things that had previously been walled off from him for so long. Taking a cue from his departed love, he often walked the narrow trail out to his new gazebo and wrote in a notebook, typing the notes up later at home. It was through these efforts that he had managed to publish his first book of poetry in years.

But now, as he finished his painful reminiscing with these ghostly photographs, Don thought about all that he had to prepare in order to complete his latest chore, his latest day to come. The weary professor walked to the white-walled kitchen, grabbed a jar of instant coffee out of one amongst the row of white-painted cabinets, and began spooning the putrid grounds into a white coffee cup. He filled the cup with water and slammed it into the microwave. Step One.

At the beep, he retrieved his morning call to arms and immediately began stirring a healthy serving of sugar into the dark liquid. As he did so, he realized with a jolt that later in the year, the verge of winter, would be the three-year anniversary of her death. Three years hence since Julie had passed . . . Could that really be? Had he really been a lonely shell for this long?

The ringing phone on the marble countertop interrupted Don's thoughts. It startled him greatly. He couldn't remember the last time he had heard it ring. It *never* rang. He couldn't imagine who would be calling him at this early hour, either, but guessed that it was probably a new student, worried and wondering about when classes would start again.

"Hello," he croaked. "Don Lipton here."

"Hi, Don," came a familiar voice. "This is Cheryl."

A short pause followed. Don was startled and still a little sleepy.

"How are you?" Cheryl asked.

"Oh, hi, Cheryl," Don finally said. "I'm okay . . . fine, I mean. And you?"

Don could hear Cheryl drawing a long and what sounded like a troubled breath on the other end of the line. "Well," she said, "things are about the same here, but I have a three-year-old who misses you. Matt keeps asking me when Grandpa Don is going to play ball with him again."

Don smiled proudly at the thought of his relationship with this little guy. "He does, does he?" he said, the broad smile on his face evident in his voice. "Well then, I guess it's about time we set up some sort of get-together."

"That's actually why I'm calling, Don. I was wonder—"

"How is little Madison doing?" Don interrupted. He was leaning heavily on the countertop as he spoke into the phone, and the position was beginning to take its toll on his back. He stood to his full height and attempted to straighten his lower back with the palm of his free hand, to no avail. "I have to make time to get out there to see her again or she'll never get to know me," he continued.

"Well, we all miss you terribly," Cheryl said, a hint of guilt lining her voice.

Don turned to walk into the dining room, where he had a mind to sit in one of the chairs surrounding the opulent dinner table. It seemed strange to have such a large and accommodating dining room when he never had anyone to dine with, but there it was. The table and chairs had been a gift from Emily's father on their wedding day, and he never could bear to part with it, even despite the long move across the country.

Just as he set foot on the tan carpet in the dining room, he remembered his coffee, and wheeled around to retrieve it. "You know, Cheryl," Don said, "I love living here in Michigan, but I miss you all terribly, too."

There was a long silence. As Don finally took his seat in the dining room, it seemed to him that Cheryl was pondering deeply her next words. Don decided to beat her to the punch.

"Cheryl, maybe you can help me with a problem. Do you have any family in Michigan? An aunt, maybe?"

"No," Cheryl said slowly. "Not that I know of . . . why?"

Don choked down a quick sip of his coffee, speaking quickly just after he swallowed. "Oh, it's nothing, really. Just wondering."

Cheryl projected a deep sigh. "Okay, then," she said, her tone becoming much lighter. "Madison is great, though. I can sure see the difference between boys and girls already. She's so much easier to take care of than Matthew was. And so loving! I'll never forget those long nights with Matt and his colic."

Don laughed. "It's hard to imagine that boy causing trouble of any kind."

"Right," Cheryl said, her voice dripping with sarcasm. Another deep breath followed, blowing forcefully through the line like an autumn wind. "Mom would have loved Madison. I wish she could have known her."

For the second time that morning, Don felt himself choking up. "Yeah," he said. "So do I, Cheryl. Your mom would have loved every minute with those kids."

Don slouched forward and rested his elbows on the table. More silence followed.

"She loved every minute with you, too, you know," he added. In a moment, the professor could hear the unmistakable sound of muffled crying. It was a long while before Cheryl spoke again.

"Don, I don't really want to get into any of this right now," she said.

Every ounce of Don Lipton longed to be in California at that instant. He wanted nothing more than to hug and comfort Cheryl, the only daughter of his former love. Tears welled up in his eyes. "I know, Cheryl," he managed. "And I'm sorry to get into it again."

"Listen, Don," Cheryl continued weakly, "the reason I'm calling is to invite you here for a small celebration we'll be having for Madison's first birthday. We don't know the exact day we'll be having the party yet, but it'll be sometime next month."

"Oh," Don said, practically giddy over the invitation despite his barely audible reply.

"I know you're already busy with college and all but . . . well . . . Tom and I would both love to have you here. I mean . . . you're such a part of the family now."

Don sighed, quivering with sorrowful excitement as he did so. Cheryl seemed to do the same on the other end of the line.

"Please say you'll come, Don. It would mean so much to the kids."

The professor sat up straight once more. "I won't make any promises that I can't keep," he said with certainty, "but I will try to come. Maybe I can find a sub to teach my classes."

Cheryl sighed with relief. Don could almost hear her nodding.

"If things go as planned, I'm going to be spending a great deal of my time later this week tying up some loose ends back at

Whinburg, anyway. So if I come again next month, that'll give you and I more time to catch up."

"Oh, Don," Cheryl said happily. "I can't wait to tell Matthew. He'll be so excited."

"Now don't jump to any conclusions," Don said, chuckling a little as he stood. "You just tell Matt that he had better practice swinging that bat I bought him."

Cheryl laughed softly. "Will do. I can't wait to see you . . . in a couple of days, right?"

"That's right. Thursday, I'll be there."

"But, Don, are you sure you're okay? You sound a bit tired or something."

"Well, it *is* early, Cheryl," Don joked. "You just caught me before I was totally awake."

"I see."

It seemed to the professor that Cheryl's voice indicated just a hint of disbelief. Perhaps his depression had become more obvious than he'd thought. "Thanks so much for calling, Cheryl," he said quickly. "And thanks for caring."

"You're welcome. And it's easy to care. We'll see you soon. And, Don?"

"Yes?"

"I love you."

"Right!" Don said, a little startled by the words. "Love you, too."

As he returned the phone to the cradle, Don realized what a treasure he had in Julie's daughter and grandchildren. Cheryl was a good and kind young lady, and had been close enough to her mother to know and understand the love she'd had for him. Most kids would have rebelled at the thought of their married mother carousing with a widowed man. But not Cheryl. From the start, she had seen the love that Don had given Julie – a love that her own father never could.

Julie's passing had of course left emptiness in both their hearts. Remarkably, the two of them had turned to each other for support, and had somehow managed to fill a part of that void with each other. For sure little Matthew and Madison could bring joy to anyone.

Anyone except their biological grandfather, apparently. Robert, Julie's husband at the time of her death – the only real reason Don's love for Julie had never been fully realized – had quickly abandoned his family following the death of his wife. Shortly before making the decision to take the job he had been offered at Michigan State, Don had learned that Robert had met a woman, had sold his business that he had been a slave to for most of his adult life, and remarried. Without a thought, he had moved several states away and only called once a month to talk briefly with his daughter.

Word from Cheryl was that her father and his new wife were doing all they could to live life in the fast lane. Children and grandchildren obviously did not fit into that part of the plan.

So Don had cancelled – or at least postponed – his plans to leave. Without even trying, he had stepped into Robert's place as doting grandfather, and he had filled the role so well. Although his spring and summer classes had kept him busy much of the time, he had always found a way to spend time with them. Even now, as he had moved halfway across the country to Michigan, he would take the opportunity every few months to fly back to California to spend a day or two with Matt and Madison.

With little left to brighten his life, Don so looked forward to these times. Being around Cheryl and the kids somehow connected him with Julie. After all, they were a living reminder of her. For brief moments, it was almost as if she was still alive. At times, Don would half expect her to come walking out the back door of Cheryl's home, smiling as she came to join the fun in the back yard.

As Don retreated to the small bathroom attached to his bedroom to begin step two of his day – brushing his teeth – the phone rang again. *Two calls,* Don thought. *Red-letter day.* This time, he let the answering machine catch it.

"Hi, Don, this is Mark. I found info on a great air show next month. I thought if we can get your Cessna ready to go by then, we might fly down and spend a few nights there. Give me a call. You know the number!"

Don reached for the phone to call Mark back. Then, noticing the time displayed by the polished chrome clock on the wall just behind the telephone, decided to wait until later. He recalled an early morning meeting he had with the other members of the English department's faculty, and realized that he would have time to do little else but get dressed and get on the road.

As he dressed in the doorway of the cluttered walk-in closet in his bedroom – tan slacks and an old argyle sweater today – he thought once more of the call from Cheryl. Such anguish in her young life. Although, he was about her age when Emily and Abby had been taken from him . . .

Blinking away the moisture in his eyes, he took one last draft of the lukewarm coffee, feeling the lump in his throat wash away. Then he pulled on his toffee-colored shoes and headed out the door, leather satchel in hand.

~~~

The traffic had been light, and Don arrived at his building with an extra five minutes to spare. As he turned the corner and entered the brightly sunlit hallway, he felt himself bathed in the natural warmth of the late summer day. It did little to calm his anxiety about having forgotten to bring the most important item from his home: his trusty thermos of coffee.

As he walked through the doorway leading into the modest lobby that headed the English department, he saw Mark standing next to the secretary's table to the left. He seemed to be having an animated and playful discussion with Marie, the secretary. Mark was a vaguely handsome man with a square jaw and slick black hair. His Roman nose rested between a pair of green, bespectacled eyes and above a set of tight and rather shrewd lips. He was the kind of man with shoulders that were amplified gaudily by the suit jackets he always insisted upon wearing. Dressed as he was, his upper body appeared triangular in shape, with his broad shoulders carving a dramatic line down to his slim waist and skinny legs. The look lent him the appearance of fitness – though Don knew the man to despise going to the gym – which in turn suggested an age much younger than his forty-nine years.

"Good morning," Don said, clapping his friend on his considerable shoulder. "I got your message earlier, but I was running a bit late, so I couldn't call you back."

"No problem," Mark said jovially with a dismissive wave of his hand. "So what do you think?"

"Depends. Where and when is this air show?"

"I don't have all the details yet, but Mike sent me an e-mail last night with some of the information. Think he just wanted to get me excited. This is supposed to be one of the biggest air shows this year. I think it's at Traverse City."

"That'd be a short flight," Don offered.

"Exactly," Mark said. "And we can enjoy the benefit of all the work we've done on your plane."

"And hope like hell that we didn't wire anything wrong!"

Mark elbowed Don in the ribs. "You got that right. But we'll have it checked out again before we go anywhere."

"It'd be nice to go somewhere where we could get new ideas from other pilots. Share flying stories." Don's voice grew dreamy. It was one of only a few things that could captivate him anymore, flying. Well, he loved flying and being with Cheryl's children.

"So does this sound like something you'd be interested in?" Mark asked with a knowing smile.

"Sounds great," Don said, checking his wristwatch. "But we'll have to talk about the details later at the hangar. I'm late."

Chapter Three

Back home that evening, Don struggled through the final paragraph of a student story that all too closely resembled the tale of Hamlet. Having finished, he took sick pleasure in being able to finally throw the awful thing to the floor in disgust. The student's grasp of narrative scope – let alone the importance of literary originality – was atrocious. And besides, Don Lipton wasn't really processing a word of it.

He had tried all through the day. He had even had the notable distraction of visiting the hangar with Mark. But despite all that, how could he think about anything else but Jill, the woman from the bookstore? Maybe her resemblance to Julie had been mere coincidence. But then, there was no denying that even their names were similar: Julie and Jilly. How could they not be related?

Maybe I'm making too much of this, he thought. After all, it had been almost three years since Julie had passed. It occurred to him that his longing to see Julie might be causing him to project a greater resemblance onto this Jill. He had read about such psychoses in the past, and of course the heart tended to play games with the mind.

Don returned to the task of grading stories, but in short order, he realized that the effort was useless. Every quip and curl of every letter reminded him of Julie. The memories flooded his thoughts. There was little he could do to concentrate on anything else.

He recalled the lighthouse. It had been raining that day, but it didn't really matter. How silly she had looked in that yellow rain coat! He could still hear her voice as she danced around in the rain.

"I'm a bird!" she had said, lifting her arms. The slicker had billowed out behind her like wings. "I'm free, and I want to fly!"

In this suddenly vivid recollection, they sat together on a granite bench and watched the beacon light up the rocky shoreline. Don smiled through tears as he watched himself get down on his knees and pledge his eternal love. He sobbed as Julie begged him not to take her home yet. She wanted to sit and cuddle – and how happy he was to oblige. He could almost feel her delicate embrace . . .

They had pledged to each other to be "forever friends." As the phrase returned to his mind, memories began flooding his heart. He recalled the porch at that old cabin where they sat side by side on the old buggy seat. How they never tired of conversing – and they learned so much about each other in such a short time together. It had been so simple back then, sharing his feelings with Julie. How he missed having someone to share his feelings with now.

He recalled that last Christmas – the one he had staged for her. He had decorated a blue spruce for the occasion with cranberries and popcorn chains, and little red feathered cardinals. He had repaired, sanded, and re-stained the gazebo – one last gift of effort to his departing love. As the Christmas music replayed in his mind, Don watched as the two of them toasted with their non-alcoholic wine. He languished anew in the sight of Julie eating the food he had prepared, despite her lack of appetite in those days. He would never forget that beautiful last dance. . .

Don rocked forward in his recliner and reached toward the computer desk for a tissue. *Even memories connected to these,* he thought sadly. As he brought the tissue to the corners of his eyes, he remembered her dying day.

"Here," he had said sorrowfully. "These are only fifty cents today."

She had not the strength even to laugh. How he burned to hear her laugh at his corny jokes once more.

As he examined the tear-stained tissue, Don chuckled despite himself. "Look at what this Jill has done to me," he said aloud. "Maybe I shouldn't see her again."

But for the memories she stirred up . . . this was exactly why he knew he *had* to see her again. There was no denying the curiosity. No denying the feeling that she could somehow fill the hole in his heart – if not with love, then with forgotten memories.

Don resigned himself to leave the papers to grade later. No one cared about grades during the summer semester, anyway. And his students could wait.

He stood warily, swinging the footrest of his recliner down with a loud, creaking thump. From the desk, he grabbed his leather-bound journal and started the walk through the tiny, unfurnished sunroom and into the back yard. The yard itself was wide near the house, ducking into a circular shape at the opposite end, where a thick brush of tree-line made a half-moon out of the freshly mowed grass. It was a shady yard, dotted here and there with deep green spruce and ancient oak trees. This had been the primary reason Don Lipton had chosen this house, this yard.

At its center was a clearing, and in this place, Don had constructed an oak-stained gazebo in honor of his departed. His bare feet caressed the smooth surface of the polished stone he had used to construct the walkway to this now sacred place. His forehead delighted at the touch of the late summer sun.

Unaccustomed as he had become to the change of the seasons, Don found himself dreading the deep humidity of the August evening. As he opened the swinging door to the gazebo, he noticed that some of the cushions on the benches, with their trim patterns of primary colors, had become dusty with disuse. He had tried to maintain this new gazebo as his private way of honoring Julie, and so his first act was to lay the journal down on the floor and wipe his bare hands across the surface of the cushions.

When he'd finished, he gazed out at the woods serving as the border to his yard. The thousands of branches rustled slightly in the breeze, serenading his arrival to this place of significance. He sat slowly, resting his shoulders against the elbow joint of one of the gazebo's six large screened windows. Then he reached down and picked his journal up off the bare, wood-plank floor.

He brought pen to paper. Immediately, and without warning, crippling grief constricted his throat. His eyes burned with building tears. Several dropped onto the page all at once.

Julie's presence, even after her death – and for the longest time – seemed real, as though Don were walking constantly with a solid, tangible person. Such was her touch on his life. But that, too, had faded over time. In the place of her presence was constructed a gap in Don's character, an emptiness he believed he could never fill on his own.

Then out of nowhere Jill had come into his life, a new physical presence and a freshly tormenting reminder. Being in her company was like seeing Julie all over again – for the first time in ages. She was a familiar, delicate beauty, so painful, yet alluring.

Sobs wracked him. He wanted nothing more than to experience that familiarity once more. He knew that he needed to visit Jill again. But in so doing, would he be insulting the memory of Julie?

The space on the bench next to him felt more vacant than ever. His arms ached to hold his love once more.

After several minutes, the sadness clutching at his chest eased, and he took a deep breath. Regardless of how difficult it might be, he had no choice but to see Jill again. He would not be able to sleep properly – let alone write or even grade a paper – until he somehow got to the bottom of Jill's strange resemblance to Julie.

Besides, he told himself, *there's nothing wrong with pretending, if only for a brief moment, that it's Julie looking back at me with those velvety brown eyes.*

Chapter Four

His latest workday now ended, Don parked the Dodge along the curb in front of the Open Book and climbed out, grabbing the file folder off the passenger seat. He had driven by the store a number of times on his way to and from the university but had never taken the time to stop in.

Being the well-read author that he was, he obviously enjoyed perusing the numerous bookstores in this collegiate neighborhood, finding gems among the dog-eared paperbacks. But the last thing on his mind at that moment was finding a new volume to add to his collection.

In the manila folder he now carried, he had dropped the various required reading lists from the handful of professors in his department. But even the lists served as secondary purpose for his visit to this place.

A string of large silver bells jingled on the door as he walked in. The sweet aroma of freshly brewed tea reached his nostrils, dancing within his senses for a brief moment before being replaced by the mildewed scent of old paper. This, he knew, was a formidable collection of books.

His eyes gazed momentarily over the half-dozen or so shelves to his left and right. Each shelf appeared to be nearly six feet wide, and stretched all the way from the floor to the vaulted ceiling above. The path that led from the doorway to what appeared to be the checkout counter was crowded, packed as it was between the two heavy rows of bookshelves.

Upon the desk, Don could see an old, 1920's-era cash register, a well-polished hand-bell, and a slender calico cat. As his eyes settled on the cat, it meowed and then sprang down to the upholstered reading chair behind the desk, where it settled, curled up, and began licking its paws. No other sound but the creaking floorboards beneath his feet came to him as he walked.

Three steps from the door, the first thing he noticed was the poetry section. Strange to see it right up front, across the aisle from the shelves of *New Fiction* instead of buried somewhere in the back, as usual. He wondered if his own volume of poetry was among the offerings, but did not wish to get caught in the vain act of checking. Casting his eyes over the shelf of new editions, he remembered the thrill of seeing his latest novel in such a display after his long hiatus. He'd had no idea just how successful it would be.

Wandering absently to the back of the store, he noticed a few tables and chairs set up in a small room to the right of the check-out counter. Ceramic tea sets with floral designs sat in a glass display case attached to the far wall. He again remembered fondly how much Julie had enjoyed her daily cup of rosehip tea. Tiffany-style reading lamps rested in the center of the three narrow antique tables. Hand-knitted afghans had been draped over the Louis XVI style chairs.

Julie would have loved this place . . .

"Well, hello, Don."

Startled, the professor turned toward the voice, part of him not wanting to see her face again, part of him wanting nothing more than to stare. "Oh," he said. "Hello there. You remembered not to call me Professor Lipton."

Jill smiled knowingly. "Well, you seemed so adamant about it the other day."

Don chuckled. "You're right about that. I don't like to use the formal title when I'm not in the classroom. Even then, I don't care for it."

Jill nodded. "Don it is. Anyway, can I help you with something today?"

Don's eyes lingered a bit too long upon those deep, intoxicating brown eyes of hers that seemed so familiar. "Yes," he said, snapping suddenly out of his trance and sliding the small bundle of papers out of the manila folder. "For one thing, I have those lists of books for the next term that you asked me to bring. I know you've been waiting for them."

"Ah, yes," Jill said, taking the lists from the professor. "I was hoping you'd bring these."

Don watched for a moment as Jill's striking eyes panned across the list on the top of the bundle. She nodded dreamily, as though confirming the selections in her mind.

"I'm also looking for a good book," he added.

Jill's face came to light. With her thin, light eyebrows arched, she beamed up at her much taller customer. "What sort of book?" she asked.

Don laughed. "Nothing too heavy," he said. "It's for a mini-vacation I'm taking. I'm thinking fiction. Has Richard Gehrig or Howard Paquette published anything recently?"

Jill squinted and thoughtfully placed her index finger against her delicate chin. "As a matter of fact, I think Gehrig does have a new book out this month. Let me check here." The young woman turned and walked to a small desk to the left of the checkout counter. It was a desk that Don hadn't noticed. Upon it rested an old, boxy computer.

"No card catalogue?" Don asked with a playful grin. "In *this* place?" He motioned to the antique furnishings in the tearoom behind him.

Jill smiled as she looked up from the computer, her hands still braced against the keyboard. "Not *everything* can be preserved," she said. "They don't make cataloguing cards for new books anymore. Besides, these things are much more efficient."

"But not nearly as timeless," Don said dreamily as he took to examining the nearest row of books, which was the psychology section. *How quaint,* he thought. All at once, he was taken with the entirely homey atmosphere of the Open Book.

"All good things must come to an end," Jill said.

The comment cut straight to Don's heart. "You're right about that," he managed.

The silence that followed was broken only by the intermittent clacking of the keys beneath Jill's long, slender fingers.

"Yes!" she shouted suddenly. "I was right! Gehrig's new book, *An Island to Remember*, came out on the first of the month.

It looks like a contemporary romance." Jill glanced at Don, her long, silken eyelashes fluttering. "Sound interesting?"

"Sure," Don said casually. "But I only read that kind of book if the author's one of my favorites. In this case, it sounds perfect."

Jill's gleeful expression melted quickly into a frustrated frown as she looked back at the computer screen. Her face glazed over with the bluish hue of the screen's glow. "Oh, but I don't have it in stock."

"That's all right," Don said, strolling over to stand next to the ever-more fascinating bookstore owner. "I'm not leaving for a while. Could you place an order for me?"

"Absolutely."

Don rubbed his bristly chin with his thumb and forefinger. The rough gray strands of his beard danced and swayed at his touch.

"You're in luck," Jill said in a sing-songy way. "I can put the order in before I go home this evening. It'll arrive with the shipment of professors' books on Thursday. Is that soon enough?"

"Absolutely!" Don echoed with a smile.

The younger woman smirked. Then she began clacking away at the keyboard again. Don assumed that she was placing the order for the Gehrig novel.

"So, Ms. Larkins," Don began, a little uncomfortably. "It *is* 'Miss,' isn't it?"

Jill looked up from the screen, her lips pressed into a mischievous half-smile. "Well, if you insist on my calling you Don, I must insist once again on you calling me Jill. But, yes, it is 'Miss.' Always has been." Her tone carried in a charmingly light-hearted manner.

"What made you open a bookstore in these parts?"

"You assume I'm not from these parts?"

Don chafed slightly. "I suppose I do assume that, yes."

Jill stood, apparently finished with placing the order, and rested her hand on her hip, which she jutted casually to one side. "Well, you assume correctly. I'm originally from Minnesota."

"Why did you move from Minnesota?"

"Wow! Three questions!" Jill said with a grin, melodramatically placing the back of her hand against her forehead. "Why Dr. Lipton, is this an inquisition?"

Don's heart skipped a beat. "No," he said. "I'm just curious about the new kid in town."

"Well, in short, I was born here. My parents moved to Minnesota when I was just a year old. I guess I got a little tired of the old haunts. So I decided to give this place another try . . . forty some years later."

"Forty some?" Don said in surprise. "You don't look a day over thirty!"

"Why, Donald. You do flatter me."

As she pursed her lips and her cheeks grew rosy, Don Lipton felt as though he was sinking into the floor. "It's a nice place to live," he said quickly, diverting his attention from whatever significance the moment was beginning to hold. "And it's a great neighborhood you've chosen here. I've gotten acquainted with many of the people around here through the college. Most of them are very nice to know."

"Yeah, as you can imagine, I get a lot of them in here every day. Though I guess you wouldn't be able to tell by this evening." Jill motioned to the empty space all around them. The shop was indeed vacant.

"They've been good to you, I hope." Don moved closer to his companion, nearly close enough to embrace her. The tension in his heart was building.

"Oh yes," Jill said, clearly comfortable enough with the closing gap between herself and this relative stranger. "They've all been very kind and helpful. A couple of them even asked me to dinner. One offered to show the new girl around town."

"So did you go?" Don asked, almost pleadingly. Then he calmed himself, correcting his tone. "To dinner, I mean."

Jill smiled. "Not yet," she said. "I'm a little gun-shy, so to speak. I've had some bad experiences with men in the past. I like to take my time before getting close to new people." She stopped herself, placing her palm against her cheek and sighing. "I can't believe I'm talking like this to you, actually. Talk about keeping your distance."

Don, a little startled, took a quick step back. "Oh, I'm sorry," he said. "I didn't mean to impose."

Jill shook her head once, emphatically. "No, no. You're not imposing. I was just saying . . ."

Don felt his blood warm as his heart fluttered. His muscles tensed – even in his jaw – as he began to form his next words in his mind. "Perhaps you'd let me be the one to show you around town," he cooed. "Or dinner, maybe . . ."

Jill looked at the ground, disguising her glowing smile. "That's very kind of you, Profess—Don. Maybe your wife could come with us."

"Oh, I'm not married right now," Don said, fumbling for his words, immediately realizing how crazy he must have sounded. "I mean . . . I was married. But my wife has passed."

Jill placed her hand against her heart, clutching at the lacy blouse that she wore parted at the neck. "I'm so sorry, Don," she said solemnly. "I didn't mean to . . ."

"It's okay," Don said sheepishly. "You've done nothing wrong. You were right to assume that I was married. Strange that I'm not married, I guess. It is strange that *neither* of us is married, really. You're such a pretty young lady." Don chided himself inwardly. He was rambling out of bounds.

"I'm not all that young," Jill said, now seemingly incapable of holding Don's gaze. "But thank you for the compliment."

Don shook his head. "Where are my manners?" he asked himself. "You have things to do. I should get out of here so you can place that order."

Jill appeared more guarded now. She certainly seemed to be having trouble casting those misty eyes upon her customer, anyway. Don felt wretched. He had crossed the line already.

Suddenly, her mood seemed to shift. All at once, her expression lightened and she looked Don in the eyes once again. "Think nothing of it," she said cheerfully. "You can stay as long as you like. The order won't take long."

Don nodded appreciatively.

"Can I get you anything? Help you find a book, maybe?"

"No," Don said with an appeasing wave of his hand. "I'm sure the couple hundred other customers you have waiting for book orders would be angry with me if they knew I was keeping you from your duties." He chuckled at himself.

"Well, I suppose I *should* get back to that. Closing time's coming soon."

"I understand."

Jill turned back to the computer and started typing once more. She would occasionally look over at a sheet of paper resting next to the keyboard on the tall, flimsy looking desk that supported the computer. Don assumed it was a list of ISBN's for the clearly giant order. She looked so like Julie, hunched as she was over a keyboard. There had to be a simple explanation to this uncanny resemblance, but what was it?

Don glanced at the large antique clock behind the checkout counter. Its lightly golden, ornate face and long, intricately fashioned brass hands indicated that he had darkened the doorway of the Open Book for more than an hour. Time now ran scarce. And those soon-to-be-late papers wouldn't grade themselves.

Still, his heart pounded, begging him to stay. He almost felt as if walking away from Jill now might cause her to disappear from his life forever. As she was still focused on the computer, Don took a final look at her. She wore a hunter green skirt and jacket to go with her very professional beige top. She carved an alluring figure. And the color caused her hair and eyes to dance in their beautiful dark brown. *Julie. . .*

He hesitated for a moment more, but knew that it was time to leave. If he didn't find something to do with himself quickly, he would have crossed into the realm of gawking suitor. And so he turned.

As he did so, he heard that sweet, melodic voice carry once more. "By the way," Jill said, "I just ordered twenty more copies of your book. Ever since the *Times* added it to the bestseller list, I can hardly keep it on the shelves."

Hearing the laughter in her voice, Don turned back. A slight smile lifted the corners of her lips, and her eyes sparkled with mischief.

"I bet that just drives you crazy," she continued. "Thousands of housewives across the nation gobbling up your work, meeting in little book groups to pick apart the brains of your characters like a board of doctors working on a troubling patient."

He scoffed playfully. "It pays the bills," he said with a shrug. "I can't complain."

"Well, you deserve every cent you make from that book. The last hundred pages kept me up until two in the morning."

Don felt a grin spread unbidden across his face. "Now if I could just finish this new manuscript I've been working on . . . I'll make a proper insomniac out of you yet."

Her brilliant smile was like a sunbeam reaching all the way into his heart. "I'm counting on it," she said.

Feeling a little dizzy, Don pushed the door open and stepped into the growing twilight. Before he could even begin beating a path away from the store, he took a few deep breaths of chilly fresh air to clear his head. He suddenly felt rejuvenated . . . re-born.

Chapter Five

Jill rinsed the last teacup under scalding hot water and set it in the dish rack alongside the others left earlier by the unexpected afternoon crowd. Drying her hands on her apron, she grabbed a damp rag and began wiping the indelible chalky brown stains from the tearoom's tall counter, moving aside the displays of caramels and lemon cookies as she did.

She had been pleased by the turnout this month, even on weekdays. Students had begun to flock to her little store to study and socialize. Her dreams had reached fruition already, she realized.

Opening an independent bookstore was always risky, she knew – especially in these days of big chains, with their coffee bars and national reputations. She had added the teashop to her business plan because she had always enjoyed a warm cup of tea while reading and hoped it would draw more lingering and repeat customers. As she finished her nightly cleanup routine, she realized that it had proven to be a shrewd business move.

Her mind traveled back to her life from only a few months ago. Still living in Minnesota, she had always loved being around books, and was employed at the time by a national book warehouse. It was far from a glamorous job, but it gave her the chance to see fresh novels before they even reached the stores. The pay had been fair, and while they were not the greatest, she did enjoy a few insurance benefits.

She had been content.

That all changed, however, when she and her boyfriend Michael split up. They had been together for almost a year, and had even set a tentative date of marriage. She had bought her wedding dress, and even had a couple of bridal showers before she discovered that he was seeing other women behind her back. When she confronted him about it, he became violent.

In an instant, her girlhood dreams of marrying Prince Charming were obliterated.

Michael had begged her to give him a second chance, saying that he was "only human" and that he had simply "made a mistake." But those words did little to heal her broken heart. She knew that she could never trust him again.

For the weeks that would come, he would follow her around like some sort of lovesick puppy, and he called her so often that she had to get an unlisted phone number. She told him flatly that it was over forever between them, but that only seemed to make him that much more determined.

"It will never be over," he had vowed, and something in his eyes told her that he meant it sincerely.

Jill grew more frustrated with each passing day. Her life seemed to be stuck in neutral, and with Michael's continuous badgering, she felt she had little hope of ever moving forward. Before long, she began to harbor almost constant thoughts of running off alone somewhere and starting her life over again. Maybe she could relocate to another country, she fantasized. Or at least to a different part of America.

As fate would have it, when she finally did make her "big move," it turned out to be much less dramatic. She had come across a monthly newsletter that arrived at the warehouse where she worked. The letter listed the names of small bookstores all across the country that were for sale.

As she had some savings stashed away, it occurred to her that now was the time for her to pursue her dreams of working and living independently. When she found a listing that she could actually afford, she was both delighted and disappointed to learn that it would be in Michigan – in the town of her birth, no less. It was still in the Midwest, but far enough away from Michael that she could hope to put him out of her life for good.

And so she gathered up her courage and decided to give it a shot. *After all*, she had reasoned, *how many chances does someone get to start fresh?*

It was difficult leaving Minnesota. It was the only place she had ever known. So she made the primary flight to examine the store and sign the papers, shifting title into her name.

When she arrived in Michigan for good, the first thing she did was survey her new bookstore. The previous owner had died, and she was disappointed to see that all of the bookshelves were empty. She assumed that they had been sold along with the rest of the old woman's estate. But still, even on that day, strolling through the dark, empty store, her footsteps echoing off the spackled, sepia-colored walls, she could visualize the Open Book filled with classics both old and new. The teashop she would put in the far corner.

She knew she had her work cut out for her, but work had never intimidated Jill. She accepted the challenge willingly, putting all her heart into this new venture.

Dropping the rag in the sink, she moved to the bookshelves to complete the task of replacing and reordering all the errant volumes that students and other customers usually left in piles at the end of each row. As she straightened the shelves, she found her mind wandering to Don Lipton. She grinned as she remembered his bright blue eyes on her, the mouth beneath that neatly trimmed beard – always so serious, even when he smiled. He was actually very large, his frame twice her size, at least. But he was quite a handsome man.

She recalled his pleading gaze. Clearly, his curiosity about her had been intense. Jill was, of course, accustomed to getting long glances from men, but something about Don had been different. He seemed to be more soulful and caring.

In some ways, it frightened Jill to think that Don might be interested in her on a romantic level. She knew that she just wasn't ready for that sort of thing. Yet there was something about Don . . . She couldn't help but want to see him again, hopefully soon.

Feeling exhausted, Jill suddenly felt like skipping the rest of her cleanup efforts and heading home to draw a long bath. She walked to the back of the store and grabbed her jacket and handbag. She then strolled to the front doorway, flicking the series of light switches and then swinging outside the door to grab the wooden sidewalk sign on which she had scrawled the new arrivals and drink specials earlier in the day. She propped the sign inside against the wall just to the left of the door, then stepped outside and locked up, checking the door twice to make sure it was secure.

She savored the thought of returning to an empty apartment. The thought of being alone made her heart flutter with the kind of joy only freedom and independence can bring.

It was a quick walk to her modest, silver Mercury Sable. Just as she was settling behind the wheel, her cell phone rang. The caller ID announced that it was Kate – her best friend from back in Minnesota. Missing Kate terribly, Jill was excited to take the call.

"Kate!" she hollered into the phone. "Is that you?"

Infectious laughter rang through the line. "Yeah, this is Kate. Is this Jill? Jill Larkins?"

Jill giggled. "Oh, Kate, am I ever happy to hear from you. How have you been?"

"I'm just fine. How about you? Boy, I miss seeing you at work."

"Yeah," Jill lied. "I still miss that place in a strange way." The new bookstore owner went on to tell her friend about the recent grand opening, the college students who were beginning to frequent the store, and her tiny apartment.

Kate, for her part, listened quietly – which was certainly unusual for this boisterous best friend. "That all sounds great, Jill. I'm so happy for you."

"Thanks," Jill said modestly.

"But I'm not happy for me. I don't have anyone to hang out with anymore."

"I know. I get lonely, too. But . . ."

Kate suddenly cut in. Her tone seemed guarded. "Jill, I had an idea I wanted to run past you. I have some vacation time from my job coming up in about a week. I was thinking maybe I'd come out for a visit."

Jill hesitated, opened her mouth to speak, but then stopped.

"What?" Kate asked, sounding slightly annoyed. "Don't you want to see me?"

The last thing in the world that Jill wanted to do was to insult her old friend. In fact, she missed her so much that she could hardly stand it. But she just wasn't ready for a guest yet. She felt the need to fully cut the fetters with her former life before revisiting anything that might remind her of how things had once been. "No, Kate," she said. "No, it's . . . it's nothing like that."

Kate didn't sound convinced. "Then what is it?" she snapped.

"It's hard to explain. It's just . . . well . . . it seems like not enough time has passed yet. I want to see how I do on my own."

An awkward moment of silence followed on the line. Finally, Kate spoke up. "I know you too well. Something's up. What is it? A guy?"

Jill's mind shot to an image of Don. No, there wasn't a man in her life, but why, then, did she think of him? "Well," she said reluctantly, "I did meet someone, now that you mention it. But there's not any big relationship or anything. And it's not that I don't want you to visit. I just want some time to, well, you know, settle in some more."

Kate laughed. Clearly, she thought she had Jill's secret now. "It's a guy," she said confidently. "And you probably want to get to know him better before your old friend from back home comes over and messes everything up."

Jill smiled at her friend's good intentions. She played along. "I never could hide anything from you," she said.

"I wish things could be different," Kate said with a sigh. "I guess I'll put off that trip for now. Remember, though, if you ever need me for anything, just call."

"Thanks, Kate," Jill said warmly. "Just keep in touch, okay? And always be my friend. I am lonely and miss our fun times. And I'm sure we can get together soon."

They carried on with small talk all the way through Jill's drive home, and she enjoyed every minute of it so much that, for a while, she reconsidered her decision to tell Kate not to come.

As she pulled up to her new apartment and clicked off the phone, deep sadness gripped her heart. She wondered then if running away from her past was really the best way to embrace her future.

"Who knows?" she said inside her empty car. "I sure don't."

Chapter Six

"Hi, Don!" Cheryl waved and greeted him with her usual cheerful smile as he strolled across the grass toward her, squinting in the sun. She sat on a bench near the edge of a playground, where Matthew was jostling with other young boys for a turn on the corkscrew slide.

Don languished in the moment as he quickly checked his watch. If he hadn't arranged for a trade in classes with a colleague, he would be teaching his Creative Writing 101 class, and especially in summer, the lower-level, casual writing students were always the worst.

"The perfect choice for a meeting place," Don said with a smile, remembering how he had been worried that he might not be able to find the park that Cheryl had given him directions to. He had never heard of the place before – and it was quite a stretch from Cheryl's house. More of a stretch than the tired college professor had anticipated, in fact. As the weather was sunny and a nice breeze was blowing, Don had opted to have the cab drop him off at Cheryl's house so he could drop off his overnight bag. From there, he would walk to the park.

He had left the bag on Cheryl's expansive back porch. Normally, he would have been a little uneasy about leaving his things in plain sight, but Cheryl's house was in a quiet, safe neighborhood, and her yard was fenced in.

As he approached his old friend, he couldn't help but gaze up at Matthew, who was so intent on waiting for his turn on the slide that he hadn't noticed the arrival of his surrogate grandpa. The boy had his grandmother's dark curls and a giggle that melted Don's heart. Over the past three years, Don had grown extremely fond of Matthew and had spent many lazy summer days tossing a ball with him or teaching him to throw a Frisbee while Cheryl's husband was at work. It had become a ritual he depended on, a way of indulging the grandchild he had once hoped to have. Seeing Cheryl and her children always provided him with a much-needed connection to the woman he loved, keeping Julie's memory alive and fresh.

However, his best friend Mark had left California to pursue a job at Michigan State. It had been he who recommended that Don take a look at the job opening in the English department. While Don felt so connected to Cheryl and her family, he couldn't shake the notion that a change of scenery was exactly what he needed.

It had been even harder to leave Cheryl and the kids behind than he had imagined. But he had felt compelled to seize this new opportunity, promising that he would come back as often as he could to visit.

"Don't look so sad," he had told Cheryl on the day of his leaving. "I'll come back so often . . . and you'll be so sick of seeing me, you'll want to throw me out!"

Both of them laughed dispassionately, knowing that it would never happen.

As Don reached the bench on which his young friend sat, he could see the tiny bundle in Cheryl's arms, wrapped in a pink blanket.

"How's Madison today?" he asked, grinning like a love-struck schoolchild as he always did when in the vicinity of Cheryl's new daughter.

"Colicky," was all Cheryl had to say. The dark circles under her bloodshot eyes said the rest.

"So not all is good with girls, after all," Don said with a smile. "Has she been a little too much like her older brother lately?"

Cheryl grunted mildly.

At the moment, the baby was acting the part of a perfect cherub, her eyes closed beneath a little pink bonnet as she napped.

"I don't know. She looks pretty sweet to me," Don said, unable to wipe the grin from his face as he and Cheryl shared a quick hug.

"Yeah, well, you didn't see her last night when she screamed at the top of her lungs from midnight until two. By then, I hadn't slept in twenty-two hours. I thought I was going to pull my hair out."

Don sighed sympathetically. "I don't know how you're even sitting upright."

Cheryl shrugged with resignation. Don knew that she had been through it all before with Matthew.

"By the way, she's 'Maddie' now," she added with a raised eyebrow. "Matthew's begun calling her that. I think it's easier for him to say."

Don chuckled. "Maddie? Hmm . . . I like it."

"Mom would have gotten a kick out of it." Cheryl paused. "She would be so proud of him. He loves his preschool class. He's been making leaps and bounds in reading. He must take after his grandma."

Don laid a hand on Cheryl's shoulder as she wiped her eyes. Every now and then, when Matthew reached a particular milestone, Julie's absence hit hard. Don knew it must be difficult for Cheryl not to have the benefit of her mother's advice and support as she raised her children.

"How was the flight," Cheryl asked, doting over Maddie's blanket as the tiny baby slept.

"Oh, fine," Don said sleepily. "It seemed long, as always."

For the next few minutes, they watched Matthew chasing a little girl around the swings, both of them giggling hysterically. Eventually the girl tripped, braids flying. After a moment of stunned silence, the crying began, and the girl's mother hurried over, murmuring consolation. Cheryl remained still as a Buddha statue, unwilling to risk sacrificing her few moments of tranquility by waking the baby.

Suddenly in the commotion, Matthew finally noticed his eldest friend and went running up, arms outstretched, to greet him. "Grandpa Don!" He hollered through an open-mouthed, toothy grin.

"Why, Matthew!" Don said, returning the ferocious hug as gently as his heart would allow. "My, how you've grown!"

"I know," Matthew said with a chortle. "I'm so very tall now."

Don laughed. "It's great to see you, my boy."

"Grayda see you, too, Grandpa Don. Wanna see me go down the slide?" The boy spoke so quickly that he barely stopped to breathe. He hopped in place as he waited for Don's reply.

"Absolutely!" Don said, pride glinting in his eyes.

Matthew ran off, a light skip in his step as he approached the large plastic structure that supported the slide and an attached jungle gym.

As he waited for his would-be grandson to get into line for the slide, Don recovered from his infatuation with Matthew long enough to remember the questions he wanted to ask Cheryl. "Julie doesn't have a sister nobody knows about, does she," he asked with a joking tone, not expecting an answer.

What he got was a sideways look from Cheryl. "Where's that question coming from?" she asked, narrowing her eyes at him. "You said something about this on the phone, too. Are you trying to hook up with my mother's long-lost twin or something?"

Don laughed and waved his hand dismissively. "Of course not," he said, wondering just how close to the mark she was.

Cheryl said softly, "She's not coming back, Don . . . and no one is ever going to be able to replace her."

"I know, Cheryl. No, no . . . It's just that . . . well, I met some-one who looks remarkably like her. You wouldn't believe it. I thought maybe she was related somehow."

"Really?" Cheryl wrinkled her nose a bit. "Coincidence, I guess."

Don shrugged. "Must be." Despite his instincts to the contrary, the professor knew he might just have to accept that there was no solution to this little mystery.

Just then, Matthew got to the head of the line on the slide. "Grandpa Don!" he yelled in his adorably high-pitched voice. "Washme slide!"

Don turned away from Cheryl's imploring gaze and beamed up at Matthew. "Okay!" he hollered, immediately worried that he may have woken Maddie.

"Weeeeeeeeee!" Matthew squealed as he plummeted down the slide, wheeling his way around the central support post. When he reached the bottom, he stood up straight, raising both his hands above his head. "Didja see me, Grandpa Don?"

The professor chuckled proudly. "I saw you, Matthew," he said in a low tone.

Matthew hopped over next to Don and yelled, "Whadjou say?"

Don laughed as Cheryl shushed her son. "Maddie's sleeping," she said softly.

"Oh," Matthew whispered, bringing a tiny, extended forefinger to his lips, his eyes wide with wonder. "Shhhhhhh!"

Don looked down at his watch solemnly. "I hate to leave so soon, but I have to meet someone back at Whinburg in half an hour."

"Did you rent a car?" Cheryl asked, carefully looking around as she cradled Maddie.

"No," Don said. "I took a cab to your house and then walked here."

"You walked here?" Cheryl said with clear disbelief. "You must be exhausted!"

Don scoffed in jest. "These old legs still have a few miles left in them." He patted his thick, muscular thighs.

"Well, you won't be walking to Whinburg," Cheryl said, standing slowly. "C'mon, we'll drop you off."

Don stood, too, his palms raised. "Are you sure?" he asked. "I could just catch a cab."

"Nonsense," Cheryl said. "You're our guest. And we don't get to see you often enough." She paused as she gathered Maddie's diaper bag. "But we'll be seeing you later today, won't we?"

"Of course," Don said, leaning down to place his hand on Matthew's narrow, delicate shoulder. "If I remember correctly, this young man needs to show me whether he can hit my curveball."

Matthew giggled and nodded. "Yeah, Grandpa Don! And I can frow you a curffball, too."

"That'd be great!" Don smiled and turned his attention back to Cheryl. "Yeah, the meeting won't last long. And then I'll take a cab over to your house. When Tom gets home, I'll take all of you out for pizza."

Matthew tugged on the leg of Don's slacks. "Wiff lotsa cheese and no onions, right Grandpa Don?"

"Right on, Matt. Lots of cheese."

"Are you spending the night with us, too?" Cheryl asked warmly. "We have an extra bed, and it's already made up."

"I already made reservations at a Sleep Inn nearby. I suppose you could convince me to cancel. If . . ."

"If what?"

Don looked sidelong at Cheryl, a sheepish grin on his face. "If you don't stick me with the midnight duties with Maddie."

Cheryl's face lit up. "That's a deal." Then she slung the diaper bag over her shoulder. "I guess we should get going. It takes some time with two car seats, diaper bags, and toys."

"I bet it does," Don said, taking Matthew's hand. "Come on, big boy. I'll give you a horsy back ride to the car. Up we go!" He then carefully lifted a cheering Matthew onto his back, grabbing hold of the boy's legs on either side. He felt Matthew's tiny arms tighten around his neck.

With their things all gathered up together, the four of them went to the freshly paved parking lot adjacent to the playground. It only took Cheryl a few minutes to load everything up. Don opened the door for her to get in the driver's side, then walked around and sat in the passenger seat beside her.

"It is so good to see you again, Don," Cheryl said as he sat down. "Sometimes I wonder who misses you most, the kids or me."

Don placed his hand atop Cheryl's. "The pleasure is mine, Cherrie. Thanks for keeping me in your life."

Cheryl started the car. "Did you give any more thought to that cookout for Maddie?"

"Yeah, I have," Don said thoughtfully. "I still hope to be able to make it. Remind me again when it gets closer, okay?"

"Sure."

"If I come, what would you want me to bring?"

"You don't have to bring anything. You know Tom; we'll have enough leftovers to eat for weeks."

After an all-too-quick drive, the van pulled up to the main staff lot at the familiar old college. Whinburg beckoned like an old friend. Don unbuckled his seatbelt, and then turned around to look at Matthew. "How about a hug, little fella?"

Matthew threw his slender arms around Don's neck. "Will you come over ta play again tonight, Grandpa Don?"

Don eased away from the hug and gently tussled Matthew's hair. "I sure will." Then he leaned down and kissed Madison. He bent to his side and kissed Cheryl last. "I'll see you all later, okay?"

"Thanks, Don," Cheryl said. "We love you."

Don swung open the door, climbed out of his seat, and started walking toward the college. Then a thought occurred to him and he turned back to face the open passenger window of Cheryl's van.

"Ah, by the way," he said, "would it be okay with you guys if I brought a friend with me to the cookout . . . if she can come?"

Cheryl looked puzzled at first. Then her face glazed over with understanding. "Of course," she said. "Any friend of yours is always welcome here."

Don smiled and nodded, then started to walk away again. Just before he reached the front entrance to the red-brick Whinburg faculty building, he turned and waved goodbye. He felt so blessed to have this little family in his life.

Chapter Seven

Don and Mark had been working most of the morning on Don's four-passenger Cessna. The professor had always wanted a plane, and had finally given in to his whims after years of yearning. The day had been hot, and the heat was radiating from the walls of the metal hangar. Since there was no air conditioner, Don had asked Mark to open the overhead window, hoping to get some fresh air. The task called for Mark to go outside and climb a ladder along the north façade of the hangar and then crank open the window with a long, heavy iron rod.

Don took the opportunity to enjoy the moment alone. He wrung his greasy hands with an equally greasy dish towel. The towel had once been pristinely white and soft, but now appeared as a brownish ball of mess that vaguely resembled a towel.

"Yeah, that's no job for an old man," Mark hollered as he walked back in through the massive door of the hangar. "Good thing you sent me out there. That rod's heavy."

Don just shook his head genially. From his kneeling position, he looked up at his old friend, who wore a smile of admiration as his blue eyes traced over the freshly polished fuselage of the plane. Don knew his friend well enough to know what was on his mind. Buying and rebuilding this increasingly beautiful plane was certainly a valued hobby, but nothing would thrill his friend more than finally getting it up in the air. Mark had flown planes in Desert Storm, and Don knew that he would be eager to make his next journey into the skies a far more pleasant one.

"There you have it," Mark said, gazing at the exposed portion of the engine. "Just a few more wires to hook up, and then we can take your baby up and see what it does in the air."

Don smiled and wiped a sweaty forearm across his sweaty brow. Despite his attempts with the towel, his hands remained caked in grease.

Mark shoved both hands into the front pockets of his jeans. "Have you decided who's going up with you when you take it up for the first time?" A hint of hopefulness provided a clear current in his voice.

Don furrowed his brow. "What kind of friend would I be if I didn't allow you the honors?"

"I never dreamed of doing something like this," Mark said, beaming. "Overhauling a single-engine plane . . . doing the maintenance."

Don stood. "Yeah," he said, "and who knew it would take us such a long time?"

Mark laughed amicably, rocking back and forth on the balls of his feet, his hands still crammed into his pockets. "We should be right on time for that air show."

"Now, now," Don said, raising his hand as if to slow Mark's pace. "Let's not put the cart before the horse. We've still got to take a look at some of these engine mounts. They're a little old for my taste. And that piston's not going to replace itself."

Mark waved his hand dismissively. "Aw, the piston's fine."

"Yeah, tell me that when we hear sputtering once we're in the air." Don's eyes lit with the camaraderie of the moment. "You're just overanxious, my friend."

Mark laced his hands behind his head, like he was so apt to do. His slender arms formed perfect triangles to either side of his head. "That's because this air show is going to be amazing," he said. "Traverse City, old man! One of the best shows ever, I hear."

Don chuckled, shaking his head.

"Blue angels, the F-15C Eagle, and the E-2C Hawkeye. You know, that one's fighting in Iraq right now."

"If we can get the piston replaced . . ." Don said slowly.

"C'mon, Don," Mark paced away as though frustrated. His friend knew that it was all just an act. "We've had a long summer at school. We could both use some time away before the fall semester."

Don kept his tone noncommittal. "I'll think about it." Then he took a few steps back, standing to the side of the wing opposite from Mark. "She sure looks nice."

"She," Mark asked with a prodding grin.

Don knew his friend was well aware that he was talking about the plane, but still, he had come to expect getting picked on. "My plane," he said. "When you stop to think about it, this plane is forty years old. For a woman in her forties, she sure looks great."

"Most of the women I know don't hold up that well after forty years," Mark chimed in as he walked around the long wing to stand next to his friend.

Don, used to his friend's silly and somewhat chauvinistic jokes, just ignored the comment. "Did you ever think we'd figure out where all those wires were supposed to go?" He pointed vaguely at the wiry mess jutting out from beside the exposed portion of the engine.

"I still can't figure out how we did it."

"Or how we managed to contort our hands into all those tight places," Don reminisced. "There were times I thought my hands would be stuck in there forever."

Mark nodded proudly.

"I think we owe ourselves a pat on the back," Don said.

Mark patted his friend on the back of the shoulder. "There," he said, "how's that?"

Don smiled, staring dreamily into the distance. His breathing slowed and became more methodical.

"So, what about that air show?" Mark asked, absently bending down to pick up the heavy pair of pliers Don had been using only minutes before. "I need to get word to Mike as soon as possible."

Don failed to hear his friend. His mind had drifted off to far gentler places than this. Still, he offered a response as best he could. "Yeah, sounds good." The hesitation in his voice was clear.

Mark threw the pliers down on the floor in obvious frustration. It startled Don out of his reverie. "What sounds good?" Mark asked, almost angrily. "You're not even listening to me."

Don's face sank knowingly. He'd been caught red-handed.

"What's going on, my friend?" Mark continued. "You've been lost in space for days. You think I wouldn't notice?"

Don sighed and reached down to pick up the discarded pliers. He fiddled with them, holding one arm of the tool in his hand and then rocking it back, tossing the other arm up in the air and then waiting for it to crash down to its closing point. "I'm okay, Mark," he said, still flicking the pliers open and closed. "I just have a lot on my mind."

Mark reached out and placed his palm over the pliers in Don's hand, preventing the fidgeting from continuing. "A lot by the name of Jill, maybe," he said with a smile. "You're thinking about that Jill chick, aren't you?"

Don averted his eyes. "Could be." He'd hoped that visiting Cheryl during his brief trip to California might bring some sort of closure – or a little relief, at least – from the thoughts of Julie that kept haunting him, and his growing obsession with Jill. He hadn't really expected Cheryl to shed any light on the amazing resemblance between Jill and Julie. But he'd thought that being with Cheryl and her children, if even for a short time, would make him realize that the resemblance had been merely a figment of his imagination, after all. There was no such luck.

"Damn it, Don," Mark said, grasping his friend at the shoulder, near the base of his neck. "We've been friends for a long time and been through a lot together. Why the big secret now?"

"There's really no secret," Don said distantly. "There's not much to talk about, actually . . . that's the problem." Don picked up the dirty rag from the floor and attempted once again to clear his fingers of oil. It was no use.

"You, my friend, are being too hard on yourself."

Don threw the rag to the floor. "See, that's just it," he said, his arms slightly extended, palms to the sky. "I really like Jill. Sometimes, I get the feeling she likes me, too. But, Mark, I'm scared to death. I mean, it's been years since I've truly dated. I don't even know where to begin."

Mark frowned suddenly. "This isn't really about Jill, is it?" he asked. "It's about Emily and Julie. You're afraid they wouldn't approve."

Don sighed again.

"Look, man, you know as well as I do that neither Emily nor Julie would ever want you to spend the rest of your life alone. You've told me time and again that they always put your happiness before their own."

"I know . . . it's just that . . ."

Mark slapped the back of his hand lightly against Don's barrel-like chest. "It's just nothing," he said playfully. "If you ask me, you're long overdue for a little romance. If Jill doesn't work out, there are plenty of women out there for you. If you keep comparing them to Julie, you'll never get anywhere."

Don's face flushed slightly. *If only Mark could appreciate the irony in that,* he thought. "I know, I know," he repeated. "It's just that . . ." All at once, he stopped as if out of breath. He couldn't bring himself to tell Mark about Jill's resemblance to his departed love. Mark's reaction to such a revelation would be predictable – and certainly wouldn't be favorable. "I guess I just don't know how to date," he said finally. "It's been too long."

Mark chuckled and rolled his eyes. "For God's sake, Don, just ask her out," he said. "What's the worst that could happen?"

She could say yes, Don thought. *Or I could accidentally call her "Julie." Or I could fall in love with her and then find out she's got a year to live . . .* "I guess you're right," he said eventually, turning to his tattered jeans as a source to clean his hands. He ran his greasy palms over the rough fabric and actually felt as though they were a bit cleaner this time.

"Of course I'm right," Mark said briskly. But when he spoke again, his voice was much gentler. "Don, I know you've had a rough time. I won't pretend to know how it feels to lose someone like that, but if anyone deserves to be happy, you do."

Don smiled, surprised by this unexpected moment of affection from his old friend. "Thanks," he said, turning back to face the plane.

Don heard the sound of his friend clapping his hands together, as if cleaning them off. "You think we should wrap it up here and call it a day?" Mark asked. His voice sounded uncomfortable and guarded. "I've got some yard work to finish up before dark. It's supposed to rain tomorrow."

"Sounds good to me," Don said, bending down to begin the task of picking up all the tools from the dusty, concrete floor and returning them to the massive red metal box in the northwest corner of the hangar. "Thanks again for your help on the plane . . . and for the advice." He glanced over to his friend and sensed that Mark could somehow read his deepest feelings.

As Don finished picking up the tools, Mark returned outside to close the overhead window he had just opened. By the time Don had finished and walked outside, Mark was scaling back down the ladder. Together, they walked across the airstrip and out to the small parking lot. Before parting, they agreed to talk the next day about taking the trip to Traverse City.

～～

On the way home from the hangar, Don found himself turning down a winding road he had found not too long after moving to the area. After a ten-minute drive through woods, past some secluded homes, he came into a clearing, where he saw a lighthouse on the edge of the shimmering waters of Lake Michigan. The clouds were blowing off to the north now, revealing a brilliant orange sun that lit up their undersides and threw ripples of color across the sky. This lighthouse, with the now-placid lake stretching out before it, was truly a sight to behold.

As he gazed upon the structure and reflected on the joys and tragedies of his life's path, he knew in his heart that Julie would have encouraged him to take chances and make the most of every minute he had. If that meant pursuing a relationship with Jill, the professor realized that he would encounter unknowns as well as risks, even within himself. Still, whatever cautious predisposition gripped him, he could not ignore the fact that he thought about Jill night and day. Something, he realized, would have to be done.

The sun dwindled to a tiny pinpoint of light and then sank behind the silhouettes of distant trees circling the lake. Don took a deep breath of the clean air and decided that he would put out of his mind all thoughts of Jill's resemblance to Julie. Life was too short to second-guess his own feelings and deny himself a chance at happiness.

Chapter Eight

The next morning, when Don opened the door to the Open Book, he was overwhelmed by the bustling sound of the many patrons within. The café at the opposite end of the store hummed with conversation. As he approached, he noticed that all the reading chairs in each aisle were taken.

He then looked ahead to the checkout counter. His heart skipped a beat when he saw Jill. The beautiful younger woman was ringing up the purchases of an elderly customer with tightly permed silver-gray hair. Jill was smiling and nodding politely as Don approached. She did not notice her suitor, however, as she seemed locked in a conversation with her elderly patron.

"Oh, you should have heard that girl play Vivaldi," the old woman said.

"Vivaldi?" Jill said with a gasping smile. For a moment, she placed her hand over her heart. "That's pretty complex. How old did you say your granddaughter is?"

"Seven!" the proud patron said with a slow nod. "Can you believe it?"

Jill just laughed and shook her head in an impressed sort of way. As she did, her eye caught Don, which, to the professor's delight, caused her smile to grow wider.

Don nodded his silent greeting before turning his attention to the book displays. His powerful jaw clenched as his nerves tensed. *What on earth am I going to say to her,* he wondered almost audibly? He caught his lips moving and worried for a moment that he may have actually voiced his trepidation. To save face, he wandered over to the one place he knew he'd never see anyone who would trap him in a long conversation: the children's section. As it was a small room off to the left side of the checkout counter, Don took the opportunity in passing Jill to smile. Jill returned the smile with a roll of the eyes that said, *enough about piano recitals already, lady.*

Don chuckled inwardly and then stepped into the children's section. The little half-room was embellished with fanciful, brightly colored decorations, toys, and stuffed animals. The shelves, too, were smaller and shorter to accommodate tinier hands and diminutive reach.

Before he could even begin searching through the books, he heard the silver bells on the front door jingling, which suggested to him that the elderly patron had finally left. He could finally enjoy a moment alone with Jill. So, he edged his way back out of the children's section and strode back over to the counter, where he lingered for a moment, admiring Jill's beauty and remarkable resemblance to Julie. She was wearing her hair up, and it lent her a look of careful, striking intelligence.

"Uh, excuse me," Jill said, waving her hand in front of her face. "Professor? Do I have a horn growing out of the middle of my head or something?"

Don shook himself back to the present and laughed.

"You look as if you've seen a ghost," Jill added with a smile.

"I'm sorry if I was staring," Don said distantly. He cast his sorrowful eyes down and pressed his chin against his neck. In this light, the curved scar just above his eye paled to a pure white against his forehead. "I was just in deep thought, I guess."

Jill cocked her head to one side playfully. "Not to worry," she said. "I get caught up like that sometimes, too."

Don thrust his hands into his front pockets, which caused the tails of his plaid suit jacket to jut out at each side.

"So," Jill said, breaking the awkward silence, "what can I do for you today?"

"Oh yes," Don said, lightening up considerably. "I'm looking for a book for a little boy in my life. He's having a birthday soon, so I want to get him something special."

"Is this young man your son?" Jill asked, her eyebrows arched in a quizzical sort of way.

"No, I don't have a son." Don thought suddenly about Abby's porcelain-like face. "Never did."

Jill frowned sympathetically, "A nephew, perhaps?"

"No, not a nephew, either," Don said, rocking back onto his heels and looking up at the arched ceiling for a moment. The plaster was peeling at the corners, near the latticework, he noticed. He then wondered why he would notice such a thing at a moment as tense as this. "Matthew is the son of a . . . a friend . . . just a friend." The tone of his voice was intentionally vague. "He's quite the young man. Almost four, I believe. I'm trying to help his mother put together a library that will account for years of bedtime stories."

"That's wonderful!" Jill said, the mauve of her cheeks lighting up. She turned and started walking toward the children's section, motioning pleasantly back over her shoulder for Don to follow.

The professor obliged.

"Here are a couple of my favorites," Jill said, handing her older companion a short stack of three books. One had a glossy cover that featured a picture of a lion. Another was bound in the familiar old cardboard of earlier generations of children's literature. Its cover had been decorated with a train of the deepest and liveliest blue. The third was small and fat, its entirety fitting in the palm of Don's hand. He recognized none of the titles or authors, a fact that he found both strange and compelling.

Jill first pointed out the book with the glossy cover, which she opened as Don held it in his flattened left palm. Her sinewy hands turned the pages just a few inches in front of him. The professor's heart raced.

"This is one of my favorites," Jill said, "not only because it's so imaginative, but just look at these lustrous illustrations!"

Don nodded, focusing more on Jill's delicate fingers as they traced across the page than on the page itself. He longed to hold this hand in his own. He longed to weave his own fingers between hers.

"Look at this lion," she said, pointing excitedly as she finished turning the page. "See how he almost reaches out of the book and pulls you back into that toy box with him?"

"Yes," Don said as he turned toward Jill with an admiring smile. "Marvelous."

Jill looked up at the professor, her soft face suddenly mere inches from his chin. She blushed and backed away slightly, the otherwise tense muscles at the base of her neck relaxing as she sighed.

Don turned his attention to the book, running his rough, slightly grease-stained hands over the page in exactly the same way Jill had just done. "No, I've never seen anything quite like this," he said. "What age do you think a child would need to be to enjoy this book?"

"Oh, I've seen kids from two years all the way up to seven or eight years reading this book. It was chosen by Edison School, in fact, as recommended reading for the second and third grade students."

"Sold!" Don said with a wry grin. "Now how about these?"

Standing close to each other, Don and Jill looked at the other two books in Don's right hand, and then inspected others. Jill seemed to have a way of making each one come alive, and it was difficult for the professor to choose only a few.

"I never realized there were so many children's books," Don said. "I thought this would be an easy task, but I can see where this might take days."

"I'm sure your young friend would like almost any of these in this section," Jill said.

Suddenly, a soft young voice came drifting in from the check-out counter. "Jill!" it said. "I'm here."

At the call, Jill turned her body but not her gaze away from Don. She extended her forefinger in the air as she walked slowly toward the counter. "You know, you can buy a few, and if your young friend already has any of them . . . or if you find he doesn't like them . . . you can always bring them back and exchange them."

"In that case," Don said with a kindly expression that seemed as if it wanted to reach out and hold Jill in place, "I'd better make sure I get one or two that he already has . . . that way, I'll have an excuse to come back and bother you again."

Jill stopped in her tracks and turned back to face Don. "Bother me again?" she asked curiously. "When did you bother me the first time?"

Don smiled. "Just a figure of speech." Then he summoned up all the courage he had within him and looked Jill straight into her beautiful, frolicking brown eyes. "I don't mean to sound forward . . . but actually, I was wondering if . . . well . . ." Don's words faded. He took his handkerchief out of his suit jacket and wiped the sweat from his forehead. This had been so easy, so natural with Julie. *Why should it be any different now?*

Right then, there was then the sound of a phone ringing. Shortly, it was broken by the soft young voice from the direction of the counter. "Jill! You've got a call."

"Just a minute, Don," Jill said. "I've got to take this. But we'll continue when I get back." Jill then shuffled quickly out of the room.

Don rifled through the small pile of books he and Jill had created, settling on four of them to take to Matthew. For the moment, it was all he could do to focus on anything but the words he would use to ask the beautiful bookstore proprietor to dinner.

He gathered up the books, holding them to his chest with his forearm, and carried them to the counter. Jill had apparently taken the call in the tearoom, because the only person at the counter was a young lady who looked strangely familiar. She had wispy, rather thin blonde hair that she had pulled back into a ponytail. Her horn-rimmed glasses lent her that bookish sort of look. Her slight chin and pale complexion did little to combat the assumption that this young woman, here in this bookstore, was well within her element.

As Don set the books on the counter – which was cluttered with fliers about upcoming sales, poetry readings, and lecture series – he noticed the young woman smiling up at him in an oddly friendly sort of way. "Correct me if I'm wrong," he said, suddenly making the connection, "but aren't you one of my creative writing students?"

"Yes I am, Dr. Lipton," she chirped. "My name is MacKenzie. I have you in the mornings on Mondays and Wednesdays. Modern Creative Writing." She blushed and glanced down, her eyelids fluttering constantly. "I suppose if I tell you that I enjoy the class, you'll think I'm fishing for an A."

Don laughed to himself. The poor girl looked almost frightened. "Not at all. What do you like about the class? The reading or writing?"

"Both," MacKenzie said with a strange and barely perceptible little quiver. "I love to read, and hope to become an author someday."

Don nodded respectfully. "Good answer!" He craned his neck to see if he could see over the tall counter at the head of the tearoom, hoping to catch a glance of Jill. "Do you like working here . . . for Jill?"

The young lady perked up. "Love it!" she said. "Love her. She's so much fun to work for. She keeps us busy, though."

Don smiled dreamily as he thought about working with Jill. *It would be fun*, he realized. In the process, almost without noticing, he had taken out his debit card and paid for the stack of books. He snapped out of his reverie the moment MacKenzie handed him his receipt.

"Two more books, and you get five dollars off the next one you buy," she said in a sing-songy sort of way.

"Now *that's* a deal."

Don glanced quickly to the tearoom once again. At that moment, Jill stood, revealing herself over the tall countertop, the phone still pressed to her ear. It would seem strange now, the professor realized, to linger in the store until she finished speaking. He felt compelled to leave. *But without saying goodbye . . .* His heart ached. Yet there was no denying the sense of relief he gleaned from the realization that he would not have to ask her out today. He felt like a teenager again.

"Well, good-day," Don said, turning and taking the bag of books that MacKenzie was holding aloft over the counter for him. "Thank you for ringing me up."

"No problem," MacKenzie said with an awkward little nod. "See you in class."

"Yes, yes," Don said absently as he turned. His eyes lingered on the tearoom counter. "Take care."

Don left through the jingling front door and climbed into his car. He started the engine, and almost without thinking, drove several blocks away from the store. Then it hit him. *Do it, old man! You'll never find a better opportunity than this one.* He stomped on the brake pedal and then pulled a U-turn. Determined as ever, he wheeled back over to the store.

When he walked back in, his heart fluttered at the sight of Jill alone at the counter.

"Forget something?" Jill asked, looking puzzled.

Don found himself fidgeting, still holding onto the bag full of books, for some reason. *Why didn't I just leave these in the car,* he chided himself. "Well, actually . . . yes . . . sort of." He stumbled with his words like a flustered schoolboy. A quick glance at Jill informed that she was looking rather perplexed. "I . . . ah . . . I forgot to ask you if you would like to join me for dinner later this evening. You must be hungry after working all day, and I just thought it might be nice if we ate together." Immediately, he hated himself for not having something more poetic – or at least intelligible – to say. *You're an author, for godsakes.*

Jill pressed her palm to her chest, just above her heart. She seemed momentarily short of breath as her cheeks flushed. To the professor's delight, a wide smile briefly crossed her face. But then, without warning or reason – and much to his dismay – the younger woman seemed to become completely preoccupied. A look of reserved consternation replaced her beautiful smile.

"No, I'm sorry," she said quickly, softly. "I really can't . . . I can't go with you tonight." There was a long, heartbreaking pause as Jill looked to be searching for her next words. "I have plans."

Don nodded in embarrassment – which he tried and failed to hide.

"Well," Jill continued, "what I'm trying to say is that I've had a long day, and I plan to go home and retire early tonight."

Don, crestfallen and confused, nodded a second time before turning and walking out of the bookstore, never looking back. As he stepped outside, he felt all energy leave him, and he slumped into the familiar driver's seat of his car.

How could this be he asked himself. *How could I have misread her so completely?* It was just like he had told Mark; an old man out of the dating scene too long . . . he just didn't know what to do. Clearly, he had done something wrong, assumed too much, *asked* too much. Apparently he wasn't even competent enough to tell if a woman liked him or not.

His spirit crushed, Don started the car and drove away.

Chapter Nine

Don shoved the pile of essays into his satchel, snapped it shut, and followed the last student out of his classroom. Despite his otherwise disconcerting morning, today had been a good day in World Literature. Several students had even answered his questions about the reading – correctly! Over the past few years, he had actually begun to enjoy encouraging his students and fanning the sparks of enthusiasm when he saw them. Some time after meeting Julie, he had realized that being the most hated instructor on campus no longer brought him any satisfaction. He used to enjoy his reputation as a fire-eater, even as a very rude person. He had liked the feeling of power it granted him to see fear in his students' eyes. But that, like so many other things, was part of his past now.

He had planned on grading papers at lunch to make up for the time he hoped to spend with Jill, but sadly, it now looked like he would have as much time to himself as he needed that evening.

He recalled momentarily his morning conversation with Mark. He had just been turned down by Jill, and he wasn't sure if Mark was the best or worst person to run into in the lobby at that moment.

"Don't worry about that," Mark said dismissively. "Don't you remember how your relationship with Julie got started?"

Don had looked blankly back at his friend.

"You were a jerk, and she was determined to prove you wrong."

Don shook his head now, just as he had when talking to Mark. The words rang as true in his head now as they had several hours earlier.

"The two of you came together in spite of it all," Mark had said with a reassuring grin. "You came to love each other despite all those obstacles. I mean, if you could handle that, surely you can handle a little bump in the road with this Jill."

"I'm not so sure," Don had said. And he still wasn't sure. He only knew that his heart burned and he felt empty inside.

He reached the elevator, planning to take it up to his third-floor office, where he would drop off his satchel at his desk and pick up his newspaper, which he would read at lunch. Much to his surprise, when the elevator doors opened, he nearly ran into Jill . . .

"Well," Don said, unable to mask his delight, "I didn't expect to see *you* here."

Jill, clearly flustered, straightened her smart denim skirt.

"What brings you here this afternoon?" Don continued. "Do you have another list of books for me?"

"No," Jill said curtly. After a short, blushing pause, she added, "No, I'm here for a personal reason this time."

"I see," the professor said in a businesslike way. "Perhaps I can help you find somebody. Which way are you heading?"

"I was going to your office. I was coming to talk to you . . . but I can see that you're leaving, so . . . well . . . can you find time for me later?"

Don suddenly felt his confidence surge back within him. Here he was now, in a position of power, a familiar position of power, and it brought him right back to Julie and their tender, unabashed moment at the pond. "No time like the present," he said, motioning back into the still-open elevator. "Hop on in here with me and we can go back up to my office and chat for a bit, if you like."

"Sure," Jill said meekly. "I promise I won't stay. I just wanted to clear something up with you."

The elevator door opened, and the two walked in silence to Don's office. He unlocked the door and pushed it open. He then motioned for Jill to step inside ahead of him. "Have a seat," he said warmly, flicking on the light switch as he followed her in.

"No," Jill said. "I really don't want to bother you long. I just have something I want to get off my chest."

Don walked up to Jill, standing a little closer to her than he probably should have. He didn't want to seem imposing, but something about her refused to allow him to keep his distance.

"Yes?"

Jill shook her head sadly. "I just feel like I owe you an apology for turning you down so coldly this morning."

Don placed a hand on each of Jill's slight shoulders. "Think nothing of it," he said. "I understand."

Jill squinted her eyes. "No, I don't think you do," she said. "It's just that I have some personal things going on that are bothering me. You took me by surprise when you asked."

Don made a motion to quiet Jill, but she pressed on.

"I really did have plans for tonight," she said apologetically, leaning closer to the professor, "but I should have at least explained my answer to you."

"That's okay." Don smiled. A little of his gentle, teasing sense came bubbling to the surface. "You're not the first lady to break my heart, you know."

Jill suddenly turned her back to her companion. "Please," she said just above a whisper, "let me assure you that that wasn't my intention at all."

Don returned his hands to Jill's shoulders, and he began to softly and reassuringly run his hands up and down the sides of her arms.

"It's just that . . ." Jill continued, taking a deep breath. "I would like to take you up on your offer."

Don's heart soared.

Jill turned to face him once more. "I just can't meet with you tonight. Would you like to join me for lunch right now? Do you have time to eat with me here?"

Don smiled tenderly. He wondered if she had any clue how happy this unexpected development had made him. "That sounds like a great idea. My next class, which would have been my first of the afternoon, completed their work early last week. So I gave them a free day to catch up on their other classes."

Jill's eyes twinkled slightly. "That was kind of you."

"I tend to be that way once in a while. It's a distinct change from the character I used to be."

The younger woman smiled. "What's that?"

His grin was just short of being silly. "I was known as the ogre of the campus."

~~~

A little later, the two were back at ground level, seated across from each other in the cafeteria in the neighboring building. They had spent a pleasant lunch hour discussing everything from politics to campus gossip.

"I'm so happy I bumped into you," Jill said almost lyrically. "A few minutes later, and we might have missed each other."

Don smiled as she placed her hand atop his. He felt the warmth of her fingertips trace against the backs of his own fingers, and he found himself swimming in her deep brown eyes.

And this would only be the beginning. The pleasant lunch would lead to a later invitation to dinner – which she would freely and gladly accept. The dinner, in turn, would be even more light-hearted and endearing, as the two could enjoy each other's company without time constraints, and their conversation could carry compellingly, skirting inhibitions, fueled by a fine wine that Don would order.

Over the course of the next few weeks, in fact, Don and Jill would spent a great deal of time together, going on picnics by the lake and taking in a couple of shows at the theater. With each passing day, both seemed more eager to see one another.

~~~

One day, at a surprise lunch that Don had arranged for Jill, the professor gazed upon his comely guest and asked her a question he had been holding off for some time.

"By the way," he said, "do you like to cook out?"

Jill's eyes lit against the steadily flickering candlelight resting on the white tablecloth in front of her. Her soft facial features were warmed additionally by the sunlight beaming through the large picture window at the head of the rather swanky restaurant. She had remarked at how Don need not spend so much on lunch, but then, there was no convincing him once his mind was made up on food.

"Yes," Jill said. "I love a good hamburger or steak cooked on the grill."

Don smiled appreciatively. "Yeah, I like to cook on a grill when I find time, too. I think cooking on wood is the best, and I love to get together with people to eat."

"Mmmm," Jill said, taking a bite of her salad.

Don found himself unsure of whether the coo was for the salad or for the idea of wood grilling. He cared little, however, as the only thought now on his mind was how to best steer the conversation into an invitation to California. He decided to go with the indirect approach. "I don't suppose you would consider joining me for a barbecue at a close friend's house in two weeks?"

Jill wiped a bit of errant salad dressing from her lips. She had ordered the honey mustard, which was a deeply brownish yellow against the pink of her lips. "I can't see why not."

He put on a silly grin. "The catch is that it's on September fifth in California, so we would have to fly."

Taken aback, she paused, unable to hold eye contact with him. Her answer sounded to Don like an excuse. "Oh, that sounds like fun," she said. "But, Don, I'm scared to death of planes."

Don's look drifted from one of mild consternation to one of soft appeasement. "Oh well," he said soothingly. "Maybe if we'd made plans earlier, we could have driven out together." Then, almost childlike, he shined his eyes up at Jill and begged the unexpected question. "What do you think of that idea?"

Jill cocked her head to the side. "California's a good distance away, isn't it? I mean, how long would it take?" Without giving Don time to answer, she added breathlessly, "I can't close the store, though." Then she brought her forefinger thoughtfully to the side of her marvelously prominent cheekbone. "But I have a few friends who know how to run it, and they owe me!"

Don simply watched in admiration as Jill worked things out in her mind audibly. Despite the fact that he still hardly knew her, he had already grown familiar with this charming quality of hers. He rested his elbow upon the table, and in turn, his powerful chin upon the meat of his hand. His face glowed with innocent wonder.

"One lady I know used to own a bookstore," Jill continued. "She comes in to see me a few times a week, trying to give me advice and help with little things. She just might want a job for a short time." After locking eyes with Don, her expression became imploring. "Who is this friend, anyhow? Is she a lady?"

Don smiled.

"She is a lady, then. Do you think she would mind having you bringing another woman along?"

Don laughed. "No, no, you've got it all wrong. Cheryl's a younger lady, and she is married to a man named Tom. She is, well, she's like a daughter to me."

Jill furrowed her brow.

"Uh," Don stammered, "I used to know her mother fairly well . . . and because of that . . . Cheryl and I became close, too. In fact, you remember those children's books I bought a couple weeks ago?"

Jill nodded, still looking adorably confused.

"Well, they were for her little boy. Matthew is his name. And the cookout is in part in celebration of her daughter Madison's first birthday."

Jill rested both of her hands flat against the table, flanking her plate and half-eaten salad. "Are you sure this Cheryl wouldn't mind your bringing me along?"

Don nodded eagerly, his full eyebrows raised. "Almost sure . . . But I'll call her tomorrow just to confirm it." He then looked relieved. "So does that mean you'd like to go with me?"

Jill hesitated for a moment. The rapid movement of her eyes suggested that she was mulling over a wide range of emotion. Eventually, she turned her gaze to him, and it was an endearing one, to be certain. "Sure," she said. "You can count me in."

"Excellent!" Don leaned back in his chair and crossed his arms in front of his chest.

"Let me know what Cheryl says, though," Jill said, turning her attention back to her salad. "And ask her what I can bring along for the meal."

"I'll do that," Don said, diving into his soup as if he had just now noticed its presence. After a few quick bites, he checked his watch. "Oh my," he said. "We may have to pack up the main course, I'm afraid. It's already going on two."

Jill quickly checked her own watch, a band of solid silvery metal that peaked into a narrow little quartz face. "Oh," she said. "You're right. I have to get back to the store."

Don placed his fingers delicately against the back of Jill's free hand, which still rested palm-down on the table. "I hate to leave such enjoyable conversation," he said with a smile.

Jill blushed slightly. "I know," she said. "Me, too." She patted Don's arm affectionately. "I really must go, though. MacKenzie has class in a few minutes. She's probably ready to kill me."

"Not to worry," Don said. "I'll have the waiter box up your meal. Maybe I can bring it by the store later this afternoon."

Jill smiled and whispered her thanks as she gracefully stood and headed toward the door.

As he watched her stroll out into the sunshine over the parking lot, her skirt swirling around her knees, Don suddenly realized that inviting her to Cheryl's family barbecue might not have been such a good idea. He had actually forgotten, for the time, her remarkable resemblance to Julie. In the short time he had known her, she had captivated him with her confidence, engaging manner, and lilting laugh – a laugh that, to him, was as melodious as church bells.

But how would Cheryl and her family react when Don pulled into the driveway with Julie's veritable twin? Would they think it all some cruel joke? And how would Jill react upon seeing the many framed pictures of Julie in the Cheryl and Tom's household? Would she feel she was merely the replacement to a treasured past?

A sick feeling quickly replaced the genuine euphoria he had built on the back of his hour with Jill. He had drifted onto an uncertain path, with no way of knowing where it would lead.

Chapter Ten

Don pulled into Jill's driveway just as the sun was coming up. After a quick jaunt up the stone walkway leading to her blue front door, he was just reaching for the brass knocker when Jill swung the door open. She stood before him in white shorts and a modest blue tank top. Even though it promised to be a hot summer day, she definitely wasn't the type to wear anything too revealing – and that was yet another thing Don found endearing about the woman. Despite her often progressive viewpoints, she seemed almost old-fashioned in dress, and there just weren't too many women like her left in the world, as far as Don was concerned.

Even this early in the morning, her eyes were bright.

"I hope I didn't wake you up," Don said.

Jill shook her head. "Are you kidding? I've been up for an hour, finishing my packing." She stepped aside so Don could come in.

As the professor set foot on the freshly polished hardwood flooring of the foyer, he immediately saw the three hard-cased, matching, oversized suitcases neatly lined up on the edge of the Berber carpet in the living room.

Jill pointed apologetically. "That one's the heaviest," she said. "Would you mind carrying it for me? I can handle the other two."

Without a word, Don walked over and picked up two of the suitcases. Of course, he had no intention of letting Jill carry any of the bags. He grimaced as he felt the bag's full weight tug against his arm. "What do you have in here" he joked. "Bricks?"

Jill simply laughed. He could never get enough of that sound. "Just be thankful I decided to pack light," she quipped. "I hope there's enough room in the car with all of your stuff, too."

In the driveway, Don set the lighter suitcase down and fished through his pockets for the remote to his car. He then pressed a button and waited for the trunk to pop open. He felt Jill hot on his heels as he turned the corner around the back of his car and looked down into the trunk with a smile. In the corner was a small duffel bag, stowed away neatly in the spacious trunk. "I don't think we have to worry about space," he said, winking at Jill.

Jill blushed and shook her head. Then she watched intently as Don eased her massive suitcases into the fold.

~~~

The traffic ran surprisingly light as the two road-trippers headed toward the interstate. Don had planned on stopping at a doughnut shop to get some breakfast and coffee, but Jill had come well prepared. She had made fresh brewed coffee, which she brought along in travel mugs, and she also offered Don first choice from the half-dozen homemade muffins she'd brought along in a pink cardboard box. She held the box in front of Don, just beside the steering wheel, and watched, playfully open-mouthed, as he selected the one brimming with blueberries.

Don carefully ate a portion of the muffin as he took the ramp onto the highway, heading west. After his second bite, he turned sidelong to her and said, "You baked these yourself?"

Jill nodded proudly. "They're pretty popular at my store. What do you think?"

Quickly finishing off the rest of the muffin and licking his lips, Don said, "I think you're in the wrong business. You could make a lot more money selling these than selling books."

Jill took a sip from her travel mug and carefully placed it back in the cup holder. "Nah," she said. "Books are so much more interesting than muffins." She turned her head to look at the scenery roaring by out the window. "But I'm glad you like them."

Don concentrated on the road. The rising sun was behind them now, and the early morning traffic on the highway was picking up. A giant tractor-trailer came out of nowhere and slipped into the lane only a few feet in front of Don's car. Don gave a sharp blast of his horn.

"What a jerk," Jill said, picking up her travel mug once more.

Don pointed his hand at his own chest. "For laying on the horn?"

Jill laughed so hard she had to put her coffee down so she wouldn't spill it. "No, silly. I'm talking about the trucker that just cut you off."

Now it was Don who was laughing. "Oh, okay. I get it now. I was worried there for a second."

With a smile playing across her lips, Jill said, "It almost sounds like you're used to people calling you that."

"What? A jerk?"

Jill nodded.

Don had to think for a moment before responding. "Well, I'm not really used to being called a jerk. I don't think anybody gets used to that. Maybe 'cranky,' I guess. But in any case, not so much anymore. I think I've changed quite a bit over the past few years."

"Was there something wrong with the old Don?"

There was a long answer he could give for that one, but he wasn't yet prepared to give it. He simply shrugged and then adeptly shifted the conversation by pointing his open hand at the truck still dangerously close to his hood. "I just don't understand all this rushing around that people do these days. What's the big hurry?"

Jill shook her head thoughtfully. Don could see it out of the corner of his eye.

"I think maybe I was born a century too late," the professor said. "It would have been nice to have lived in a quieter era, when the pace of life wasn't so hectic."

Jill's eyes widened as she gazed at him. "You must have read my mind. I was thinking the same thing."

Don nodded, as if to confirm they were indeed on the same wavelength. "I guess that's why we both love books so much. They have the power to take us back there."

A long conversation about books and literature ensued, lasting until late afternoon, when they crossed into Iowa. The environment grew increasingly rural the further they traveled. The glass-lined corporate buildings that dotted the interstate in northern Illinois gave way to white-paneled farmhouses and miles and miles of waving, yellowing corn. Don marveled at how brittle the cornstalks appeared and wondered when it would be time to harvest.

Suddenly, the professor's stomach began to grumble. "Do you want to take a chance that there might be a halfway decent restaurant off one of these exits?" he asked.

Jill shifted in her seat. "Yes, let's," she said. "I'm starving."

"I just hope there's something other than fast food out in the middle of these cornfields."

"Mmmm, me too."

"Well," Don said with a slow turn of the wheel, "there's only one way to find out. Let's go exploring."

When they reached the end of the exit, at first they saw nothing but more of the endless fields. "Not much for scenery around here," Don said.

Jill smiled. "Depends on your definition of scenery," she offered. "I'm sure many people find this spot beautiful."

Don turned right, and they headed north for several miles. "I'm not sure we're going to find anything here," he said. "My confidence wanes."

Jill giggled. "Just give it another mile or so, Mr. Explorer. Then we'll turn back."

Don shrugged. "Hey, you asked for it."

A mile later, just as Don prepared to make a U-turn toward the highway, he noticed a little sign that read, *Lakeview Restaurant.* The accompanying arrow pointed down a narrow dirt road between two cornfields. As a thick line of trees sprung up along the horizon, the road didn't appear to lead anywhere.

The car now at a complete stop, Don turned to face Jill. "You up for it?" he asked.

"You're the captain," she answered with a smile. Then she placed one small hand on her tummy. "But, yes, I'm hungry enough to try anything."

Ten bumpy miles later, the two travelers arrived at the Lakeview Restaurant. "Surprisingly upscale," Don said, noting the bold right angles of the building as its glass façade jutted out over a pristine little lake, the setting sun dappling its shimmering water. Inside, through the glass, could be seen random huddles of patrons dining on small, modern tables.

The two approached the tall, wooden double-doors leading into the restaurant, and Don swung one of them toward himself, allowing Jill to lead him inside. As he stepped in after her and allowed the door to come crashing shut, the sepia-like daylight was blotted out, and all that remained was the dim glimmer of the art-deco lamps that hung from the warehouse-style ceiling overhead.

The two approached a small host table, where a bubbling young hostess with red hair awaited. "Two?" she said pleasantly.

Don nodded, and they were off. Jill suggested that they take a table outside on the deck overlooking the lake. As the weather remained pleasant and the sun still had not yet set, Don readily agreed.

After a lovely dinner of chicken for Jill and a messy meal of baby-back ribs for Don, the two sipped on coffee and gazed out at the moonlit water. Don suddenly reached over and took Jill's hand in his.

"Something about looking out at water brings out the romantic in me," he said.

Jill nodded softly and blushed.

~~~

Back on the highway, the two travelers had put another fifty miles behind them before they came to the first reasonably inhabited-looking town they had seen for some time. The blue highway signs indicated that there were several hotels just off the upcoming exit ramp – and a quick look at Jill's watery eyes indicated that it was time to stop. Don yawned and pulled off the highway.

In short order, they found a long, two-story Ramada Inn with the doorways leading to each room exposed to the outside. Through the glass front doors, the lobby appeared clean and appealing enough, so Don parked, helped Jill with her bags, and proceeded to check in.

The clerk was a tall, very thin, dark-haired man with a pleasant smile. "Good evening, sir," he said in a raspy voice that belied his youth. "Do you and your wife have a reservation?"

Don's heart fluttered at the mention of the word "wife." It had been a long time since he'd had someone in his life who could even be mistaken for his other half. The question stirred mixed emotions in him. First, he felt sorrow at his troubled marital past. Then it was replaced by a sudden twinge of excitement at the prospect of sharing a room with Jill.

Don's silence seemed to confuse the desk clerk. "Sir?" he said.

Don snapped out of his reverie. "Oh, no," he said, looking pleasantly at Jill. "We're just friends traveling together. We'll need separate rooms."

The clerk looked at him as if he had said something strange.

Maybe nobody does it this way anymore – married or unmarried, Don thought. *But I'm glad we're doing it this way.* He would never disrespect Jill by presuming they share a room.

After they finished checking in, they went up to their rooms on the second floor, and were delighted to find that they had managed to book rooms that were side by side. Don dropped his duffel bag in front of his door and then helped Jill carry her suitcases into her room. When he'd finished, the two returned to the exposed hallway outside, the night air brisk and welcoming to Don's lips.

As Jill's door swung shut, she stepped meekly toward Don and placed her hand over his heart. Her lips quivered slightly as she closed her eyes and turned her chin up to him.

A surge of thrilling energy took hold of Don, and he slid his hands up to Jill's waist and gently pulled her close. He pressed his lips to hers quickly and slightly, feeling the rush of a small and yet passionate kiss. He wanted nothing more than to linger there upon her lips, to press his body against hers, but he knew in his heart that he could not. It was not yet time.

As the two pulled back from their subtle embrace, Don felt the tingling excitement of a schoolboy at the end of a first date. He recalled his first kiss with Julie. It had felt much the same way to him. His heart pounded, yearning for more.

"Well, good night," he said softly, despite himself.

"Good night, Don," she cooed, looking up through wide, dewy eyes as she smirked and turned toward her door. She fumbled with her key for a moment, which caused both of them to laugh giddily, before she finally managed to push her way inside.

Once her door had closed behind her, Don unlocked his own door and immediately kicked off his shoes. He lay atop the lumpy bed for a moment, thinking about what Jill would be doing just on the other side of the wall. He knew that it would be wrong to push things along faster than they were meant to go, but still, he couldn't shake the notion that the night would not be complete without just one more kiss, just one more touch, just one more embrace.

He stood up with a start and laced his shoes once more. He then stepped outside, carefully and quietly closing the door behind him. The crescent moon shone in the distance, carving through the misty gray night with a calming glow. Here and there, the strongest stars glimmered through the vague light of the town. Don could not get enough of the fresh country air. He turned toward Jill's door, but then immediately second-guessed himself. Knocking now would seem presumptuous, and he certainly didn't want to come off the wrong way.

And so he stood on the balcony overlooking the parking lot, drinking in the air and sighing over the city lights in the distance.

~~~

Jill stood, frantic. Despite her overwhelming desire to sleep, she could not bring herself to even take off her shoes. She paced at the foot of her bed, throwing her hands up every now and then, fretting over what to do about her fresh new neighbor.

There was no denying her trepidation about getting involved with another man so soon after Michael had mistreated her so thoroughly. But Don . . . *Oh, Don.* She could not shake his allure, his magnetic pull, his sparkling eyes, his tender heart, his lips. She knew she would not sleep until she was close to him again at least for just one more time. She needed his presence if only for a moment.

Pulling on a zip-up sweater of thin gray cotton, she approached the door. Her slender hand reached for the doorknob and her fingers traced a gentle path over its chrome-like surface. "Don," she whispered, hesitating uncomfortably.

No. She couldn't go to him now. It would seem too presumptuous or perhaps too permissive. And still, she did not yet know Don's true feelings. What if she had been projecting his loving gaze onto him? What if her heart, her lonely, empty heart, had simply imagined it all?

For a long while, she stood next to the doorway, her arms folded tightly in front of her chest as she fretted about what to do. Eventually, she decided to remove her sweater and shoes and climb back into bed.

~~~

Early the next morning, after having breakfast in the hotel restaurant, the two hit the road early, again heading out onto the westbound interstate. The hot summer sun climbed over the horizon behind them.

As they drove along, listening to oldies on the radio, they inevitably began sharing more about their lives with each other. Don enjoyed every minute of their easy conversation as they traversed the seemingly endless fields of the Great Plains. Don skirted the issue of Julie, however, afraid of his own emotion almost as much as his perception of Jill's inevitable reaction.

For her part, Jill told him much about her childhood. As an only child, she spent a great deal of time alone, lost in the world of books. She also spoke briefly about a serious relationship she'd had as a young woman, one that had ultimately ended in heartbreak. From there, she explained her predicament with Michael, and her hesitant, careful words were not lost on Don. The professor could sense how hurtful the subject was for her.

Don took her hand in his right as he drove with his left. "I can see that Michael is a part of your life that you need to put behind you."

Jill offered a thin smile and nodded.

They were quiet for the next three miles or so, neither apparently feeling compelled to say anything.

"If there's anything I can do," Don finally said, "you just let me know."

Jill squeezed his hand. "You already have."

He took his eyes off of the road just long enough to give her an appraising glance. "I have?"

"Yes," she said, looking down at her lap. "You have helped just by being here to listen to me. You're a very good listener."

Don tried but failed in his effort not to chuckle. "Funny, that's not what my students tell me. Even in my 'kinder, gentler' mode, I'm still considered one of the toughest professors on campus."

Now it was Jill's turn to laugh. "That tough-guy stuff might convince some others," she said, "but I think it's all just a big act. I believe that hidden under all that tough veneer is a very gentle man."

Don felt hot blood rush to his face. Without words, his smile projected his appreciation.

Later that day, they began to ascend the foothills of the Rockies, continuing to climb to steeper elevations as the afternoon wore on and the sun's bending path took it behind the mountains in the distance. Jill had never been to this part of the country before, and she was clearly awestruck by the majesty of the mountains.

"These aren't even the tallest ones," Don said. He then turned off the air-conditioner and rolled down the windows. "Smell that mountain air. If you ask me, nothing is as glorious as that."

Like an excited child, Jill pointed feverishly to a sign that read: *Scenic Overlook*. "Oh, let's pull over there and see it."

Without hesitation, Don flicked on his turn signal and made his way over to the right lane, down the long, paved, and winding road, and finally into the gravel parking lot, where he brought the car to a stop. They got out of the car and walked hand in hand to a metal railing at the edge of a precipice. This windswept vista served as the perfect vantage point for a view of the entire valley and all of the purplish mountains that surrounded it. The remnants of sunlight traced their pastel hues across the rocky facades of the mountains, casting a long, dim shadow over the tree-lined valley below.

"Wow!" Jill exclaimed, taking it all in. "This is spectacular."

Don had seen these mountains before, but they always had the same effect on him – almost as if he were seeing them for the first time. "Sort of makes you feel small, huh?" he remarked as he admired how her hair gently flowed with the breeze.

Jill leaned her head against his shoulder as she continued to gaze down at the valley. "That's not such a bad thing," she said. "Creation is a big and wonderful thing. I'm content to be just a small part of it."

She again seemed to echo Don's very thoughts. His original gut feeling that this woman was special had revealed itself to be true. He was nearly certain that he had been delivered the one woman his life so yearned for – and how profound, this creation.

The two remained there for over an hour, reluctant to leave until the warmth of the sun began to evaporate and the twilight air grew chilly.

~~~

Finally, on the following day, after many long miles on the road, Don spotted the sign they had both been waiting to see: *Welcome to California.* He pointed it out to his lovely passenger, and she hooted in celebration. They both let out a cheer as they crossed the state line.

"California, here I come," Jill said, and they both broke out in laughter.

"It's still another few hours from here," Don said distantly.

Jill smiled. "I'm not in any big rush," she said.

"You're going to really like Cheryl, Tom, and the kids," Don said. "They're great people. They are so very special to me."

"Any friend of yours is a friend of mine," Jill replied.

Julie, Don thought. *She's so like Julie. That is exactly what she would say.*

All at once, his past came rushing back to the forefront of his mind. Tears began to form at the corners of his eyes as he thought about his last days with her, the times they had shared in the very wilderness he now drove through with Jill.

Then he shook his head forcefully. *But she's not Julie,* he thought. *She's Jill. Only Jill.*

He braced himself against the steering wheel as the thought occurred to him: all weekend, he would have to fight to remind himself of that fact.

Chapter Eleven

With dusk closing in, Don and Jill rolled into the parking lot of a hotel not far from Cheryl's house. As had become custom, the fact that they needed separate rooms caused a start in the young, boyishly handsome clerk's attention. By this point in the journey, it was all the travelers could do to suppress their warm and flirtatious smiles.

As it was late and Don and Jill were both quite exhausted from the drive, they decided to turn in for the night rather than pay Cheryl and her family a quick visit.

"We could drive around for a while and I could show you my old haunts . . ." Don had said. "My old school . . . old house . . . old . . . everything."

Her sighing response had been all he needed in order to know not to push the issue.

"You're right," he had quickly added. "It's getting late and we've got a long day tomorrow."

Jill had nodded silently through her yawn, winked as she wished Don good night, and then retired to her room.

Now Don lay in bed, staring at the ceiling, the thought of his captivating companion next door only secondary in his mind. On this night, his primary concern would lie with Cheryl. How on earth would she be able to come to terms with her mother's near twin paying her a visit? How would she react? And would she remain civil? Would he risk losing her friendship?

~~~

The next day, at the appointed time, the familiar rising pulse of nervous jitters lining Don's stomach, the two travelers drove down the oak-lined street on which Cheryl lived. Jill was unusually quiet as Don pulled up to the curb in front of the well-kept, two-story, modern house where Cheryl and Tom lived with Matthew and Madison. The home was as picturesque as it had been when Don had left, its sky-blue shutters serving as brilliant contrast to the wooden and pristinely white-painted siding. The gleam of the many windows on its front façade suggested to the professor that his surrogate daughter had spent the bulk of the day cleaning in preparation for their arrival.

Don's worry from the previous evening had carried over into the morning – and he had spent the better part of the day second-guessing himself about his decision to bring Jill along. Not even a visit to Whinburg had been enough to take his mind off things. Jill had indulged him as he showed off his former digs, his former stomping grounds – and for that, he could not help but admire her. But now, there they were, idling in front of Julie's daughter's home, Don Lipton as nervous as a schoolboy preparing to introduce his girlfriend to his parents.

How will Cheryl react to seeing her mother incarnate? Don wondered melodramatically as he glanced over at his lovely companion. *How can I possibly explain myself?*

Jill shined her brown, ponderous eyes in his direction, sparking him to action. He shut down the car, hopped around the front end, and opened the passenger door for her.

Grinning and feigning flattery, she said, "I'm not used to such gentlemanly gestures."

Don chuckled nervously. "Me neither," he jibed, closing the door behind her slender frame, which now stood tall in the plush grass of Cheryl's front yard.

The professor looked thoughtfully to the sky as he sidled up next to Jill and led her toward the baby-blue front door. It was a brilliant day for a barbecue, with just a few puffy clouds moseying across a deep blue sky. His nose twitched at the sweet aroma of meat cooking, and his mouth began to water . . .

As they crossed onto the stone walkway leading to the front door, Don found himself trying as best he could to keep his mind occupied. His eyes traveled quickly to the ground, watching his steps as they plodded along a little more slowly than would otherwise seem normal. The azaleas lining the stone walkway had been carefully and neatly pruned, he noticed. *Julie,* he thought. *I'm sorry . . .*

Just as they reached the front door, a familiar voice came careening in from their right, racing towards them with furious glee. "Mommy!" it called. "Look who's here! It's Grandpa Don! Grandpa Don!" Matthew had apparently heard the crack of the closing car doors and had come charging around the house. The intensity and innocence of his grin warmed Don's nervous heart. At least one member of the family had failed to immediately notice Jill's strange resemblance.

He closed his embrace around a hopping Matthew. How he had missed this remarkable young boy.

"We're all out back, Grandpa Don," Matt said, wiping his eye with the back of his smooth and rounded hand, looking only briefly up at Jill. "Who's she?"

Don smiled at the little boy. "This is Jill," he said softly. "She's a friend of mine."

"Oh," Matt said, looking impatiently at the ground and digging his toe into the grass.

"Is it okay if she stays here and eats with us?"

Matt beamed up at Jill, then quickly back at Don. "Sure!" he said. "But we can still play ball, can't we, Grandpa Don?"

Don laughed as he glanced over at Jill and winked. "Of course we can, young man," he said. "Who knows, maybe we can talk this pretty lady into playing ball with us later. First, though, let's go over and see your mommy, daddy, and little sister."

"Yeah!" Matt grunted with excitement and then ran out ahead of the other two, his lolling little steps taking him quickly around the side of the house and into the back yard. All along the route, he called out the arrival of the guests, harkening everyone to the fact that Grandpa Don and his pretty friend had arrived. "And we're gonna play ball!" he yelled as soon as he got up alongside his mother, tugging on her wrist frantically.

"Okay, okay," Cheryl was saying with a smile just as Don and Jill rounded the corner into the back yard.

The yard was a wide and sunny affair, its warm green grass dotted only here and there by the shade of oak saplings and young evergreens. Don's nose led him first to examine the waving Tom, whose tall, gangly frame had turned to greet the approaching guests. As soon as Don returned the wave, Tom turned back to hunch over his oversized charcoal grill. The man took pride in his steaks, and Don could already smell that the pride would pay off in spades.

To his left, just on the edge of the stone patio that stretched from the back door of the home all the way to Tom's custom-made grill, was little Madison, who bounced around dreamily in her baby chair, flinging soft plastic toys to the grass just below, blissfully unaware of the tense moment about to unfold.

To her right, then, standing very near the back door – which Don knew to lead into the kitchen – was Cheryl. The expression on her face caused his heart to sink as it melted from shock, to confusion, to deep concern. Such was the intensity of her gaze that Don barely noticed the other guests in the yard. The barbeque would be a well-attended event, as it turned out, but as far as Don was concerned at that moment, there were only three people in the world: the woman he had only recently come to adore, the woman who would judge her skeptically, and himself, sweating and shaking.

Don quickly led Jill over to Cheryl. "Jill," he said, extending his hand in Julie's daughter's direction, "this is Cheryl, our host for the afternoon." He immediately felt ridiculous for the formal introduction, but then whatever embarrassment he could take on was immediately snuffed out by Cheryl's uneasy sidelong glance.

The young mother nodded politely, smiled, and shook Jill's hand. The moment Jill bent down to coo a few words at Madison, however, Cheryl glared at Don. The professor's worst fears had been realized. She had quickly noticed the resemblance. Later, there would surely be words exchanged.

Soon, however, things began to settle down. Introductions were made between Jill and Tom before the two of them turned their attention to the other guests at the party. Don marveled at how quickly Jill seemed to loosen up. In no time at all, she was beginning to seem like an old friend of the family. In fact, she was doing a better job of socializing than Don was himself.

~~~

Everyone had a pleasant afternoon in the back yard. The warm air was refreshing. Don played with Matthew, throwing a ball to him as Jill stood off to the side, playfully rocking a giggling Madison on her hip as she talked with Cheryl and Tom. Only occasionally, during moments such as these, did Don's thoughts drift to Julie. *Oh, Julie . . . how you would have loved this day.*

But then here was Jill with her big, comfortable smile. The familiarity of her conversation with the strangers at the party, with Cheryl and even Tom, fascinated him. The warmth and genuine joy with which she played with the children was adorable, and so gentle and loving.

Soon would come the moment Don had been dreading, however. With Jill chasing a cackling Matthew around the yard, Cheryl seized the opportunity to seize him and yank him into the kitchen. With the dim light of the modern hanging lamps flowing over the dark stone countertops and linoleum flooring like a soft blanket, Don stood aghast.

"So this woman is the reason you asked all those questions about my family?" Cheryl snapped.

Don hung his head, embarrassed to even think about the fact he had hoped she had forgotten about the questions. Not a chance. Cheryl had an excellent memory for such things.

"I can't believe how much Jill looks like my mom," she continued. "This is really strange."

Don tried to sound matter-of-fact about it. "She does look a lot like Julie, I know."

Cheryl looked at him as if he had just made the most ridiculous understatement imaginable. "Wow!" she said with mock enthusiasm. "You know, when you two arrived, I thought for a second that Mom had somehow come back for a visit."

Don nodded, almost pleading. "I felt the same way when she first came into my office a few months ago. But now . . . well . . . I see her for who she is. She's . . . um . . . just wonderful."

Cheryl's face warmed over slightly as she broke into a crooked smile. "The famous writer at a loss for words, eh?"

Don looked sheepishly at the floor. "I guess so."

"I suppose Jill's resemblance to my mother will make it easy for you to replace her."

The professor lifted his head with a start, imploring Cheryl with his gaze. "Please don't say that," he said. "No one will ever be able to do that. Are you mad at me for bringing her with me today?"

Cheryl sighed and seemed to calm down a bit. "No, of course I'm not mad. You might say that I'm sort of confused."

"That makes two of us."

For a moment, they both gazed quietly through the kitchen window. Outside, Jill was chatting with Tom. Her musical laugh rang out as she threw her head back at something Tom had said. Her curls shone in the sun. Don took that moment and tucked it into his heart for safekeeping. Whatever happened between the two of them, that image of this beautiful woman would stay with him always.

"Well," Cheryl said calmly, "I just hope you know what you're doing."

"That makes two of us," Don repeated. Then, he and Cheryl walked silently back out of the kitchen and into the fading sunlight.

~~~

Later, as evening set in, Jill and Don said their goodbyes.

"I don't know how to thank you for this day," Jill said warmly as she embraced Cheryl. "I live so far away from most of my old friends and their families . . . It was so nice to be a part of this family for a while."

To Don's great relief, Cheryl was glowing as she received the praise. "We're glad you came," she said, and her voice certainly sounded sincere. "Maybe we'll see you again sometime before you go home."

Jill flashed an inquiring look at Don. "We're planning on spending a few days out here, so it's fine with me if it is with Don."

With a grin, Don said, "Are you kidding? Of course we will. You don't think we drove all the way out here for just one visit."

"Great!" Cheryl said. "If you come early tomorrow, I'll whip you up some breakfast."

Jill placed a hand delicately on her stomach. "Oh, man," she said. "I'm not sure I'll be able to eat all day tomorrow after all the food we've had today."

Don chuckled and shook his head. Quickly, he stole an appraising glance at Cheryl. For the first time all day, he felt comfortable that his new love interest had been accepted by the only family he had. Now, all he had to do was explain to Jill the significance of this day. The only question that remained in his mind was, would he?

~~~

On the way back to the hotel, when Don saw the gothic-style Catholic church come into view on Sierra Road, a thought came to mind. It was more like an impulse, really, but one that he was determined to follow. The impulse sent his hand turning left on the wheel as opposed to the right that would take them back to the hotel.

"Where are you going?" Jill said, perking up from her silent reverie in the passenger seat.

He cleared his throat and glanced at her, looking for signs that she was as nervous as her strangely frantic tone suggested. With no desire to frighten her, he donned his most soothing tone. "It's a place I like to go every now and then when I get back here . . . to enjoy the scenery."

"But, Don," she said, "it's dark outside. We won't see anything."

"Yes," Don stammered, "but the peace and quiet is nice, too. And since you've never been to California, I thought you might like it."

Jill shrugged reluctantly.

"We can leave whenever you want. I've been dying to get back there. Do you mind?"

Jill seemed to relax marginally. She gave him a tentative smile, but remained quiet.

Don guided the car along the winding road through the woods until they came to a lonely stretch of Pacific beach. The darkness was in full bloom by the time they arrived at this place so sacred in Don's heart, but the stars were as bright and numerous as the professor could ever remember them being.

Don took her by the hand to the old gray lighthouse on the water's edge. He said nothing as they walked, listening rather to the spray of the surf and the crunch of the sand beneath their feet.

"Oh, Don," Jill said, bringing an open palm to her lips. "This is absolutely beautiful."

Don simply nodded, though he knew that she was unlikely to see him. Her eyes seemed transfixed on the lighthouse. As they got up alongside it, she reached out to touch its rough, salty wet base. Julie's hands had graced this spot so many times before. And Emily's too . . . *Perhaps it was wrong to bring her here.*

Don began to feel that once-familiar ache gather and rise near the back of his throat. Tears began to well up in his eyes – and as they did, he felt thankful that he had chosen to bring her to this place at night.

"There is something about lighthouses," Jill said, blissfully unaware of how choked up her companion had suddenly become. "They are so exciting, and yet so comforting. They are the thought of the last resort when you're lost at sea, they are one's guiding light . . ."

Every word stabbed straight to Don's soul. It was all he could do to keep from sobbing. To his relief, peace followed, and the two of them simply stood side by side, watching the dark waves glimmer rhythmically to the dim light of the crescent moon behind them.

After a long spell, Jill playfully elbowed Don in his fleshy side. "So, do you bring all your girlfriends here?"

Don gulped the pain away and then, to his surprise, managed a laugh. "Sure," he said glibly. "Every one of them."

Jill moved in closer, brushing her shoulder into the border of his embrace. "Well, I'm glad you brought me here."

Without a thought, Don leaned in and smoothly brushed Jill's chin up toward him. He pressed his lips to hers. Warm energy surged to his fingertips before reverberating back to his toes. The light coconut scent of her hair melted into the light tea essence of her clothing, and all swirled into his mind upon the back of a salty air. For the briefest moment, he dipped into the kind of ecstasy he hadn't felt in years. He watched like an outsider as his hands worked their way down to her hips and pulled her close to him. But then, all at once, he pulled back.

"I'm sorry," he said meekly. "I didn't mean to be so forward."

She nuzzled up to his shoulder. "That's okay," she said. "I'm fine with it." Then she ran her hand across his belly. "Just promise me one thing."

"What's that?" he asked, turning all his attention upon her deep brown eyes, so bright and inviting, even in this relative darkness.

"Promise me that you'll do that again sometime soon."

His heart fluttered as he grinned. Every ounce of Don Lipton wanted to lock her into an embrace and kiss her once more, but he allowed his better judgment to get the best of him. He decided that there would be days like this to come. For now, he only needed to worry about falling too deeply and too quickly in love.

Chapter Twelve

A week had passed since returning from the trip to California. It was as if it had all gone by in a whirl. Jill was back home, with only her memories and some photographs to recall how much fun she and Don had.

She trudged across the grass in her gardening clogs, carrying a tray of vibrant pansies to the edge of the brick walkway behind her house, which was just begging for some mid-season color. At ten o'clock, an unusually hot sun was already beating down, and she welcomed the cool breeze. She had intended to be done with her gardening by this point, but an extra hour of dozing beneath her fluffy down comforter had been too tempting. Tyson had finally spurred her out of bed with a soft swat to the nose. The cat had clearly been perturbed that his morning meal had not yet arrived in his dish.

Dropping to her knees on the gardening pad, Jill began digging holes with her trowel and tucking the small clumps of flowers into the cool soil. Even with gloves on her hands, she reveled in the proximity to nature that gardening provided. Part of the reason she had closed on this home, despite its tiny kitchen and aging roof, was the small vegetable garden in the back and the beautifully tended garden out front, surrounded by a white picket fence. Cliché though she knew it to be, the picket fence represented everything she had ever wanted: peace, security, and happiness. And she had spent too many years feeling as if she lived behind the confines of chain link.

As she worked, she thought about the recent turn of events in her life. Just last month, she had been preoccupied completely with how to boost sales at the bookstore, which flavors of tea to order, and whether she should get another cat to keep Tyson company – all the while priding herself on her independence. Now, suddenly, she found her thoughts increasingly focused on a writer and college instructor who, for whatever reason, seemed to find her utterly irresistible.

She basked in the sunshine as she moved the pots of recently purchased plants from her driveway to the yard. Jill again reflected on the wonderful trip to California and the cookout and, of course, the visit to the lighthouse afterward. Through it all, he couldn't seem to take his eyes off her. At first, she had been a little unnerved by this attention, but then just mostly flattered.

As she worked, Jill's mind continued to linger on the trip and her developing relationship with Don. It had been so long since she had had such an enjoyable and relaxing time. Cheryl and her family proved to be delightful, and she had immediately felt at home with them. Matthew and Madison had found their way to the center of her heart within minutes. She marveled at Don's unique relationship with them. He had played with little Matthew with the pride of a father or a grandfather, and yet a father or grandfather he certainly wasn't. Still, there was something about the depth of his bond with them all. She wondered where Don had met this remarkable family.

Her mind turned to something Don had mentioned at the lighthouse about the losses he had suffered. He had told her a little bit about his first wife, and his little daughter Abby. How tragic it had to have been for him to lose both of the people he loved most at the same time. He hadn't elaborated on the details, but the pain in his heart was mirrored in his eyes. These deep feelings and thoughtfulness in Don intrigued her.

Jill had been nervous at first when Don had taken a detour to the lighthouse. She recalled that for a moment she'd had the fleeting thought that maybe he was going to turn out to be just like other guys who, the first chance they got, would try to get her alone to make a move. She smiled as she chastised herself for thinking that way about him. He wasn't like that at all.

She vividly remembered how thrilled she was by the beauty of the lighthouse and the soothing sounds of the ocean – and the inspiration that Don seemed to draw from it. As he held her in his strong embrace, he had talked about his love of flying and how different a sunset looked from up in the sky. She could still feel the firm warmth of his arms around her, his lips against her hair.

He had caused her to feel something growing inside her that she hadn't felt for ages. When he walked her to her room that night, she had wanted badly to invite him in, but remained hesitant to move forward with a relationship. Her past with Michael still haunted her so. Besides, she wasn't the kind of woman who thought sex outside of marriage was not a problem. In fact, it was a big problem.

Letting someone like Don into her life – and even her heart – might not be so bad, she reasoned. She wanted to trust him, but she wasn't sure that she could trust him, or even herself, at this point.

Jill continued working for over an hour before realizing that she still had some inside chores to do. She stood back and admired her garden. She complimented herself on a job well done. It was almost noon, and she wanted to go to the store for a bit to pick up a few things. She took a final look at her work, and went inside.

Stripping off her damp clothes, she stepped into the shower and turned on the faucet. As she waited for the water to heat up, Jill let the notion of romance play across her mind. She was growing increasingly tired of waking up alone, eating dinner alone, and showering alone.

She had learned from the trip that Don was intelligent, talented, and a true gentleman. She knew she shouldn't be thinking about another relationship while she was still recovering from Michael – and dealing with his continued interference in her life. She had learned the hard way that she shouldn't trust just anyone, especially men. They had to earn it. Yet her instincts told her that Don would be willing to do whatever it took. Her instincts, she knew, were seldom wrong . . .

Chapter Thirteen

Don stared down at the grilled chicken sandwich before him, which looked distinctly unappetizing in the fluorescent light of the cafeteria. The first bite had been disenchanting – hopelessly dry despite the lettuce leaf and faint drizzle of Italian dressing. As part of his fresh effort to slim down, he had opted for the chicken instead of his usual two slices of pizza or an Italian sub. He had even taken a stab at the treadmill that morning in the rec center. He couldn't explain it; spending time with Jill had made him acutely conscious of the bulge he had accumulated around the middle as a result of many evenings spent in his recliner, grading papers and watching the national news.

He wasn't cut out for health foods. Giving in to his taste buds, he retrieved two packets of mayonnaise and slathered it liberally on the bun.

Much better, he thought as he took his second bite.

Almost a week had passed since the barbecue at Cheryl's and his visit to the lighthouse with Jill. He had spoken with her once over the phone since then, telling her how much he had enjoyed the trip and that he looked forward to the next time the two of them could get together. They had joked about Tom's devotion to his grill and of little Matthew's fond attachment to Jill.

But when Don had suggested another outing the following weekend, Jill had politely declined, saying she had work to do in her garden. Although he would normally have considered this a rebuff, he had detected a flirtatious note in her voice that indicated to him she was open to future possibilities. He thought that maybe he would call her as the weekend drew nearer and suggest that they do dinner Saturday evening, as it would be hard to garden in the dark.

In fact, the only reason he hadn't been thinking about Jill constantly was because he had been extra busy this past week, grading student essays, writing, and working every spare minute on his plane. It almost seemed like the end of summer was the busiest time of the year. He did have a few weeks' vacation coming up prior to Labor Day, and he felt the need to unwind.

In any case, he would use the days off to spend more time in the air, one of the things he had come to enjoy most. Being with Jill, however, was beginning to take its place as first in his heart.

When he told Mark about the upswing in his growing relationship with Jill, Mark had said, "I told you so." His friend had also mentioned offhand that Don might consider inviting Jill along for his first flight out since overhauling the plane. Don thought it was ridiculous, knowing that she was afraid to fly, but he had nonetheless found himself mulling it over.

Now, sitting in the cafeteria, eating lunch alone and staring at the empty seat across from him, he abruptly made a decision. Taking one last bite, he folded his newspaper, tossed his trash in a bin, and headed for the elevator.

Back in his office, he called Jill.

"Good afternoon, Open Book."

"Jill, this is Don. Did I catch you at a bad time?"

Jill seemed to be in a good mood, and happy to hear from Don. "There isn't a bad time when it's you calling. What can I do for you?"

Don smiled to himself. He could picture her face, her warm glow, the phone pressed tightly to her ear. "Well, to be honest, I miss you. I was trying to think of something fun we could do together . . . something different."

"Ah!" she said jovially. "Come up with something, did you?"

She again made him smile. "You're too much. As a matter of fact, I was wondering if you would like to go for a ride in my plane this weekend. I know you have gardening and other chores to do, but we could make it later in the afternoon." When his suggestion was met with silence, he pressed on. "We wouldn't have to go far. I thought maybe we could fly to Marshall, and then eat at Schewler's restaurant there. What do you say?"

Jill sounded startled by the proposition, and Don wasn't at all surprised that she would be hesitant.

"Wow!" she said, breathing a little more rapidly into the receiver. "Is there a second choice? I am scared to death of flying, and I have never been in a private plane, with a pilot of my own."

"Nothing to worry about," Don said confidently. "I've been flying for many years now, and I can assure you that I've checked and double-checked everything on the plane – it's good as new after being overhauled."

"I don't know . . ." Jill said distantly. He could almost hear her twirling her finger nervously around the curly telephone wire.

"My friend Mark will be with us," Don added. "He flies, too . . . so you won't have to worry about our safety if I get preoccupied with you." Don immediately regretted saying the words. But just talking to Jill gave him a new sense of wanting to live and love again.

"That's supposed to make me feel better?"

"Being with you would make me feel better." If he had regretted his first statement, he certainly regretted this one. A bestselling author and he couldn't come up with something a little less corny. Still, his craziness never seemed to bother her. He loved the fact that he could be himself around her.

Jill remained quiet for a moment. Don let the silence mull, as he didn't want to push her into something that she might find frightening. But he was convinced that once they were airborne, she would realize that it wasn't scary at all. In fact, he felt certain that she would love it as much as he did. Or at least, that's what he was hoping would happen.

Finally, she spoke, drawing a long and audible breath before she did. "Okay. I'll go with you . . . but I'm holding you personally responsible if I pass out, or have a heart attack, or who knows what else."

"I should feel honored," Don said, excited. "I can't remember another woman before in my life who thought being with me would make her pass out!"

Jill giggled, though the giggle sounded terribly uncomfortable.

"No need to be afraid," Don added breathlessly. "I know CPR. And if necessary, I'm sure Mark can handle the plane while I bring you back to life." He could hear Jill snicker on the other end of the line. This time, it sounded more genuine. "Just giving you a hard time," he said. "Are you free Sunday . . . say, around two?"

"Sure," she said. "So how do I find you and the plane?"

"I can pick you up at your house."

For some reason, Jill insisted on meeting him at the airport. "No," she said shakily. "If you don't mind, I'd rather meet you there. Can you give me easy directions? I'm not very familiar with much around here yet."

"Great!" Don said. "It's really easy to find." He then offered directions in the simplest terms he could manage, finishing with the standard, "You can't miss it."

"Shoot!" Jill teased. "There goes my excuse for not showing up!"

"You'll be fine," Don replied. "I promise to take very good care of you."

"And that's supposed to make me feel better, right?"

Don laughed out loud. He really couldn't get enough of this woman. After repeating step-by-step directions to the airstrip, he said goodbye and hung up, puzzled. Why didn't she want him to pick her up at home? Maybe his decision back in California, stopping by the lighthouse, had upset her more than she let on. Or maybe she just wanted to preserve her independence. Whatever the reason, he was surprised and thrilled that he would be able to share flying, one of the pure joys of his life, with her.

Please, let nothing go wrong, he thought. He knew this meant she had made the decision to trust him implicitly, and under no circumstances would he let her down.

~~~

Jill's palms were damp with perspiration by the time she hung up the phone. She rubbed her temples, willing away the headache that was slowly creeping from behind her eyes. What had possessed her to accept Don's invitation? Did she really want to impress him that badly?

"Everything all right, Jill?" MacKenzie asked as she passed by and flashed a look of grave concern.

Jill smiled and waved her hand to dismiss the question. "Yes, yes. Just got a headache coming on." Looking around desperately for something to do, she grabbed a cart full of books to be shelved and dragged it down the nearest aisle . . .

She hadn't mentioned to Don that she hadn't flown since a terrifying trip with her high school volleyball team, when a drop in cabin pressure sent the oxygen masks tumbling out of the ceiling and forced them to make an emergency landing. She had been terrified of flying ever since.

Recalling the incident, she asked herself again: why in the world had she accepted his invitation? The answer she came up with was tantalizing. More and more, for whatever reason, she felt an exciting willingness to trust Don, but how could she know whether he was really a qualified pilot or not? Could a writer be a good pilot? How did he even have time to learn to fly? Was he just showing off? And most importantly, what had gotten into her?

She was suddenly startled out of her daydream when a customer came up from behind and asked where she might find books on self-empowerment. The irony was not lost on Jill. She directed the woman around the corner, and then headed back to the front desk, determined to call Don back and offer some excuse.

She reached for the receiver, but then pulled her hand back and slouched onto the stool behind the counter. At least she had made sure she would be taking her own car, in case she changed her mind at the last minute. Then, if her gut started churning, she wouldn't have to inconvenience the men by asking Don to drive her home.

And yet, maybe this would be the day that she overcame her fear of flying. *Either that or it'll be a humiliating experience,* she thought darkly.

Chapter Fourteen

During the twenty-minute drive to the airstrip, Don struggled to suppress the anticipation that burned in the pit of his stomach. Mark was describing one of the projects he had going in his garage, but Don couldn't make himself pay much attention. It wasn't that he doubted his abilities as a pilot or the successful outcome of the flight. Even the weather was cooperating. Early morning clouds had burned off, revealing pristine blue sky and perfect flying conditions. His nervousness had more to do with seeing Jill again . . . finally.

"So what do you think, Don? Do you think I should use the electric or gasoline engine . . . or burn the house down?"

"Uh, engine?" Don said absently. "On what?"

"That's what I thought," Mark said triumphantly. "You didn't hear a word I said!"

"I'm sorry. I have my mind on flying right now," Don replied half-heartedly.

"Is it on flying the plane, or on the passenger?"

"Both."

Mark grinned, clearly finding Don's restlessness somehow amusing.

When they arrived at the airport, they found Jill waiting in her car outside the small building where pilots checked in. She seemed to be in no hurry to get out, and they startled her when they approached and tapped on her window. After she recognized that it was Don, she calmed down and stepped out of the car.

Don introduced Mark to Jill.

Mark extended his hand. "Hi, Jill. A couple of weeks ago, I picked up a novel in your bookstore."

"Oh really?" she said, a bit too intrigued. Don could tell that she was trying hard to focus on something other than the impending flight. It was an endearing effort – but, as he could see, a failing one. "I don't recall seeing you."

"You were busy with another customer in the back," Mark explained, running a hand through his well-groomed black hair. "And I was in a hurry, so I didn't get a chance to say hello. Good to meet you now, though."

Jill nodded nervously.

With a comforting hand against her lower back, Don led Jill toward the hangar that housed the Cessna. The professor opened the big door, and he and Mark rolled the plane outside.

Hoping to ease some of Jill's clear concern about the state of the plane, Don explained to his lovely companion that each time a plane was taken out to fly a careful and detailed walk-around check was completed. With Jill watching over his shoulder, the last points he checked were the gas and oil levels, and he inspected the gas tanks to make sure there was no water in them. Mark had, meanwhile, been checking a couple of things in the hangar.

Jill seemed calmer after the walk-around inspection; at least, that was what her eyes were saying.

Don then helped his uneasy passenger into the plane, allowing her to take the front seat next to him. Mark would ride in the back, manning the autopilot controls and keeping watch over the various gauges he had recently installed.

Taking his seat next to a very tense Jill, Don said, "Well, what do you think, young lady? Front seat. Up where you can see it all."

Swallowing hard, Jill said, "Usually, I'd consider it a compliment to be called a young lady. Right now, I'm thinking age doesn't matter."

Don laughed as he helped her to get comfortable in the front seat. He put his arms around her to reach for the safety belts, and even as nervous as she was, she seemed to exhibit a twinge of excitement as his hands brushed against her.

"These aren't like seatbelts in cars, are they?" she said hopefully.

"That's true," Don said. "Much more secure," he added as he fastened the two shoulders straps and then connected them together with the belt that he had run over his passenger's lap. Once the belt was secure, he handed her a set of padded headphones. "These will help to muffle the noise of the engine . . . and I'll be able to talk to you, as well."

Outside the plane, Don ran through a mental checklist on each of his points of inspection. But now inside the cockpit, he reached down and picked up a clipboard holding a paper checklist. This list included a number of steps to go through before the engine was even started.

He realized as he explained what he was doing that it probably seemed a bit strange to Jill. Still, it had to have been at least somewhat comforting.

Once the engine roared to a start, there was still another checklist with a number of points to be checked. Jill seemed amazed as she watched Don check off all the steps in the process of getting ready to fly.

"Wow," she said into the little microphone extending down from her headset – which looked adorably oversized on her elegant head. "This is a lot different from getting started with a car."

Don just smiled as he prepared for takeoff. He got on the radio and talked to the tower operator, requesting clearance to take to the air. He then taxied down to the takeoff point and whipped out another checklist. When he finished, he sighed noticeably, flicked a few levers, and then brought the plane to full speed. So enthralled by the thrill of the takeoff, Don forgot to check on Jill's look. By the time they were in the air, he felt certain that she would be passed out – or, at the very least, a nice shade of green.

Regardless, since she was a beginner, Don knew what Jill was probably experiencing: a feeling as if she had left a bit of her stomach behind her on the runway. But as he looked over, he could see that everything was going at least reasonably well. Mild discomfort was all that he could detect in her eyes as she peered over at him and smiled.

The plane soared over the countryside, and the view was spectacular. Green plains bled into green-brown cornfields and small patches of prairie grass. Clusters of cows and huddles of barn-yards drifted past smoothly and quickly.

Jill turned to Don. "This is a lot different than anything I've ever seen before."

Don took his eyes off the controls and glanced back at Jill. "You seem a little bit tense. Are you okay?"

"Sure." It was obvious that she was trying her best to sound calm, though acting was certainly not her strongest suit.

Don continued to make conversation to help Jill relax. After a short time, it seemed that Jill was just fine and really enjoying the ride.

"We are only going to go for a short trip today. I just thought you might like to see some of the beautiful summer scenery from a different vantage point. There's one place a little south where we can get fairly low, and the field is full of wildflowers."

"That sounds pretty. I love wildflowers." Her voice carried like that of an enthusiastic child. It was music to Don's ears.

He switched on the autopilot, giving him more time to look around and point out different sights to Jill as they floated over the ground in what felt like a big soft chair. Jill wanted to know when Don was not touching the controls how the autopilot worked.

"Autopilot?" she questioned. "Does that mean you let the air-plane fly where it wants to go?"

"Not exactly," Mark responded from behind. "We tell it where to go, then sit back and enjoy the ride."

"I trust you guys, I really do, but there are some things that you have no control over . . . and . . ."

"Look at it this way," Don said. "Do you really think either one of us would get in this plane if we did not feel at least one hundred percent sure it was safe?"

"When you put it that way, I feel much better."

"Great!"

"Hey Don, look at this." Mark was motioning to something near the back of the plane. He was trying to get his attention away from Jill long enough to poke some fun at him.

"Yeah, what am I supposed to be looking at?"

"Jill!" Mark got a big grin on his face. "Are you going to ask her to join the Mile High Club, or should I?"

Don would have slapped Mark across the back if he were not in the back seat. "My friend is also a comedian," Don said.

"So, when are you going to explain the joke to me?"

There was silence over the headsets for a moment.

Don thought for a minute, and decided to change the subject.

"Oh, look, Jill," he said. "Isn't this fantastic? Look down to your left now. What do you see?"

"Well," Jill said hesitantly. "For one, I see a lot of ants."

Don laughed, looking over the side of the fuselage. "They do look like ants from up here, I guess. But those are joggers, I think. Looks like a marathon, maybe."

"No," Jill said, laughing blissfully into the headset as she peered out of the cockpit. "Oh, I wasn't talking about way down there. I'm talking about in here. There's a tiny piece of bread down there between the seats, and it's loaded with ants!"

Don looked down into the crack in the seat between him and Jill to find a piece of bread that he realized must have fallen from a sandwich he had eaten the last time he had flown. And sure enough, there was a churning pile of ants enjoying it. "Well, I'll be," he said with a smile.

They both laughed at the misunderstanding. Jill then looked outside and started to describe a little lake and some colorful trees. "Wow, Don," she said. "Some of the leaves are already turning. So soon!"

Don grinned unseen out of his side of the cockpit. "Yes, even the sky is beautiful today," he said. He then began to provide a rundown of what was happening with the plane. He told his lovely passenger how fast they were flying, and at what altitude.

Jill just smiled, seeming as though she was totally taken in by what she was seeing outside, and also by who was sitting next to her on the plane.

"How are you doing by now, Jill?" Don ventured to ask. "Feeling any better?"

After a long pause, Jill responded with a shaky reply. "Um . . . Did I mention I'm afraid of flying?"

Don and Mark teased her for a moment, but rather than angering her in any way, their lighthearted banter actually seemed to help in talking her through the flight. Before long, she clearly began to relax.

The group flew for a little over half an hour, and then returned to the airport to land. When the plane had safely come to a gentle halt, Don helped Jill out of the cockpit, and the three of them pushed the aircraft back into the hangar.

"There!" Don said proudly. "Now wasn't that nice? Did you enjoy it at all?" Before she could answer, he gave her a giant hug for comfort, and she quickly relaxed into his arms. He inhaled her scent and relished the warmth of her cheek next to his. She appeared very relieved.

"You were very brave," Don added. "Congratulations on surviving the flight and not having a nervous breakdown."

Jill laughed quietly into Don's shoulder.

"Whatever made you decide to go up with us today?" the professor asked.

"I'm not sure," Jill answered dreamily. "I guess something deep inside told me that I should trust you." She lifted her head and looked up until their eyes met. "And I'm so glad that I went today. Thank you, Don."

After a moment of blissful silence, the two of them gazing into one another's eyes, Don noticed the feeling that they were being watched. As he snapped out of his Jill-induced trance, he saw that Mark was still standing there next to them, a goofy expression on his face.

Mark looked at Jill. "Hey, what about me?" he chided. "I'm the mechanic. Don't I get a hug, too?"

Jill and Don looked at each other, and Don broke into a wide smile. "Sure, my friend," he said, turning toward Mark and throwing his arms around him. "There . . . is that better?"

Mark laughed, patting Don on the back. "Not exactly what I had in mind," he said. "But it'll do."

The three of them headed out to their cars. Just as Don readied himself to say goodbye to Jill, Mark poked his head in on the conversation once more.

"Wait, you two," he said with a smile. "Now, I was kind enough to play chaperone up there, but I absolutely refuse to drink alone this evening. Would you two like to join me down at Wings before closing time?"

Don tore his eyes away from Jill as they both laughed sheepishly.

"Sounds good," they both said at once.

"You go ahead and ride with Mark," she said softly. "I'll follow."

"That's fine," Don said. "But this doesn't excuse you from the fancy restaurant I said I was planning to take you to. We'll just have to do it another night."

As Don and Mark climbed into the Dodge, Mark remarked, "You didn't mention that she looks just like Julie. Could be her twin, you know."

Don could feel his face flushing red. Leave it to Mark to remind him why he shouldn't be falling head over heels in love.

"I hadn't noticed," he said, jamming the key into the ignition.

Mark snorted. "You're a bad liar."

~~~

Predictably enough, Wings featured a flying theme, with an antique propeller suspended from the ceiling and posters of various aircraft hung on the dark-paneled walls. The tavern was a little dingy-looking, but Jill had seen worse. She had never spent much time in bars and didn't care for the dim lighting and crude pick-up lines, but in the company of two well-built men, she figured the regulars wouldn't try anything funny.

Like Don, Jill ordered a cold beer. Despite her resolve, however, she couldn't stifle a grimace as she took her first sip.

Mark chuckled. "Not much of a beer connoisseur, huh?"

Jill shrugged. "I thought I'd try being one of the boys. I figured it couldn't be half as bad as that." She gestured to Mark's Guinness.

"How about a white wine?" Don said, casually laying a hand on Jill's thigh.

She grinned and glanced at Mark, who was politely checking the score of a basketball game on the TV overhead. "Zinfandel, if they have it," she said. "Thank you."

They snacked on greasy fried wings and a large basket of Cajun fries while Don explained what had drawn him to flying. He told her that the freedom of flight and the beauty of the Earth's splendor from on high were what most appealed to him. Despite her initial fears about flying, Jill thought she was beginning to understand exactly what he meant.

"Well, that was a nice trip today," Mark said.

"Yes, it was," Don chimed in. "Next time, we'll have to go farther!"

"What got you interested in flying, anyhow?" Jill asked, wanting to learn all she could about Don. "I mean, for the first time."

"My father used to fly, and so it was always a part of my life. After he passed away, I was so busy teaching and just living that I never got around to getting my own plane. About a year ago, I ran into a friend of mine who flies a lot, and one thing led to another."

Jill nodded and tried another sip of her light beer – to no avail. It brought another grimace to her face. At that moment, as Mark cracked a joke about Don's first, uneasy flight, Jill's heart stopped as she caught a glimpse of something she had been dreading for some time. Out of the corner of her eye, she saw a man walk into the bar and take a seat at a table across the room. Her stomach tightened into a knot, and her breathing suddenly grew rapid. The dim lighting of the bar made it difficult to be sure, but that plaid shirt, the wheat-colored hair curling over the collar, the square build and arrogant set of the shoulders . . . instantly, she recalled Michael. He had his head down, buried in a menu, so she couldn't be sure yet that it was him.

Don noticed that Jill was suddenly quiet and preoccupied.

"Are you okay, Jill?" he asked, turning slightly toward her. "You look like you've seen a ghost."

Just as Don spoke, the mysterious man at the other table turned to talk to the waitress, and Jill's fears were dispelled. It wasn't Michael. Still, her heart raced.

Now I'm seeing things, she realized. The cycle had begun again. This kind of thing was exactly what she had hoped to escape when she left Minnesota. She hated the constant vigilance, the uncertainty, and the feeling that no place was safe. Why her? Why did this have to keep happening? Now, in this moment, even if he wasn't there in Michigan with her, Michael was interfering with her life all the same. She didn't want to hate him for it – but it was hard not to.

Jill attempted to assure Don that everything was fine. "Oh, it's nothing. I just thought that I saw someone I know."

His expression showed that he knew there was more to it than that.

Jill tried to engage with the conversation that Mark had rekindled. Comforted though she was by Don's subtle affection, after her scare, she couldn't concentrate.

Finally, realizing that she would be unable to enjoy the rest of the meal, she pushed back in her chair. "I want to thank both of you again for a wonderful afternoon . . ." She squeezed Don's hand, her words beginning to sound frantic. "I'm sorry, but I'd better get going. I forgot that I need to be somewhere in about an hour. But I hope to see both of you again very soon."

Don hurriedly stood. There was concern in his eyes. "Do you want me to escort you home? It's no trouble. Mark can take my car."

"No, no," she said with an appeasing smile. "You haven't finished your beer. Please stay."

Don appeared crestfallen as the three of them said their goodbyes. He hugged her gently and kissed her on the cheek. Even in the midst of her low mood, the touch of Don's lips graced her with excited chills. "You have my number," he said. "If there's anything . . ."

Jill's heart melted as she noted the concern that remained in his eyes. "Thank you," she said. "I will."

On her way out, passing the bar patron who looked all too familiar, Jill was hit once more by a vivid memory of Michael the day he had accosted her on the sidewalk outside her office building. His blue eyes had been gentle at first as he begged her to give him one more chance, but when she tried to shrug away, he had grabbed her so tightly that she later found hand-shaped bruises on her arms. Her days in Minnesota hadn't been the same afterward.

Jill turned her eyes away from the look-alike and pushed the door open, taking deep breaths of fresh air. Her heart rate gradually slowed. If only she could erase the past. She felt that it was the only thing standing between her and the happiness she had almost forgotten could exist in life.

Chapter Fifteen

After dropping Matthew off at preschool and putting Madison down for a mid-morning nap, Cheryl found herself enjoying a rare moment of downtime. She made herself a cup of hot chocolate and settled into her favorite chair by the bay window. But as was always the case, her busy mind began drifting away from peace and solitude and toward something to keep herself occupied.

She reached out for the large photo album on the tall and narrow end table next to her chair. When she had it in her lap, she set down her tea on the table and dug into the album. She had been putting together a family tree and scrapbook of mementos and pictures of her mother. It was the only thing she could think to do to help Matthew and Maddie understand what their grandmother was like.

She flipped through the completed pages now, simultaneously admiring her work and grieving her mother anew. It was painful labor, but a labor of love nonetheless. But on this occasion, she found it difficult to dwell on either of the typical emotions that often wracked her as she carefully placed pictures and snippets of her mother's writing into the fold. Despite her best efforts to stay focused, her mind kept wandering to one person: Jill. *Jilly Larkins*. The mysterious but entirely endearing friend Don had brought to her door.

With such a distraction, pouring over a project that she usually thoroughly enjoyed working on seemed like little more than a chore. Confounding though it was, she couldn't help herself. She had to put the album down and busy herself with something else.

She saw the morning paper lying on the coffee table to her left and decided to look at it. She didn't always have time to read the newspaper those days, but it had once served as a relaxing ritual for her every morning. Although most of the mothers in the play groups she attended seemed to have little interest in current affairs, Cheryl's mother had always encouraged her to educate herself and exercise her mind the same way she did her body.

Julie may have seemed like a traditional mom, but Cheryl had learned in her mother's final years that her ideas about women's roles were anything but conventional. Her mother's drive to push forward and pursue her dream of a college degree – despite her husband's skepticism – inspired Cheryl. She was deeply saddened that her mother had never seen that dream materialize.

As coincidence would have it, at the bottom of the front page of the newspaper, Cheryl spotted an article about a sister and brother who had been separated at birth, given up for adoption, and reunited after forty years. The fascinating story, which recounted the extraordinary circumstances that had brought the two siblings together, reminded Cheryl of Jill and her uncanny resemblance to her mother.

This confounded her further, as she recalled the conversation she had recently had with her father on just such a subject. He had been little help in shedding any light on his former wife's childhood, and he seemed completely disinterested in talking about any matters dealing with the past.

That hadn't been enough to satisfy Cheryl, so out of curiosity, she had looked up her mother's birth certificate. To her relief, it confirmed that her grandparents were indeed her grandparents. Still, something burned in her – a desire to dig deeper, a knowledge that she had not yet uncovered all that was to be uncovered.

So, in the hopes of putting this silly idea out of her head, Cheryl decided to write a letter to the California Department of Social Services, inquiring about how she might track down the information necessary to contact her mother's long-lost relative. She figured that the curiosity couldn't possibly hurt anybody, what with her mother gone. And yet, why did she feel guilty? Why did she feel an embarrassment so deep that she had purposely neglected to mention her actions to Tom?

She was sealing the envelope just as the sound of Madison's crying rang through the baby monitor on the coffee table. She stepped onto the porch and dropped the letter in the mailbox before heading back to the nursery to attend to her motherly duties. Five minutes later, Maddie squirmed happily in her arms, and the letter was forgotten.

~~~

"Hi, Jill," Don said, feeling the warmth of his voice creating moisture against the telephone's receiver. "You just get home?"

Jill's sigh rang true across the line. "Oh, no . . . I've been here for an hour or so. I had a few places to stop on the way home; some errands to run, you know? How about you?"

"I just got home, yeah." Don paused for a while, forgetting his train of thought. "So anyway, I've been thinking about you . . ."

"Is that so?"

Don wasn't certain, but he felt fairly sure he could hear Jill's smile being projected over the phone. "That's so . . . So I was wondering if you would like to go out for dinner tomorrow. Maybe go to a movie." For the briefest moment, he felt a little awkward. To be certain, this would represent his first date with Jilly in the traditional sense, but he had traveled halfway across the country with the woman; why was he so nervous? His nerves were compounded when it took Jill a good long minute to reply.

"Dinner together sounds great," Jill finally said, a little conspiratorially. "But I have another idea. Why don't you come over here?"

Don felt a little short of breath. "You mean . . . to your place?"

"Absolutely. My grandmother taught me how to cook when I was just a teenager. I really enjoy doing it, but I have so few chances to now that I live alone."

"I'd hate to put you to the trouble after a long day of work."

"I don't consider cooking to be trouble, or even work! Besides, I can get one of the girls to cover for me and leave a bit early."

Don beamed. "That sounds great to me. Can I bring something along to add to the meal?"

"No . . . well . . . yes."

Don chuckled. "Which is it?"

Jill returned the light laughter. "Well, it isn't for the meal, but you could pick up a couple of good movies we can watch here."

"So we're skipping the theater, too?"

"Yeah," Jill said slowly, thoughtfully. "I always enjoy movies more when I can stretch out. I'll see you at about seven then, if that's okay with you."

"Seven it is."

Don hung up, still grinning. This would be the first date the two of them had had without being surrounded by people all the time. A true chance to be alone. Something for which he'd been yearning for quite a while now.

~~~

When Don arrived at Jill's, he marveled at the grace with which she even handled the minor tasks like opening her front door. His breath left him as he saw that she wore a pair of black slacks and a scoop-necked, hunter green top. On her feet was a pair of matching black sandals.

Absolutely beautiful, Don thought. He marveled at how she could look so dressed up, yet seem so relaxed and comfortable at the same time.

"Hi there," he finally said, mechanically looking down at his watch but finding himself too flustered to remember to read the time. "Am I on time?"

"Close enough," Jill said with a disarming grin.

"Sorry I'm late," Don said. "I had a tough time picking out a movie . . . so I got four of them."

"Great! If you like, you can set them on the entertainment center, and come out and chat with me while I finish the gravy. Do you like roast beef?"

"Love it. I can't remember the last time I had a home-cooked meal. This is such a treat."

Don did as he was told, placing the short stack of movies atop the wooden crown of the understated entertainment center. He then walked the short distance into the kitchen, admiring the dainty wallpaper and simple décor as he traveled. Once in the kitchen, he took a good long look around. Immediately, he noticed that everything seemed to have a place. All but the utensils Jill was using to cook was neatly stashed where it belonged. The curtains were full and a light brown, and covered all of the windows from top to bottom. The granite tiles beneath his feet were so shiny that Don could almost see his reflection in the floor.

As Jill finished dinner preparations, they made small talk. Eventually, she announced that everything was ready. Don helped her carry the serving dishes into the dining room, where he found that she had already set the long, oak wooden table with what looked to be fine dinnerware. He set the tray he was carrying down on the table and then immediately went over to Jill's side and pulled her chair out for her. He then took his place across from her.

"Thanks!" Jill said sheepishly as he sat.

"Thanks for what?"

"You know, for pulling my chair out for me. A lady misses those little things."

Don raised his chin slightly, nobly. "A gentleman likes to do those things for a real lady."

The food was everything Don could have ever hoped it to be. The roast was perfect, the whipped potatoes looked like clouds, and the gravy was delicious. Jill had baked corn – and candied yams to go with it.

Don ate too much, and then took a little more.

"Don't forget to save room for dessert," Jill said pleasantly, placing her silver fork down next to her plate.

"No way," Don said rubbing his belly under the table. "I already ate too much."

Jill smiled and cocked her head to one side. "That's not fair. I was planning on using my lemon meringue pie to reach your heart."

For a moment, Don's face became quite serious. Imploring. "Even without this delicious food, you've already touched my heart in many ways."

The light in the dining room being dim, Don was not sure whether he saw Jill's soft cheeks blush. "I'll tell you what," she said. "If you want me to, I can send a piece of the pie home with you. You can eat it later."

Don patted his belly audibly now. "That'd be perfect. That meal was amazing, Jill. Truly."

Jill nodded appreciatively and then got up to start clearing the table. Don stood to help.

"Oh, no," Jill said, playfully smacking the back of Don's reaching hand. "That isn't allowed in my kitchen. You go look at the movies and decide what we're watching. I'm just going to load these into the dishwasher."

"What makes you so sure I'm going to leave?" Don said over his shoulder as he walked through the open doorway in the dining room and into the living room. He laughed at his own enthusiasm. "Only teasing," he added.

Ten minutes later, Don took *The Bridges of Madison County* out of the box.

"Have you ever seen this one?"

"No, but I've read the book," Jill said. "And I've always wanted to see the movie. Good choice."

"More luck. I saw it years ago when it first came out and always wanted to watch it again."

Don put the movie into the DVD player, and Jill pushed the play button on the large remote resting on the coffee table. Don then turned and headed for the couch, where he took a spot that would keep a small distance between the two of them.

Even as the movie began, and Don was pulled headlong into the story, he couldn't help but notice and fret over the fact that Jill was sitting only an arm's length away. Something about Jill's body language suggested that she was worried about it, as well.

About halfway through the film, Jill excused herself and left in the direction of the kitchen. In short order, she returned with two small glasses of wine.

"Did I miss much?" she asked.

"No," Don said thoughtfully. "I put it on pause just as you got up."

Jill handed one of the glasses to her guest and then quickly took her seat, this time a little closer to Don. "I remembered you telling me once that this is your favorite kind of wine."

Don took a small sip and nodded enthusiastically. "Thank you, Jill. This is excellent – and very thoughtful." He reached forward, set the glass on a coaster on the counter, and then pushed the play button on the remote.

Leaning back into his spot, he slowly raised his arm and gently put it behind Jill, resting it on the back of the sofa. A few minutes later, she put her hand on his knee as if to say, *that's fine.*

Don found himself touched by the movie, and was more than a little embarrassed at the fact that he had tears in his eyes. A quick sidelong glance at Jill suggested that he wasn't the only one, however. So, as usual, he decided to make light of the situation. "Are we having fun, yet?" he asked.

Jill laughed through her tears, which of course lent the laughter a kind of muffled quality. "Fun?" she asked. "No, not exactly fun . . . but I'm sure having a good time. I haven't relaxed like this in so long." Jill wiped a tissue across her eyes.

"Sorry about the movie," Don said. "I certainly didn't mean to make you cry. Can I get you anything?"

Jill dabbed the tissue against the corners of her eyes. "I know," she said. "I'm sorry. You didn't make me cry. I always get moody over love stories. Can you forgive me?"

Don pulled his arm tighter over Jill, squeezing her slightly. "Forgive you for what? If you watched this movie and didn't feel anything, then I'd be worried."

The two of them huddled tighter after Don slid the second movie into the slot of the DVD player. Despite the late hour, neither of them seemed to want to part. By the time the second movie ended, however, Don could hardly recall the plot. Having Jill snuggled up next to him under the afghan was incredibly distracting, and the low-cut top hadn't helped.

Don stood up and stretched. "That was good, but the first one was the best." He fired an appraising glance at Jilly, whose eyes were as pleading and confused as his own. "But I think it's probably time for me to get going. I had a wonderful evening, Jilly. I hope you'll let me repay you soon."

Jill grinned. "You mean, you cook?"

Don couldn't help but laugh loudly. "Oh no, that's definitely not what I meant." He waved his open hands in front of him a few times, shaking his head as he did so. "I thought I could take you out to din—"

Jill didn't let him finish. "I would love to go with you somewhere."

"Then we have a date," Don said hopefully but reluctantly. "Well . . . sort of."

Don slipped his coat on, and together he and Jill walked to the front door. They stopped and faced each other, both remaining quiet for a while. Don mulled over the prospect of leaving without kissing this remarkable young woman. But soon, instinct would get the better of him. He pulled her close and leaned his head down against her face. He gently kissed her, and then squeezed her again.

"Good night, Jill. Thanks for everything."

"Thank you," she said, short of breath.

From here, their ways would part for the evening, but Donald Lipton would descend Jilly Larkins' front stoop with a certain spring in his step that had not been there before. His heart would flutter all the way down her darkened walkway. His mind would race with possibilities throughout the slow drive home.

Chapter Sixteen

Winter wasn't about to loosen its grip. Though the days were getting longer and the accumulated snow pack was slowly shrinking, the air was still chilly enough to make even the thought of going outside without a jacket seem like just a whimsical wish. Yet the dreary weather did little to dampen Jill's and Don's spirits. For them, it was as though spring had already arrived. Don felt twenty years younger, as though this newfound romance was bringing a long-dead part of his soul back to life.

The two of them had begun to adapt to new routines in their daily lives that increased involved time together. At first, it was just an occasional dinner date, or perhaps a casual lunch. Soon, however, lunch became an everyday occurrence. For the spring semester, Don had been sure to arrange his schedule so that he had time available to pick Jill up at her bookstore and walk with her to one of the many quaint little restaurants downtown.

They both preferred to walk, regardless of the weather. Whether it was because a drive seemed to go by too quickly or there was that indefinable something about walking, neither of them could say – but still, walking always proved more intimate for both Don and Jill.

One particularly cold afternoon, as the two walked along hand in hand, Jill turned to Don and said, "I can't wait until I can't see my breath anymore. I'm tired of winter."

Don smiled. "I don't mind seeing your breath," he said. "It's kind of cute."

She turned and made a face at him that suggested she might suspect him to have gone mad. "It's just mist," she said. "Mine looks the same as everyone else's."

As always, the professor had a quick answer. "It's not the same as everyone else's. It's special to me because it's the air that *you* were just breathing. It's the element that just got done providing you life and vitality."

Jill giggled. "Gee, you author types sure do analyze every-thing, don't you?"

Don smiled silently.

"Well, to me, it just means that I wish it weren't still so cold anymore." Jill nodded her head contentedly and tightened her grasp on Don's hand.

Don returned the squeeze of her hand with one of his own, and the two continued to walk along in comfortable silence. Their relationship had lately entered that wonderful phase where little gestures could say so much, and words were not always necessary.

They soon arrived at a little bistro that had become one of their favorites. The waiters there had come to know them by name, and would always reserve their preferred table for them in a quiet corner. The couple no longer needed to look at the menu, either, as by now they had already cultivated their favorites. Don's was chicken alfredo and Jill's was linguine with wine sauce. The waiters even knew their wine preference, and lately had begun to bring it to them without asking. It was the kind of familiarity that Don hadn't had with a woman since . . . well, of course, since Julie.

I have to stop making those comparisons, he said to himself. This was an exciting new woman, not a re-creation of someone who was irreplaceable. He was determined to get to know Jill for who she truly was, and not for anything else.

The budding couple held hands across the table as they waited for their lunch to arrive.

"So how's the book business?" Don asked.

"I was going to ask you the same thing," Jill quipped. "I just sell them. You're the one who writes them."

Don took a sip of his wine and made a contented sound to show his approval of it. "True. But without your bookstore, there wouldn't be any audience to receive what I write."

"I never really thought of it that way," Jill said, wrinkling her nose. "Your creativity is still more important than my sales, though."

He lavished in the opportunity to tease her a little. "Creativity is overrated."

"What?" Jill said, oblivious to the fact that she was being put on.

Don made a dismissive gesture with his right hand. "All that stuff about the spark of imagination and where ideas come from. There's really not that much to it. An author reads a lot of stuff and then basically just borrows from the parts that he likes."

Cocking her head a bit, Jill said, "You're not serious, are you?"

Holding back his smile for as long as he could – which by now wasn't too long – Don finally broke into a grin and said, "No. I'm just toying with you."

Jill lifted her hand off Don's and playfully slapped it. "You're crazy! You really had me going for a minute. I thought you were serious."

Still smiling, he replied, "Don't you know by now that I'm never serious?"

She seemed to ponder the question deeply. Don could see her thoughts jolting delightfully behind her gorgeous brown eyes.

"No, I don't know that," she said. "Actually, I believe you can be quite serious when you want to be."

Wow, she really is getting to know me. Don leaned back slightly in his chair, raising the legs less than an inch off the ground. "Okay," he said. "I admit it. But, still, I try not to get serious about things unless there's a real good reason for it."

The moment he finished speaking, Don was overcome with desire to push the conversation in a deeper direction. He had allowed himself the perfect in to discuss how serious he was about Jilly's companionship. But just as he opened his mouth to voice his desire to become something more than just her regular companion, the food arrived and broke the spell of romantic tension that seemed to be hanging over the table.

"To my favorite little couple," the tall, thin waiter said in his classic Italian accent.

Don had come to like this elderly server – and Jill had recently mentioned her endearment to the kindly old man, as well. He was certainly quite a character. He always had a wry comment for them whenever they'd come in, when they would leave, and of course, when he would present them with their food. He'd say, "Love is in the air," and other corny things. At first, it was embarrassing, but by this latest meal, they were used to it.

Both Don and Jill smiled and nodded to the waiter before digging intently into their food.

~~~

As it always seemed to do on these lunches, the time they had together went by too quickly. Soon, they were once again out in the cold air, walking back to Jill's bookstore, hand in hand.

"I'm sick and tired of all this snow and ice," Jill said.

Don didn't really mind it too much, but if it was bothering her, it certainly mattered to him. "So you're not a winter person, I take it."

Jill shook her head. Even with the wool cap she was wearing, the professor could see the way the action made her hair flip back and forth, undulating in the wind. He swore he could look at her hair all day and never tire of it.

"Not really," she said sweetly. "It's too confining. I can't get outside and exercise."

With a bit of a wolfish glare, Don gave her a once-over and said, "You don't look like you're suffering from any lack of exercise to me, toots."

Jill playfully punched Don in the arm. "You *would* say that. You're such a man!"

The two rounded the corner, and the bookstore came into sight. Don stopped abruptly. "Well, aren't you glad that I am?"

"That you are what?"

"A man."

Jill shook her head and then laughed. "Maybe you're right. You're not serious very often."

Don grinned appreciatively. "See. You're finally catching on. But I am serious about what I said regarding winter."

"About exercise?"

"Sure," Don replied. "There's no reason we can't get some indoor exercise."

"*Indoor* exercise?" Jill asked, eyeing him suspiciously. "Are you getting fresh with me, Don Lipton?"

Actually, that wasn't where his mind was going, but he liked the fact that Jill would even insinuate it. "What do you think I am, some kind of crude jerk, he asked, doing his best to fake sincere incredulity.

They started walking again as the cold wind picked up and blew determinedly against them.

"No," Jill said softly. "Just a man."

"Guilty as charged." Don then shook his head in thought as he stared at the snowy ground before him. "But what I was talking about was indoor tennis. Down at the campus, they have these great facilities. I have access to use it anytime I want, at any time of the year. Of course, that's assuming you play the ga—"

Jill interrupted mid-sentence. "Play the game? I'll have you know, I was district-wide champion back in high school."

Don beamed. "Well, sure, but that must have been," he spread his hands apart, just about shoulder width, "a good five or six years ago. You're probably *really* rusty by now!"

Again, Jill delivered a jocular punch to the arm. "It was slightly longer than that, but I play every summer . . . and I'm still pretty good at it."

Just then, they stepped up to the bookstore, the four panes of glass upon its door glistening with frost. With a step and a jangle of the bell, they were standing inside, overcome immediately by the comfort of incredible warmth. Don marveled in how good it felt to take off his jacket and indulge in the well-heated air. As he did so, Jill flipped the *Closed* sign to *Open*.

"So you accept the challenge?" Don asked.

"What challenge?"

"To see if you can beat this old man at tennis next Saturday. How does eleven a.m. sound?"

"It sounds perfect," Jill said, foisting her chin up in mock bravado. "It also doesn't sound like much of a challenge. But it'll be a pleasure to beat up on you a little bit and put you in your place."

Don languished in her playfulness – a part of her that she had only recently made apparent to him. He wasn't sure whether it meant that she was finally opening up to him or he had been enough of a presence to bring the quality to fruition in her, but either way, he swelled almost with pride whenever she cracked a joke or jabbed at him.

Don said nothing in reply. He simply gave his companion a smile and a light kiss and then started to put his jacket back on.

"Leaving so soon?" Jill asked in a somewhat dejected tone. "Back into the deep freeze?"

"I have young minds to inspire," Don quipped. "I can't let them down now, can I?"

"Must be a burden being such a highly sought-after genius," Jill said as she moved behind the cash register and began to organize some paperwork.

"It is," Don deadpanned. "But somebody's got to do it."

~~~

Saturday soon arrived, a day Jill had been greatly looking forward to. It was chilly, overcast, and drizzly, but the climate-controlled environment of the indoor tennis courts made it feel like the pleasant month of May. The only thing that was missing was the warm sunshine.

As she followed her new tennis partner into the complex, Jill was delighted to see that the courts were first class, the newest type of red clay. Without much warm-up – apart from a little playful taunting from both ends of the court – Jill and Don launched right into a few practice volleys. In no time, Jill could see that this would be a fast-paced game. The ball was lively.

"Wow," Jill said. "Look at that bounce! I'm more used to the old fashioned, outdoor courts."

Don grinned, and Jill could sense a kind of leering just behind his eyes as he looked her over. Her heart fluttered as she thought about how she must look in her sparkling white tennis dress. She had worn the slightly revealing outfit just to toy with him. The fact that the bottom of the skirt cut just long enough to cover the tops of her thighs had already proven to work to her advantage. She allowed herself the briefest moment of pride: Her legs were indeed shapely and she knew that she carved an attractive figure in the outfit.

Shortly, Don's leer shaped into a grin. "Are you copping out on me, Miss District Champ?" he asked.

She took up the challenge with one of her broadest smiles. "Bring it on, smarty pants. Bring it on."

As the points were played, it became immediately apparent that both were having an extraordinary time. Some of the volleys were endless, as each concentrated deeply on their strokes. Each with their own commitments to doing well and besting the other, they played hard.

In no time, they had worked up a sweat. A shine of perspiration covered them. Despite what Jill might have thought, the glimmer of her sweat actually added to her sex appeal – and this fact was in part responsible for the fact that the game began turning in her favor. Don's eyes simply wandered a bit too often. But mostly, Jill began to win more points because of her sheer will to beat her older competition.

That's when she lunged too far for a return shot and pulled a leg muscle. She meekly cried out in pain, doing her best not to make too much of it. Despite her resolve, the pain was so sharp and sudden that she was unable to conceal her groan.

He ran to her, reeling around the net. "Are you okay?"

She pressed the tip of her racket on the clay as she massaged her calf with her free hand. "I just pulled a muscle," she said through slightly gritted teeth. Then she did her best to tough it out and trivialize the matter. "I hate to be a party pooper, but I'm afraid I'm done for the day."

Don knelt down and ran his hand over her calf. Although his touch was certainly pleasant, Jill could sense that it was strictly clinical in scope and execution. She liked the attention, but was truly regretful about the whole thing.

"Damn," she said. "I hate to have to cut our time short."

Without smiling, he scooped her up in his arms. "We don't have to cut it short. I have some wonderful liniment at my place that will fix you right up."

She felt her heart race. Protesting mildly, she said, "Okay, Don, but I really *can* walk. Or at least limp. You can put me down."

Now the grin had returned to his face. "A gallant fellow like me? Never."

~~~

An hour later, Don had set Jill down on the divan in his living room. She gazed around the place, finding evidence of his taste and manner in every corner, upon every bookshelf, and surrounding every furnishing. In short order, Don returned with a blanket, which he used to cover her bare legs.

"Not a good idea to get chilled," he said. "Need to keep the injury warm." He disappeared once more.

A few minutes later, he returned, looking rather distraught. "I'm sorry. I don't seem to have the liniment I promised . . ." Then his face brightened a little, like that of a hopeful child. "But I can go down to the drugstore for some."

Jill grinned. "Is this kind of like the old, 'I ran out of gas' ploy?"

Don bellowed a singular laugh. "Yes, I suppose it's similar," he said. "But alas, I don't get much chance to use it." He raised a solitary finger in the air, his bushy eyebrows arching. "Let me get you a nice stiff brandy. Brandy is soothing. Great for any injury."

Jill didn't object, as she actually liked watching Don fussing over her. She couldn't deny it.

When he returned from what must have been the kitchen, he sat beside her and produced two large snifters, handing one to her. They each took several quick drafts.

"Ooh," she cooed. "That feels so warm in my tummy."

Don furrowed his brow and ran his hand across the blanket, just along Jilly's shin. "Look," he said, "where you really need warmth is on that leg."

"And what do you suggest?" Jill asked, pointing her nose in the air and smiling suggestively.

"Hot water therapy," Don said matter-of-factly. "I feel terrible about that liniment. At least let me treat you to a dip."

"A dip?" She cocked her head. "Hot water?"

"Yeah. I have a hot tub."

An awkward silence followed.

"I don't suppose you have a bathing suit for me," Jill said, looking down at her nearly empty glass.

"No, all I have is my Scout's honor," he said, grinning winningly and holding up his fingers in the Boy Scout salute.

Unexpectedly – even for her – Jilly immediately warmed to the idea. *Must be the brandy,* she thought. The truth was, though, the idea titillated her. Just as quickly as the desire came, it was shoved to the side by a sudden burst of guilt. She didn't want to seem prudish, but still, she felt the need to hesitate.

Don seemed to sense her apprehension. "Look," he said, "I don't have to get into the tub with you." Quickly, however, that now familiar impish grin replaced his expression of sincerity. "But it would be nice even if I did have to honor my Boy Scout oath."

She lifted the brandy snifter for another sip. "Will you honor it?" she asked as she finished swallowing down the warming liquid.

"Yes, of course. I'll even dim the lights if you're shy."

"You will?"

"Yes." Don seemed almost on the edge of his seat.

Their eyes locked, exploring each other. She read sincerity and honor in them.

Finally, she said, "Okay."

He led the way, careful to reach back and offer his arm in the apparent hopes of ensuring that she could limp without too much discomfort. Both carried their brandy. True to his word, Don immediately dimmed the lights as they stepped into the granite-tiled yard on the U-shaped northern side of his house.

It was a quaint little spot nestled between the two turret-like structures that framed the front and back of Don's house. With the small patch of grass paved over and then crowned with marvelous slabs of pink granite, the patchwork courtyard marched several feet to the west, where a tall and wood-lined tub beckoned. When its removable neoprene cover was unfurled, the bluish water of the tub churned invitingly from below. At the touch of a button, it began frothing white and effervescent in the soft light cast by the antique streetlamp that stood at attention just on the edge of the stone flooring.

"I'll go first," Don said reassuringly. "I'll turn my back so you can have your privacy."

She nodded coyly.

"But I want you to be sure to hang on to the safety rail," Don added. "Because if I think you need help, I'll turn."

"I'll be okay." Her face was flushing now.

She closed her eyes and listened to the sounds of Don removing his sweater and then allowing his light khakis to fall to the floor. The buckle of his belt clunked clearly against the cold granite below. She shivered at the sudden and chilly wind. Then, the sound of Don's feet trudging through the surface and down into the depths of the tub strangely startled her. Her heart leapt and then sank as she realized that there was no turning back now. She couldn't simply leave her host nude in a tub.

So with nothing left to do, she checked to make sure Don wasn't looking, and then quickly slipped her tennis dress over her head. With another deep shiver, she slid out of her underwear. And with one last imploring glance at the back of Don's head, she hastily removed her sports bra. She was delighted to see that not even when her toes touched the water and she slid softly inside did her companion move even a muscle. He stared without wavering into the darkness beyond the slight glow of the streetlamp.

"Is it okay to turn around?" he asked.

Jill quickly looked down at herself, seeing that the frothing water was properly lapping high enough above her breasts to allow her to maintain her decency. "Yes," she said, more confidently than she had intended.

Don turned slowly and sank down in his spot, which was on the complete opposite side of the tub from Jill. At first, she respected the show of honor that his distance presented, but then, as she let the allure of the swirling hot water take over, the feeling quickly evaporated. It was replaced by an overwhelming desire to get closer to him. For a long while, Jill concentrated on the water. She luxuriated in it, letting it swoosh around and caress her naked body, bringing her senses alive with the tingling sensation of tiny bubbles traveling the peaks and valleys of her womanhood.

When Don spoke, his voice had the effect of breaking a trance. "How does that calf feel?"

"I feel wonderful," Jill murmured, her eyes closed contentedly.

"I mean the leg."

"Hmmm?" she cooed.

"How's the leg?"

"Oh," she said, feeling only a little silly. "Much better. Much."

At that moment, snow began to fall softly from the sky, melting instantly on the sides of the tub, in the water, and upon Jill's warming face. She languished at the touch of the quick moist cold against her glistening hot skin. With each dropping flake of crystalline beauty, her inhibitions lifted. Not even the welcome flicker of the brandy within her stomach could touch such luxury. She felt wonderful, relaxed, and utterly content.

She stretched her arms up and held onto the edge of the tub. The movement pulled her torso slightly higher out of the water. The full bend of the tops of her breasts came into view, but she found herself relishing the opportunity to be just a bit more suggestive; to show just a bit more skin than she would normally dare.

Without opening her eyes, she could feel his admiring gaze upon her. It warmed her along with the water and the brandy, which she sipped once more. As the burn trickled down her throat, she felt the coquette in her come to the surface. She opened her own eyes and watched him intently. "You sure you didn't see anything?" she teased.

He grinned. "I don't think so, tied as I am to my oath of honor."

She became downright playful now. "You believe in that Boy Scout honors stuff?"

"Absolutely," he said – and he said it with such seriousness that she wondered if she had insulted him with her little quip.

She lowered her eyelids slightly. As she did, she could feel the perspiration from her brow lilt down and settle upon her rosy cheeks. "I don't think your oath precludes you coming over here to be closer to me."

Don's voice seemed to waver boyishly. "How close?"

"As much as honor allows," she said with a seductive smile.

Although she wasn't really worried about Don losing control, when he got near her, she began to wonder if her little flirtation was going to get out of hand. But before she could even rethink herself, she felt her knees go limp and her skin ache for his touch. All at once, Don was kissing her, his lips hungry, his tongue soft and forgiving against her own. Her heart raced, sensing the warmth within her, churning against the rolling heat of the water and the roiling presence of her desire. She returned his kiss with ardor.

Their bodies had not yet touched, but she longed to feel his embrace. A quick glance revealed that she had allowed herself to come far enough out of the water to partially expose her breasts to the cold night air. Only the occasional lap of water would pre-serve her modesty.

Suddenly, without another touch beyond their lips, they parted, both of them breathless – white hot and dripping with the heat of the tub and the intensity of their desire. As she gazed at him, she lost her grip on the feeling, wondering quickly why he looked so confused. His confusion melted into what appeared to be shame.

"Do you feel better?" he asked, his voice croaking slightly. "Do you want to get out?"

A numb kind of discomfort rushed from her heart to her fingertips and back again. "Yes and no," she said, every ounce of her passionate half wishing the answer to be no. "But I guess I don't want to get waterlogged."

"No," Don said rather mournfully. "You can turn around if you like. I'm getting out . . . But I'm not all that bashful, so you don't really have to turn if you don't want to."

She took a deep breath. "I'll turn."

She listened longingly to the sound of his body plowing through the water and then his feet swishing over the still-surging surface.

In a moment, he called for her to turn. "I'll turn my head," he said, "but I want you to grab my hand when you get out. You can get so relaxed in these things that your injured leg might give out under you."

She turned and immediately grinned at the sight of Don standing half-naked in an oversized towel. His body faced away from the tub, but he had reached his hand back and extended it toward her, urging her to take hold.

With an inaudible but appreciative laugh, she took his hand and climbed as daintily as possible out of the tub. She grabbed the towel that Don had placed on one of the wooden stairs leading up to the tub and turned her back to him. But instead of immediately wrapping it around herself, she began patting her face dry. She wondered if he was watching, and was a little surprised to discover that she cared little one way or the other. "Are you still on your honor?" she asked.

"Yes," he muttered with a soft sigh, "I'm afraid I am."

Her heart melted with admiration for this respectful man. Why, though, had she hoped that his answer would be a reluctant no?

Chapter Seventeen

Jill parked her Sable in the small parking lot behind the bookstore and opened her umbrella as she stepped out into the rain. The air was chilly, and with her free hand, she pulled her sweater around her more tightly. A dentist's appointment had occupied most of her morning, so MacKenzie had been scheduled to come in earlier than usual. Normally, Jill would have never asked one of her employees to open the store, but business was usually light in the mornings, and so she gave in to the pressure of an otherwise full schedule.

"Good morning," MacKenzie said cheerfully. "How was your trip to the dentist?"

Jill smiled with mock exasperation. "There are a lot of other places I'd have rather been this morning."

MacKenzie giggled. "Yeah, I hate going there myself."

"Well, it was just a cleaning today. Painless." Jill shook her umbrella out and folded it up. She then took off her overcoat and hooked it over the antique rack near the door. "So, how are things going here?"

"Just fine." MacKenzie pensively pressed the flat end of the ballpoint pen she was holding against her cheek. Her curly blonde hair framed a tiny, porcelain, adorable face. "Well, there weren't too many customers, but Mr. Bishop did come in to pick up that large order . . . so, sales-wise, it was great."

Jill gave a single emphatic nod. "Good."

MacKenzie's face brightened suddenly, and then her eyes grew fretfully excited as though she were a witness in one of the crime thrillers so popular amongst the casual customers of the Open Book. "You did get a rather crazy phone call, though," she said.

Jill's body immediately went rigid. Her gaze froze upon her comely and bubbly employee.

"Some man that I didn't recognize . . . and who wouldn't give a name . . . called and was looking for you." MacKenzie started rolling her hand in the air in a clockwise fashion, as though grasping for her next words. "His voice sounded urgent, but he wouldn't leave a message."

Jill tried to stay calm. "So you said urgent," she said, her voice quivering only slightly. "What made you say that?"

MacKenzie's tone intensified and her eyebrows arched almost comically. "Well, he just kept asking me if I was sure I didn't know how to reach you, and he insisted I tell him when you would be back. I mean . . . you know . . . he wouldn't accept my telling him I wasn't sure."

Jill could feel her face run white. "Did he sound like an older or younger man?"

MacKenzie shook her head slowly and squinted, clearly unsure of the answer.

Jill moved closer to the counter, her expression imploring, pleading. "Are you sure it wasn't just one of the college kids playing a prank or something?"

MacKenzie straightened up, her lips pursed. "No," she said. "I'm not sure, but this guy sounded older. He had a very deep voice . . ."

Jill's head began swimming.

"Oh!" MacKenzie said, her hands bobbing up and down rapidly at her sides. "And he used the words 'come on' a lot."

From the description, Jill was sure it was Michael. Without a word, she crossed behind the counter and looked down at the old rotary phone. Beside it, she had fixed an LED display that reported the Caller ID of all callers from the day. The only number that showed was from "Private Caller." The words chilled her to the bone. They were familiar words, as Michael had long ago figured out how to block his information from showing up on the other line. Worse yet, there was no way Jill could know whether her estranged former lover had called locally or long-distance.

She had already gotten a restraining order on Michael in Minnesota, but it occurred to her suddenly that that restraining order did not apply in Michigan. She would have to get a new one now.

But then, just as suddenly, doubt crept into her mind – doubt that a restraining order would be enough to stop Michael, anyway. He had become so controlling and so unruly that he most likely never gave any thought to the law. Would it even do any good to threaten him with arrest if he came anywhere near her?

She had seen the horror he was capable of before. How he was capable of going from perfect date to monster in a matter of minutes. With all the ills he had brought her, she knew she could never trust him again, even for a moment.

Still, a part of her cared for him. She knew he needed help – professional help – and she burned with the fact that getting him such help was out of her control.

Regardless, right now, she had to find a way to hide so he couldn't surprise her with a visit. If he knew that she was at the bookstore, he could walk in at any moment.

She started to quake from her joints to her limbs.

MacKenzie placed a steady hand on her employer's shoulder. "Can I help you, Jill?" she asked soothingly. "You look like you've seen a ghost. Can I call someone for you?"

Jill took a deep breath and calmed herself marginally. "No, MacKenzie," she said. "I'll be okay. I'm just a little shaken up by that call." Her gaze began darting around the room erratically, mindlessly looking for things she would need to take with her. She heard herself speaking. "Would you mind putting those books into inventory for me today? Do you remember how I showed you to do it?"

MacKenzie's voice had a distant quality, as though she was deeply troubled by what she was witnessing. "Sure thing," she said. "But I still think you should sit down for a bit."

Jilly nodded reassuringly. "I will." She walked to the back room, near the children's section, opened a bottle of water from the miniature refrigerator, and took a sip. Her thoughts went immediately to Don. In her unquiet mind, he represented an island of acceptance, security, and comfort – everything Michael was not, and everything she needed right now . . . but their relationship was still so new. She didn't want to do *anything* to make him pull away.

She knew she had to give herself time to calm down. So, in an effort to take her mind off the problem, she sat down behind the counter to sort through the box of used books acquired during the previous week. She focused her mind on the binding of each book, the print, the musty smell of old volumes, and the sleek cover art of new paperbacks. Since childhood, books had served as an escape, and the best she could hope for at the moment was just such a distraction.

~~~

Since he didn't teach morning classes on Friday, Don had used his free time to stop at the supermarket and pick up a bouquet of white roses before swinging by the bookstore. He had already spent several hours working on his book, and so he had found contentment in the notion that lunch with Jill would cap off a good, productive morning.

Jill was sitting behind the counter with a cardboard box in front of her and a large hardcover book in her hand, yet her gaze seemed fixed on a distant point. She jumped as Don shut the door behind him, its string of bells jingling. Her normally rosy face was white.

Her eyes widened with surprise when they met his. "Hi there," she said, clearly forcing her smile as she accepted the bouquet. "What's the occasion?"

Don felt uneasy as he looked her over. "I just thought we could have lunch. Jill, what's wrong?"

Jill glanced in the direction of the few other customers in the shop and then sighed. "I think I'll take you up on that lunch offer. Let's go someplace where we can talk."

"That sounds good to me. There's a little café over on Front Street. I think it's still early enough to beat the noon crowd." He offered his arm in a charming and carefree fashion, but his heart still held a good deal of concern. "What do you say?"

"Great." Jill turned to MacKenzie. "I'm sorry to do this to you, honey, but I'm going to step out again for a little while. Call me on my cell if you need me for anything."

"Okay," MacKenzie said with a chipper little nod. "But I think I'm starting to get the hang of things around here."

Jill darted into the back room and returned with her purse.

"I'll drive," Don said, "Unless you want to walk."

"Not today," Jill said, a little too quickly. "I'd rather ride, if that's okay with you. I just got a big order of books in, and they still have to be put in the computer before we can call the customers who're waiting for them. I don't want to be gone too long."

Don nodded, smiled grandly, and offered his arm again. This time, Jilly took it. Her movements were delicate but her grip was unusually tight. He led her out to the sidewalk and into his car, which he had parked in the metered space closest to the door.

Minutes later, Jill and Don were seated in a nearby café. They sat next to the big floor-to-ceiling windows near the sidewalk. What was left of the snow outside was melting against the rain. Both ordered a soup and sandwich combo, and Don smiled with concern at his companion as she looked nervously outside.

"So, how has your morning been?" Jill asked suddenly, her voice quivering. "What do you usually do on Fridays?"

Don answered distantly and quickly. "Fridays are usually catch-up days for me, but today I had time to write . . ."

"It's good that you take time to write," Jill said, looking once again out the window. "I suppose you're wondering what I wanted to talk about."

"It did cross my mind." Don placed his hand on Jill's. It was cold, clammy, and stiff. "So what's bothering you?"

Jill's words came slowly at first. Her hesitation to share such vulnerability was apparent. "Well . . . do you remember when I told you about . . . well . . . about Michael . . . the guy . . . the *idiot* who insists on bothering me?"

Don nodded. He could feel his face flushing, too.

"Well . . . he's somehow traced me to my store. I guess he called me there today."

"You guess?" Don tightened his grip around the back of Jilly's hand.

"MacKenzie took the call. I was at the dentist." Jill shook her head and pressed her free hand to her forehead.

Don took a long, audible breath. "That would scare me, too," he said, wishing he could think of something more reassuring to offer. "You just never know what that kind of guy has in mind."

Jill's face squinted, looking very much like she was on the verge of tears. Instantly, he regretted his oafish words. *You're an author,* he chided himself. *Be more tactful.* "What can I do to help you?" was all he could think to say.

Shimmering tears began to form at the corners of Jilly's reddening eyes. "I don't know if there's anything anyone can do," she squeaked. "I just don't know what to do. I think I'll die if he shows up at my house."

Don's protective instincts kicked in. His heart surged with the warm and commanding sensation of honor and chivalry. "You can't be at your house alone," he said. "We have to do something about that."

Jill raised both hands beside her head, causing Don's palm to slap limply against the counter. "Sure," she said with clear sarcasm. "You have anything in mind?"

Don was silent for a moment, deep in thought. "Well," he finally said, "I have a little cabin near my house. It's hidden in the woods . . . and hardly anyone knows it's there. That would make an excellent place for you to hide until it's safe to be back at home."

Jill shook her head emphatically. "No way! I'd be scared to death alone in the woods . . . and in a strange cabin, too."

Don looked down at the table, searching for the most appropriate turn of phrase. "Ahhh . . . I didn't mean you'd be there . . . alone." He looked up almost childishly from under his brow. "I have afternoon classes today, but I can give you the directions and the key to the cabin . . . and I can meet you there later. There's a sleeper sofa, and I can sleep there. You can have the bed."

There was a long silence as Jill looked down at her hands, kneading them together.

"Well," Don implored, "what do you think?"

"A cabin in the woods?" Jill said, rolling her eyes. "With you there to protect me? How could I possibly turn down an opportunity like that?" The stress left her face as she smiled. "You're kidding me . . . of course I'll go."

Don's heart soared. Still, he felt the need to add a few reassuring words. "I've never been more serious, Jilly. Very few people know about the cabin. This Michael would surely have no way of finding it . . . or you. You'd be safe." He smiled sheepishly. "Unless, of course, you're afraid of me."

Jill chuckled, tears still lining her eyes. "Funny," she said. "Maybe I *should* be . . . but I'm not."

Don smiled and placed his hand back on hers.

"Okay," Jill said. "I'll take you up on your offer, at least for tonight." Jill brought her other hand and rested it on Don's, creating a small stack of hands on the edge of the table. "Thanks so much for caring."

"Easy to do," Don said with a grin. He reached into his pocket and took out his key ring. He slid a rusty key off of it and handed it to Jill. "Here's the key to the cabin. Do you happen to have a pen on you?"

Jill absently began rifling through her handbag. "Sure do . . . here." She produced the pen.

Don took a clean napkin from the table and sketched a map for Jill. "It's really easy to get there." He began tracing the tip of the pen along the picture he had just drawn. "All you do is follow this road along the woods to the end, and then take a right. Then another left. You'll see several rolls of evergreens before you come to a clearing in the woods. That clearing's right before the cabin."

Jill carefully grabbed the napkin when he handed it to her. Her eyes fell upon it and lingered there. "Sounds like an adventure," she said. The tone of her voice suggested that a weight had been removed from her shoulders.

"Could be," Don said with a smile. "The two of us alone in the middle of the woods overnight." At the words, he noticed doubt and uneasiness creeping back into Jill's eyes. She shifted tensely. Don offered a placating hand. "I'm only kidding, of course. You'll be safe from Michael . . . and if you play your cards right, you should be safe from me."

Jill's face melted into a pensive frown. "It's been a long time since I've had to play cards."

"Me, too," Don said with a sigh. "So, what do you say?"

Jill slumped back in her chair. Her face grew warm and bright once more. "A knight in shining armor offers to protect me from the villain? How could I say no to that?"

Don chuckled. "Great." He then looked at his modest wristwatch. "I hate to end this, but I do have to get back to the college. My friend Tom had to take the day off for some medical things, and I'm subbing for him."

Jill stood without a word. She still seemed rather uncomfortable and shifty.

With a second glance at his companion, Don walked to the counter and paid the bill. Together, they left the restaurant and walked to the car.

"I should be done with my last class by three-thirty," Don said as he took his seat beside Jilly. "And then I have a few errands to run. So I'll meet you at the cabin a little after eight. Take your cell phone with you, and if you have any trouble finding it, call me."

"You are so thoughtful," Jill said, never taking her eyes off Don. "I owe you."

Minutes later, they were parked in front of the store. Jill reached for the handle to get out.

Don took her hand and pulled her over to his side. He kissed her briefly on the lips. "You're amazing," he said. "I know you can handle anything that comes your way."

As she exited the car, he could see that she seemed a little more secure. He hoped that meant she believed in her security . . . and him, too.

Chapter Eighteen

Night had descended by the time Jill had left the bookstore and stopped by her house to pack a few things, change her clothes, and fill the automatic feeder for the cat. She had intended to leave while it was still light – since she preferred not to drive in unfamiliar territory in the dark, especially with Michael possibly lurking in the area. But business at the store had required her attention, and after her conversation with Don, her resolve had formed anew. She refused to let the threat of an unstable ex-boyfriend keep her from her responsibilities or turn her into a phobic shadow of herself. She would fight for the right to live her own life, if that's what it came down to.

For now, though, she had to admit that it was nice to have a retreat where she could go to release some of her worries, if only for a few days.

Using the map light she kept in her glove compartment, Jill followed Don's directions to a one-lane road surrounded by pines. She could see the sunset in the distance, cresting behind a hill above the valley, over the trees. The night would be peaceful.

As she rolled slowly down the dirt road, a thicket to the left came into view. Her instincts suggested that this would be the place where she would find Don's cabin.

For a moment, as the small wooden vacation home came into view, she wondered whether it was real or a dream. None of it seemed likely – running to a cabin in the woods to avoid a former lover; driven into the arms of a new man on the back of a stalker.

She parked and stepped out of her car, feeling the chilly wind glide across her forehead. She brushed the hair from her face and started towards the porch.

The size of Don's cabin was certainly modest, but it appeared quaint, even in the eerie purple twilight that huddled all around it. Large logs had been arranged horizontally to form its four rectangular walls, harkening back to pioneer days, days of plentiful natural resources and human simplicity. It appeared as though the cabin was identical on all sides – with similar sized walls and two four-paned windows on each facade. The windows themselves looked quite dirty, as the brown of their grime rang true against the backdrop of the pitch black within the cabin.

Jill approached the small covered porch that jutted out several feet from the screen-covered front door of the house. The surface beneath her feet as she stepped onto the porch consisted of a series of well-stained but well-worn planks of wood. They creaked ominously under her feet. Above her was what appeared to be a triangular structure fashioned out of plywood and added to the home post-construction. The whole conglomeration had been painted over with thick brown-gray paint and was held up by two slender posts on either side. The posts appeared to be stripped and varnished tree saplings.

She paused before opening the door to take a deep breath and collect her thoughts. She still wasn't sure if she should have come.

The screen door, too, creaked into the night as she swung it back and allowed it to come to rest on her shoulder. She fumbled with the key that Don had given her, a little uneasy about the fact that she could now see absolutely nothing to her right despite the purplish light from the sunset that still radiated into the forest.

All at once there was an unfamiliar sound. It sounded like a twig snapping. Immediately, she backed away from the screen door. Her vision darted in the direction of the sound. In one quick moment, it seemed as if all remaining light from the sun had been blotted out. What was left was the strangely brown cover of early nightfall. Her eyes had not yet adjusted. She could get no bearing on the distance.

Then she heard another sound. It was closer this time. It must be the rustling of leaves.

She dropped the key, feeling her heart roar within her as she bent down to fumble over the porch, running her shaky hand over its surface. The wind began to pick up, kicking up more rushing leaves, drowning out any hope she could have had in uncovering the presence she now distinctly felt to her right.

Oh God, she thought, feeling her fingertips move over the rough boards in search of the key, *he followed me here.*

Then, in a dull flash, her eyes adjusted to the darkness and she felt her fingers graze against the cold rusty metal of the key. She vaulted to her feet, took a quick and terrified look into the woods to her right, saw nothing, and then began her quivering attempt at the lock to the front door.

More wind. More leaves. A whirling torrent seemed to be picking up next to the cabin. And still, the key fit securely into the lock. A surge of hope carried within her. She could lock herself inside, away from her pursuer.

Jill's heart beat rapidly as she twisted the knob and forced the door open. Total darkness surrounded her as she stepped inside and quickly locked the door behind her. She leaned over and laid her overnight bag near her feet.

He had said there would be no electricity.

Where the hell is that flashlight? She slipped her small hand into the pocket of her jeans and felt the light with her fingertips. *Here it is,* she thought, the fear now pulsating as far as her fingertips as she reached to switch on the beam.

Strangely, she closed her eyes. She felt almost certain that she would not want to see whatever the light revealed. Then she peeled them open. The tiny stream of light from her flashlight focused on the opposite wall . . . a wall made of logs and packed together with what appeared to be mud.

Circling the room slowly with the tiny beam, she was astounded by the objects that surrounded her. It was like stepping back in time. She found everything from an antique icebox to an old-fashioned cooking stove, complete with the warming oven. She remembered her grandmother talking about one of these.

To her right was a beautiful stone fireplace. Despite her remaining fear, her body suddenly imagined cuddling in front of it on a cold winter's night with Don. She knew all at once that she wanted it to happen for them. She was tired of waiting.

She panned the light over each window that she could see from this vantage, checking whether they had been locked. Immediately, she realized that it would mean little, as the windows could always be broken by anyone trying to force their way inside. For a moment, she listened for footsteps on the porch. All she heard was the wind.

All at once, the last place she wanted to be was standing with her back to the cabin's door. So she rushed toward the fireplace, where she found a box of long-stemmed matches lying on the hearth. She picked them up and then flashed her light around for a lamp. There, on the wooden table near the two windows on the north side of the cabin, she saw an old oil lamp.

Walking toward the table, she refused to allow her eyes to fall upon the windows. Little would be seen through them, she realized – they were so very dirty – but she could not help but feel his presence. It was a familiar feeling, as though her stalker were watching her every move. The pain and fear of it all was almost too much to bear as she unsteadily lifted the lamp to eye level and shined the flashlight upon it.

The base of the lamp revealed happy news: the reservoir was full of oil. So she lowered the wick into it and brought it back up. One scratch on the carton with the match and the flame began to glow. She lit the lamp and put the match out, then quickly turned her back to the windows, feeling a chill wash over her spine as she peered at the now-lit and still-locked front door.

What if he's out there? She thought. *I'm alone in this place. No one knows where I am except Don . . .* She checked her watch. Only six-thirty. *Why did he say he'd be here so late? How long could his errands possibly take?*

With the lamp held aloft in her left hand, she still held the freshly extinguished match in her right. She opened the metal door on the stove – cringing at the noise – and disposed of the match. This way, she could be sure that nothing caught on fire.

Shining the light back toward the stone fireplace, she noticed the stacks of kindling and a pile of dry wood. It was a chilly night, and the cabin was certainly not well insulated. If she was to wait nearly two hours for her protector, she reasoned, she might as well do so by the fire.

The only trouble was that she had never built a fire. She had seen it done many times, of course, but she had never had any experience. *Can't be that difficult,* she thought.

Despite her confidence, she remained moderately surprised at how true the sentiment was. With the help of the dry kindling, the pair of logs she had set in the fireplace was alight in no time. Soon, the fire was crackling as the resin oozed from the wood.

She felt strange to admit it to herself, but having a fire going certainly did calm her nerves. With the light flickering inside, there would no longer be any hope of seeing through the windows to the outside – and to her, in fear, ignorance was bliss. And the walls may have been sturdy, but they were certainly faulty when it came to blocking out noises from the outside. If she remained quiet, she would be able to hear anyone approaching the cabin – or skulking around the outside.

And so her attention turned to admiring rather than dreading this tiny, quaint, painfully empty space. Looking around, on the wall opposite the fireplace, Jill spotted a little flower on a small wooden table that rested beside a narrow rocking chair. After closer examination, she realized that it had been dried for some time now.

Why would a man keep a single dried flower . . . unless . . .

A little diary lay on the table beside the flower. Jill was suddenly gripped by the urge to open it and explore its contents. She was looking for answers, and a deep gut feeling suggested that some of them might be within those pages. She knew that reading the book would be invading his privacy, but she wanted to know about his world as much as she wanted him to become a part of hers.

She sat down in the rocking chair and ran her hand over the surface of the journal like a child examining the wrapping paper covering his gifts in the days leading up to Christmas. An owl hooted outside, startling her, jarring her hand away from the book. She laughed at her own cowardice.

Her attention turned back to the fireplace, and she noticed for the first time that it was not part of a full wall, as she had first imagined. No, the fireplace had been built into a wall that ended several feet from the front wall of the cabin. Jill stood and walked around this half-wall, realizing that the stone of the fireplace continued on to a small bedroom behind. This quaint little bedroom featured two windows, just like every other wall in the cabin. The far window rested just above the head of a surprisingly large Jenny Lind bed. It seemed to occupy almost all of the room. Running parallel at the foot of this bed was a little dresser, dusty from disuse.

She grinned at the sight of it all. *Like stepping back in time,* she thought again. Then she turned to grab her overnight bag from beside the front door. She brought the bag back into the bedroom and set it on the end of the bed. Opening it, she rifled through for a nightgown. She had packed a beautiful silky pink dressing gown that clearly revealed her attractive figure – and she now relished the opportunity to put it on before Don even arrived.

She slipped out of her clothes and pulled the nightgown over her head. She folded her clothes and placed them neatly back in her bag, which she set on the floor at the foot of the bed.

Looking around, she noticed the candle lanterns that had been fastened to the walls. So she walked back to the dining table to grab the matches, and then returned to the bedroom to light the lanterns. With the room well-lit, she climbed into the bed, pushing the quilted coverlet and thick down blanket past her feet. She sighed dreamily when she saw that the sheets were made of flannel.

She pulled the covers over herself and snuggled up beneath them. It was so cozy and warm. She realized that she was still wearing her wristwatch, which was a happy mistake, since she suddenly wanted to check on how much longer she would have to wait for Don's arrival. *Seven p.m.*

Oh, how long must I wait? She thought this as she removed the watch and set it on the little bedside table to her left.

She yawned. It had been a very long day, and the bed was so welcoming. Maybe she'd just lie here a while and wait for Don to arrive.

Her thoughts of Don made her realize how much she missed him. She wished he would hurry. She was so anxious to see him again. She had to admit that, earlier, as she drove to the cabin, she had felt surprisingly hopeful that this little getaway would become something more than just a way to hide from Michael. She had very deep feelings for Don, and although she hadn't allowed herself to accept it, she knew she was falling in love with him.

Suddenly, footsteps on the porch caught her attention. Every inch of Jill tensed beneath the sheets. Like a child, she covered her head with the blankets, quivering beneath.

Don, she thought, *please let that be you.*

She reached her quaking hand out to grab the wristwatch. It was still only seven-thirty. *Too early for it to be him . . .*

The sound died down for a moment. The visitor to the cabin seemed to be stalling. The tension washed over Jilly, crippling her, numbing her to something beyond simple fear.

Then, she heard the sound of a key being inserted into the lock.

Don, she thought. *It's him!*

She flung the blankets down to her ankles and sat up in bed, forgetting that she was dressed for sleep – and dressed rather suggestively.

~~~

Don opened the door and walked in. His heart had already been warmed by the sight of her car parked outside, and was warmed further by the crackling fire that greeted him on his arrival.

"Jill," he called, "are you here?" No response. "Where are you? Talk to me."

He stood a moment in silence, waiting for an answer.

"I'm in here, Don," came the reply. "It's okay. I've been waiting for you."

He turned to his left and walked through the narrow gap that
led into the bedroom. The candlelight cascading from the walls
reflected the image of her slender, shapely, nearly naked body.
She had let her hair down, and it was flowing below her shoulders. Tiny curls framed her face. She was beautiful.

"Well, I see that you found this place okay," he said with a
grin. "How long have you been here?"

Jill turned onto her hip and patted the bed beside her. "We can
talk later," she said. "All I want now is to have you come in here
and hold me." She then scooted to the side and made room for
him. "I'm scared and cold. Please hold me and take the chill off
my body."

Don could feel the force of her eagerness pulling at his heart. He
wanted to go to her and hold her at least forever. But what if . . .
What if he was still chasing after Julie, what if all these feelings
were for her, not Jill? He took a few steps forward, and then stopped.

"Are you coming?" Jill cooed. "I've been waiting so long.
What're you afraid of?"

Don stood stiffly, stretching his hand out in a placating
fashion. "I'm not sure that you want this any more than I do,
but then . . . I'm not sure that *I* want it, either." He sighed, letting his tensed shoulders drop. "This is all so crazy. I walk into
my cabin, find a beautiful lady waiting to cuddle with me, begging me to come to bed with her, and I freeze."

Jill smiled as she looked up at him. "Then why don't you just get
over here closer to me? We'll make each other secure and toasty."

Still, Don hesitated. He felt his concern spreading to his eyes,
then down to his lips. He was certain that he looked quite the fool.

"I realize that I love you, Don," Jill said – and her voice
sounded utterly sincere. "I honestly love you. Does that help you
make up your mind?"

Slowly, he walked over to the bed, leaned down, and gave her
a gentle kiss on the cheek. "I love you, too," he said, feeling his

very soul fill with warmth and light as he did so. "But I'm not sure yet that it is *this* kind of love I feel . . . or maybe I'm not sure that this is the time and place to share it."

He leaned down again, and she pulled him close to her. He could feel himself relaxing, knowing that it would not take much to get him to surrender himself to her.

"Lay with me," she whispered. "Just for a moment . . . please."

He stood up, carefully pulled his sweater over his head, and laid it on the end of the bed. Next, he removed his slacks, allowing them to fall heavily to the floor. He then slid under the sheets beside her and settled into her open arms. She pulled his head close to her own and leaned in to kiss him. He felt her warm tongue slip between his lips. He returned the pressure, his body surging with desire.

~~~

Jill could feel her breasts against his bare chest, wanting to stay that way forever. She thought it would be okay if time stopped right then.

The kiss lasted for only a few brief and intoxicating moments before Don pulled himself away. "Did you like that?" he asked meekly.

Jill's heart beat so loudly she feared he might hear it. "No," she whispered. "I loved it!"

Don sighed. "I did, too."

She reached for him, placing her hands on the backs of his shoulders. "Then let's do it again and again . . ."

Don pulled her into his arms and kissed her again. Jill could feel the force and passion of the kiss from the top of her head to the tips of her toes. If he could make her feel that way with a simple kiss, she could only imagine what it would be like if they made love. She closed her eyes, trying to hold on to the feeling for as long as she could. They continued to hold each other for a while longer, and then Don slowly pulled himself back once more.

"This is wonderful, Jill," he said. "I love laying here with you. You're stirring up feelings I haven't known in years . . . but . . .

Jill stared deeply into his eyes, searching for clues to what he was thinking. "But what?" she asked softly. "Did I do something wrong?"

"No, my love," he said. "You did everything right. That's what I'm trying to tell you." He paused for a long time, rolling onto his back and gazing at the ceiling. "It's just that I think we should take it slower."

Jill placed her hand on Don's powerful chest. The sparse but coarse hairs tickled between her fingers. "Slower?"

"You're just getting over a bad relationship," he said, turning to look her in the eyes for the first time in what felt like hours. "And it's been at least forever since I've felt this way and been . . . well . . . intimate with a woman . . . and . . ."

Jill nestled her cheek against his soft shoulder. Her heart went out to him. She wanted to make all his pain and trepidation go away. At that moment, she realized that she would do anything for him. Including honor his wishes to slow down. "Do you have somewhere else you would rather I slept tonight?" she asked.

"No," Don said emphatically. "What I want is for you to stay right here. This is where you belong. I want to fall asleep holding you . . . and wake up with you still right here in my arms."

Jill let out a soft, contented, and completely involuntary moan.

"Do you think that could be arranged?" Don asked with a half-smile.

Jill couldn't think of anything to say. She simply snuggled closer to Don. Without another words, they fell asleep in each other's arms. She felt content. Secure. Safe from the dangers that lurked outside.

~~~

Several hours later, Don awoke. A faint shade of orange was just beginning to light the sky between the curtains, and birds chirped noisily outside. Disoriented, he rolled onto his back, wondering briefly how the window had managed to move to a different wall in his bedroom while he was sleeping. Then, he realized that he was at the cabin, and the events of the previous day came flooding back to him. He remembered happily the solid warmth against his side was a beautiful woman not a mere dream to be dissolved in the harsh light of morning . . .

He took a deep breath and inhaled her scent. Jill stirred slightly as he carefully got out of bed, allowing her head to fall softly from his arm and back onto the pillow. Returning with a glass of water, he watched Jill sleep in the dim light. At that moment, he realized that what he had said was true. He did love Jill with all his heart.

He marveled at how peaceful and angelic her beauty was as she slept. Now, when he looked at her, he didn't see Julie. He saw only a very special lady, someone he could imagine sharing his life with.

She was sleeping so soundly, and the thought of resting longer seemed like a great idea to him, too. So he quietly slipped back beneath the covers beside her. Curled against her warm back, he soon became drowsy again. His last thought before he dozed off was a hopeful wish that, soon, he would be waking up to this bliss every day.

Chapter Nineteen

When Don woke again, bright sunlight was peeking between the curtains. He guessed it was late morning. Feeling a cool draft on his back, he rolled over in the space where Jill had been sleeping. The house was quiet. He wondered if she was always an early riser. There were so many things still to learn about each other . . .

After slipping on a pair of slacks and a t-shirt from the duffel bag he had placed next to the bed, he shuffled into the living room. There, he found Jill in front of a familiar open box. Before he even saw her face, his heart dropped into his stomach.

In her upturned hands, Jill held open a small picture album that Don knew to contain all his photos of his time with Julie. On the floor beside his love was a framed portrait of Julie and a family photo, Julie's and Cheryl's smiling faces beaming back.

Don's otherwise cheerful greeting died on his lips. It was replaced by horrified silence.

Jill looked up at him. Her moist and reddened eyes told him everything he needed to know. He should have been up front with her. He saw in her now the same doubt he had struggled with for so long – the fear that he was in love with Jilly only because he was still in love with the past.

"Who is this?" Jill snapped. The pain in her eyes was clear as she spoke. It cut straight to Don's soul.

Every inch of Donald Lipton wanted to explain the pain away. But flustered as he was, and try though he might, he couldn't find the proper words. As they sputtered out of his mouth, he regretted them more and more. "Her name is Julie," he said carefully, his voice shaking. "She was a student of mine. I met her right before she died of lupus, and yes, in our own limited way, I was . . . in love with her . . . but believe me Jill, it was mostly platonic. I mean . . . she was married." His voice trailed off. He could see that this wasn't working. His tortured attempt to make sense of things for her had only made it worse.

She shook her head, putting the items away in the box. "What's wrong with men?" she muttered. "Do you really think you can justify *anything*? Do you even care about me, or are you trying to recreate some fantasy with this woman you never got to have?"

Her words were like arrows in his heart. He tried to approach her, still fumbling to explain, but Jill stormed right past him and into the bedroom.

"You're just as obsessive as Michael!" she yelled. "What a fool I am! I should've known better."

Don followed her into the bedroom and watched helplessly as she tossed her things into her bag.

"Please don't leave like this," he pleaded. "We should talk . . . Julie's in my past." He tried placing his hand on her delicate, furiously jostling shoulder, but she jerked it quickly away. "You've had others in your past. That doesn't lessen what I feel for you . . . what we feel for each other . . . at all."

She glared back at him. His heart wrenched as he saw that tears now streaked her face. He would do anything to make her stop crying, yet a part of him knew that there was absolutely nothing he could do.

Jill marched past him, not meeting his eyes, and walked stiffly through the front door and toward her car. Don followed her to the porch, pleading with her, hoping that the right words might just change her mind. He wished he could somehow convince her that his love for her was genuine. His mind raced as he searched for answers that simply would not come to him.

Without even a look back, she got into her car and roared away.

Heart pounding, Don sat down on the top step and tried to breathe. As he watched the tail of her car make its way around the bend and onto the path leading back to the highway, he felt as if the bottom had just dropped out of his soul. He sensed his cheeks moistening with his own tears. It had been so long since he had cried . . . so very long. The last time had been . . . *Julie.*

~~~

Don left the cabin a little after noon. His gut twisted with pain. Such was his misery that he could hardly make it to his car without stopping in befuddlement, wondering what in the world he could do to make things right. He couldn't remember feeling this hopeless in a long time.

How could something so right turn out so wrong? He drew in a long breath and felt it stutter. *It's all your fault, you idiot . . . you should have told her.*

He was mixed up. No hope of figuring out what to do next. He had to find a way to make his heart stop hurting so badly. In fact, as he sat down in his car, he was amazed that it was beating at all.

~~~

He spent that Saturday afternoon at home, staring at the wall and thinking of Jill. Now and then, he would work up the courage to pick up the phone and call her. But then, before he could even dial her number, he would place it back on the hook. What could he say to her? What if she wouldn't talk? What if she wasn't home? What if she *was?*

He debated the issue until six o'clock that evening. Then, finally, he decided to call. He had every intention of leaving a message on her machine, but to his surprise, Jill picked up the phone.

"Hello?"

"Jill?" he said desperately. "Please don't hang up on me. I need to talk to you. Please listen to me."

A sigh of exasperation came through from the other end of the line. "I'm really busy, Don," Jill said coldly. "I have a lot to get done this evening, and I want to get to bed early . . . I'm not feeling the best."

Don's insides ached. He had caused this pain. "I understand," he said. "Truly, I do. I don't feel too good myself right now, either. As a matter of fact, I think I feel worse than I ever have in

my life." He was startled suddenly at the truth of the statement –
as if he couldn't possibly believe it until he heard it pass through
his own lips.

Jill's voice betrayed no emotion. "I'm sorry to hear that."

"Don't be sorry, Jill. Just give me a few minutes . . . please. If
you want me to beg you, I will."

"No need to beg. But I can only give you a few minutes."
Again, her voice was neutral.

"Thanks." Don realized that he had a few moments at best to
find the right words to convince Jill of his feelings for her. He
gathered every bit of the poet within him and strung his words together with care. "I understand how you feel, Jilly," he said,
frustrated that the words in his mind did not match the words
ringing through his voice. "I do. But I cannot help or change anything about my past. If it meant keeping you in my life . . . no . . .
wait . . . that would be a lie. Look, Jill, I understand and respect
your pain, but Julie was a part of my past. The past is just that . . .
it's over and done."

Jill's breath plowed forcefully to Don's ear. "You don't have
to tell me about the past."

"But I do," he pleaded. "Because you saw those pictures of
Julie . . . and whatever you conjured up—" He stopped himself.
This wasn't her fault. "I mean, the fact that I didn't tell you about
your resemblance to Julie turned a beautiful time into hell for us."

A long silence followed.

"I can't and won't lie to you and tell you that Julie meant nothing
to me," Don continued. "She was a very warm and loving . . . a very
beautiful part of my life. And Jill, even if I could forget her, I
wouldn't *want* to."

He could hear Jill swallow hard. "That's exactly why there's
no future for the two of us."

"No, Jill," Don said forcefully. "That's where you're wrong.
That might be all the more reason why there *is* a future for the
two of us. Before Julie, I had made up my mind that I could never
love again. You remember the accident . . . how losing my wife

and little girl tore me up inside. After that, for years, I was unable to feel again. My life was *empty*. My heart was shattered. Then I met Julie . . . and learned that I was able to love again."

He could hear the intermittent sound of muffled sobs. Still, he decided to press on.

"Jill, please try to believe me. Is there anything on earth I can do to convince you to give me a chance? More than you could ever begin to know, I want to continue our relationship. God, Jill, my love, if you only knew how I feel about you . . . you wouldn't have a single doubt."

Jill chimed in, her voice clearer and more certain than Don had expected. "I hear what you're saying, Don. I *want* to believe you." Then, her voice began to break down, to waver. "But for me, trust is the most important thing in a relationship. . . and it should be obvious to both of us that I don't feel that with you yet."

Yet, Don thought. *What a beautiful word.* It meant that he hadn't screwed things up so badly that she never wanted to see him again. Still, there was something cold about the way she now spoke to him.

~~~

Sitting on the couch in her quiet home, holding the phone with one hand and petting her cat with the other, Jill's mind drifted back to the past men in her life. She had been through the wringer, to be certain. Her love life had not been kind.

Even as she was speaking with Don, she felt a chill ripple through her as she had a vision of Michael lurching from some corner and grabbing her. But Don was so different from all the others. He never asked anything of her; he respected her feelings, and he had never attempted to cross the line with her. Still, her feelings remained ambivalent. How could she ever be sure that he loved her and not a memory?

"I think I understand how you feel, Don," she said, choking back her extraordinary desire to sob. "And I love you and care for you the best that I know how. But I need time alone to figure out where I stand first. Please, don't take this the wrong way . . . but I would appreciate it if you'd stop calling me . . . at least for now, anyhow."

~~~

It was the last thing that Don wanted to hear, but what could he do? He had no choice but to respect her wishes. As he hung up the phone, the weight of despair settled over him. He was surprised to notice that his eyes were wet again. Prior to that morning, it had been years since he had cried over a woman, and he hadn't intended to do so again.

He thought darkly on the idea that, after this day, he would never be the same again. A cold wind swept over his heart as he swept a shirtsleeve across his eyes. Then he stood and stormed through the back door.

I should have known better, he told himself. *I was stupid to think I could love again. You're simply too old, Don, and too bitter.*

~~~

Madison was already fussy by the time Cheryl got into the checkout line at the grocery store that evening. This was her final errand of the day, and it had certainly been a long afternoon. Maybe the next time, she could get Tom to watch Madison instead of Matthew. At least she wouldn't have to carry her son. It wasn't exactly fun shopping for produce while her crying child drew the ire of every customer within hearing range. Besides, Cheryl had forgotten the baby sling at home, and her arm wouldn't last another hour without it.

As the woman in front of her in line argued with the cashier about a coupon, Cheryl gently bounced the squirming baby and pulled out the envelope of pictures she had picked up earlier at the drugstore's photo lab. She had dropped off the film she had taken during the barbecue weeks ago and had completely forgotten to pick it up until this day.

She grinned as she unfolded the envelope and looked at the first picture. It was of her adorable son Matthew sitting on a blanket in the yard, proudly holding his little sister. He certainly seemed to take pride in being the big brother. Although there were times when her children were a handful, seeing pictures like these always reminded Cheryl that they were a nice handful that she wouldn't trade for anything in the world.

As she reached her hand gingerly around her daughter and slipped that photo to the bottom of the stack, a picture of Don and Jill surfaced. It was so good to see Don with his new friend, smiling and relaxed. He was such a great person, and he needed someone like this Jill to do things with.

Cheryl thought of her mom, and felt certain that she, too, would be happy to know that Don had started living again.

The next photo was a close-up of Jill alone. Cheryl blinked her eyes and looked again. The resemblance between Jill and her mother was uncanny. Julie had been a little thinner, but then, she had been sick, after all. And her hair was a little darker, but those eyes, lips, cheekbones, and smile made them look almost like twins.

"Are you ready to check out now?"

The voice of the teenage clerk jolted Cheryl back to the present. She quickly stuffed the pictures in her pocketbook and began to struggle getting her groceries onto the counter. A young man stepped up from behind and offered his help. She smiled and accepted.

Soon, Cheryl was walking back to her car, groceries bagged, another mission accomplished. She would go home, feed the kids, and put them down for a nap. Then maybe she could do a few of the things she had been hoping all day to do for herself. . .

She got to her car and fastened Maddie into her car seat in the back passenger side. The tiny baby was starting to settle down and looked like she would be sleeping any minute.

Slipping behind the steering wheel, Cheryl glanced down at the stack of mail she had picked up earlier at the post office. It looked like the usual ads, credit card applications, and junk. She shook her head as she thought about how many trees had been

hewn down to clutter her life. Near the bottom of the pilc, however, there was a long white envelope sticking out. She reached
with her right hand and pulled it out a bit so she could get a better
look at it. The return address was bold and caught her eye at once.
"CDDS . . . California Department of Social Services." The envelope looked important, so she stuck it on top of the pile so she
wouldn't get it mixed up with the rest.

She turned the radio on low and headed toward home. Her
thoughts went back to the picture of Jill. How strange it seemed
that Don would have found a friend who looked so much like her
mother. Or maybe it wasn't. Maybe fate had intervened.

Chapter Twenty

Jill was already running late when traffic came to a sudden stop on Ninth Avenue, trapping her between a bus and a Suburban half a block from the next side street. She slammed her hand on the steering wheel in frustration and forced herself to take deep, calming breaths. She had been in a bad mood all morning, ever since she realized she had forgotten to set her alarm. Then, the technicians assigned to install the alarm system on her house showed up an hour late, throwing off her entire day. Now she would be late to the bookstore, and her newest employee, Sandi, would be gone by the time she arrived. She hoped MacKenzie would be able to hold down the fort by herself for a while.

A blaring siren interrupted her thoughts as an ambulance appeared in her rear-view mirror, weaving its way through the snarled traffic. It was a car accident. Jill pitied the victims, but with her gloomy mood, part of her couldn't resist blaming them for her bad day, too.

Half an hour later, Jill was parked behind the bookstore and hurrying inside. MacKenzie stood shelving books, and the sole customer sat hunched over a paperback and sipping a hot drink at a table in the back. Jill tossed out a brief greeting and apology for her tardiness before disappearing into the office, thinking of all the things that she needed to get done.

Before long, she had immersed herself in her work, which always helped to push her worries far from the forefront of her mind. She was just beginning to leaf through a catalogue of new books she wanted to acquire when MacKenzie poked her head into the office.

Jill looked up. "Yes?"

"Phone call," MacKenzie said cheerfully.

Probably just more sales calls, Jill figured. The blitz of telemarketing seemed endless. They were selling everything from

155

mortgages to health insurance. It wasn't in her nature to be rude, but she hated their frequent intrusions and sometimes was tempted to simply hang up on them. With a sigh, she asked, "Is it anything important? Just tell them I'm busy."

MacKenzie nodded and left. Jill returned to her work, but her perky underling soon reappeared. "Actually," she said, "he says it's important."

There was something in the young woman's voice that was disturbing. "What does he want?" Jill asked.

"I don't know. He just said he's been trying to reach you for a long time."

Jill took a deep breath. *It* couldn't *be Michael. He would have no way of knowing where she was. Or would he?* Her heart began to race.

MacKenzie stood staring, apparently waiting for an answer. "What should I tell him? To call back again later?"

"Yes," she blurted, but then she caught herself. What good would putting off the inevitable do her? If he knew where she was, sooner or later, she was going to have to speak with him . . . and talking with him on the phone at least seemed a better alternative than speaking with him in person. Besides, maybe it wasn't even him at all. Maybe she was worrying about nothing.

"Wait, MacKenzie," she called toward the girl's back. "I'll take the call."

MacKenzie had reached the phone when she heard her boss, and she looked confused now. With her best professional voice she said to the caller, "Hold on a moment, sir. I think she's available." Then, she handed the phone to Jill and walked away.

Jill's voice delivered a small and meek "Hello."

"Finally, darlin'," said the caller. She instantly recognized Michael's Southern twang. "I thought I'd never find you."

Jill swore she could feel the blood stop circulating in her veins. In her panic, she almost hung up, but she couldn't. She froze.

"Probably a little surprised to hear from me, huh?" he said – and he said it as if everything were perfectly normal between them.

"Uh . . . What do you need?" was all she could bring herself to say.

Michael's voice sounded confident and arrogant. Obviously, some things never changed. "We need to talk," he said.

Jill gulped, and it felt like she might choke. "Okay," she muttered.

"No. Not on the phone. This is important, darlin'. It needs to be in person."

Now she felt like she might faint. He wasn't going to give up easily and let this go with just a phone call. This man clearly still wanted to possess her, to control her. She was sure of it, and she knew there was nothing that she could do about it. Even over the phone, he was incredibly intimidating to her.

"Please, Michael. Given . . . given the circumstances . . . let's just get it over with right now." She surprised even herself a bit with how forward she had been. But it didn't seem to matter to Michael. He obviously wasn't going to take no for an answer.

"It's important that we meet," he said with a tone of finality.

Jill could feel herself quivering. Mindlessly, she walked into her office with the cordless phone she had just installed. She shut the door behind her. She hated that he could frighten her so. Again, she felt a strong impulse to just click off the phone and throw it at the wall, or even to swear at him, but she knew that wasn't going to happen. The most she could force herself to do was to stall him for time.

"I'm not sure, Michael," she stammered. "I have to think about it."

"Well, don't think about it for too long, Jill. I want this to happen soon. I'll call you back."

Before she could say another word, he hung up. Jill sat there and listened to the dial tone. Her mind was a jumble of emotions. All she wanted to do was sob.

Jill had no idea how much time had passed when there came a gentle rapping on her office door. She looked up to see MacKenzie standing in the doorway. She motioned her inside. Trembling and drenched in sweat, she smiled weakly at the young woman.

"Jill, what's wrong?" MacKenzie exclaimed, eyes wide. "Does it have something to do with that phone call? Is somebody threatening you? I—"

Jill asked her to close the door, and she did.

"I'm okay, MacKenzie," Jill said, trying to keep her voice low. "Actually, there's something I need to talk to you about. How about lunch? We'll close up and take an hour."

She hadn't planned on confiding in her young assistant, but sometimes it helped to have another woman to talk to. Her best friend was back in Minnesota, and Jill would certainly be calling her later, but talking on the phone was never the same as the comfort of speaking to somebody face to face.

Unless, of course that somebody was Michael.

Chapter Twenty-One

Don set his pen down on the side table and shook the cramps out of his hand. He glanced at the clock; three hours had passed since he had sat down. Over the past few weeks, he had been spending more time on his manuscript, finally printing out a solid second draft. Now he was making another pass through it, embellishing and tightening the prose here and there by hand. He found that a more casual setting – his well-worn recliner, to be exact – helped him relax and see the story in a new light. The task had kept his mind occupied since the falling out with Jill.

Of course, keeping his mind occupied wasn't exactly the same as forgetting. He couldn't forget about Jill, even if he had wanted to. Though they hadn't known each other for very long, she had already become an incredibly important part of his life. He was not about to give up on her, but she had said she needed some time to think things over, and as much as it went against his instincts, he wasn't going to push. He knew this was a time for patience, though with each passing day, living in her absence ate away at him more.

He finally stood up and decided to head into the kitchen for a snack. He had been doing pretty well with his dieting, but sometimes he just had to splurge. Don was one of those people who sometimes compensated for problems in his life by indulging in food. Right now, some mint chocolate-chip ice cream seemed like a great way to shake off the blues.

He never made it to the kitchen. The phone rang.

Jill! He thought hopefully. He rushed over to answer it. To his surprise, it was another familiar voice. Cheryl's.

"Hi, Don," Cheryl said. "Did I catch you at a bad time?"

He smiled. "For you, my dear, it's never a bad time. What's on your mind?"

"Oh, nothing really. I just thought maybe we could talk."

Don knew his friend well enough to realize that she was hiding something. He was certain that he heard something in her voice like a certain tension or uneasiness. Something that was quite uncharacteristic for her.

"Cheryl, something's not right, is it?"

She hesitated before replying. Then she said, "It's not necessarily a bad thing. It's just very important. For some reason, I feel kind of uncomfortable talking about it on the phone."

Her tone of voice was making him nervous. He hated to think of her being so troubled by anything. "Well, I'm not too thrilled about talking on the phone for big things, either. I wish we were still just down the street. Then I could pop right over to talk."

Again there was silence as he waited for her to speak. "I'm sorry, Don. I really shouldn't be burdening you with this."

"It's no burden at all," he said. The last thing he wanted was to make her feel like he didn't want to be there for her. Then a thought popped into his head. "You know, it's not like we're living back in the days of wagon trains. It's really not that hard for us to meet. If I book a flight right now, I could see you by tomorrow afternoon."

This time, she answered immediately. "Oh, that's very nice of you, Don. It is also very crazy. I don't expect you to fly all the way out here."

He didn't let her finish. "Ah, but you forget. I love flying. Even when I'm not at the controls, I just enjoy being in a plane." He paused to see if she would respond. Her hesitation told him to continue. "Besides, we've been having nothing but cold and snow here, and I'm getting sick of it. I miss that California sunshine. Tomorrow's Saturday. It'll be a nice little weekend trip."

Cheryl sounded dumbfounded. "Are you serious?"

"Sometimes too serious," Don said. "But let me hang up now so I can make a reservation. I'll call you back with the info on when to meet me at the airport."

Cheryl reluctantly agreed. Don could tell she was feeling both relieved and a little bit guilty for imposing on him.

~~~

The following afternoon, Don hugged Cheryl as she met him at the airport terminal. They got in her car and headed off to a small restaurant a few miles from Cheryl's house. The place had always been a favorite of both of theirs. It had a kind of relaxed diner appeal, but without all the loud and sometimes obnoxious fare that came from things like open kitchens and cafeteria-like dining areas. That, and the service was always attentive.

"Tom's watching the kids," Cheryl said as they sat down at a small, checkerboard tablecloth-covered table in the corner of the restaurant.

Don smiled. "I'll see them later, then, I guess," he said. He was really looking forward to it, too.

Suddenly, Cheryl tensed up, seeming nervous. They caught up on some small talk for a few minutes and ordered their meals, but Don knew something was amiss. She asked him about his latest book and he told her that it was going well, and then she started to talk about the weather. By that point, Don had had enough. "C'mon, Cheryl, please," he said. "We both know I didn't come out here just to be jealous of the great California weather. It's time to open up."

Cheryl smiled without much enthusiasm – more of a nervous gesture than anything else. She then reached into her pocketbook and retrieved a large envelope. Don could see that it was from the Department of Social Services, but he couldn't even imagine what it might contain. Cheryl placed it on the table and pulled out several documents. Don raised an eyebrow.

Cheryl's eyes met Don's. "I know this all seems kind of weird," she said. "And it is, but, Don, this concerns my mother, so in my mind, that means it concerns you, too."

At the mention of Julie, Don's attention became even more riveted than it had been before. "Go on," he said, sipping on his water as his mouth had gone immediately dry.

Drawing in a lot of air, Cheryl started to tell Don everything that she had discovered so far. She began with the bombshell. "My mother was adopted."

Don's jaw dropped. Cheryl continued. "That means my grandparents are not my biological grandparents."

"Did Julie know?" Don asked, leaning in closer to her over the table.

Shaking her head, Cheryl said, "I don't think so. There was a letter included in the file with instructions to give it to Mom or her children in the event of her death. It was from her birth father and stated that her mother died in giving birth to her."

Don tried to comfort Cheryl as tears became visible in her eyes. He didn't know how to feel about this. It really affected Cheryl and her family more than him, but then again, they were like family. "I'm surprised that Julie never knew," he said. He felt foolish for not thinking of something more eloquent to say.

Cheryl slowly regained her composure. "I guess it's a generational thing," she said.

"Generational?"

She nodded as she took a tissue out of her purse and blew her nose. "Yes. You know, back in those days, adoption wasn't talked about as freely as it is now."

Don tried to lighten up the situation. "You mean back in my generation? The olden days?"

Cheryl smiled, but after a minute, the impact of what she was saying began to sink into Don's brain: *This does make it more possible that Julie and Jill could be related.*

Before he could contemplate it further, Cheryl told him that there was more. "Mom had a sibling," she said slowly. "A sister. She was a few years older. Separated from her at birth. They were adopted out to different families."

Feeling himself begin to sweat, Don asked, "Is there anything else?"

Cheryl shook her head. "Isn't that enough?"

Don tried to absorb what he had just heard, but it was all so overwhelming.

Cheryl finally opened up and told him the rest of what was on her mind. "Don, I'm convinced that Jill and Julie must at least be related." She then handed him the photos from the barbecue and a photo of her mother for comparison, apparently in case he'd forgotten.

All of it overwhelmed him. He recalled as if it were yesterday the day Jill had walked into his office and how he had actually thought she was Julie at first. Hearing Cheryl validate his instinct made him even more certain that their resemblance was no mere coincidence.

He wiped a tear away and glanced up to see that Cheryl was doing the same. Reaching across the table, he took her hand. Words failed him, but his mind was racing with the possibilities.

Chapter Twenty-Two

Don tried to enjoy the rest of his visit to California as much as he could, but there was just so much on his mind. That evening, he had fun at a barbecue with Cheryl and her family, and as he always did, he had a great time playing with the kids. Yet, his mind remained distracted. How on earth was he ever going to explain this to Jill?

~~~

On the plane ride home, somewhere high above the snow-capped peaks of the Rockies, Don had decided that maybe it would be best not to call Jill right away. This was such a big step . . . maybe he needed to give it some more thought. Though all of his instincts were telling him to call Jill, he instead decided to wait. He had a serious dilemma to wrestle with. Would it be the right thing to tell her? Did he have an obligation to tell her? What if it damaged – or even destroyed – their already faltering relationship? The thought of that happening almost made him physically sick.

Yet, it was a risk he was going to have to take. Don felt in his heart that he was falling in love with Jill. If that love was real, it had to be based on total honesty, which he now knew should have been a given before this moment. Anything short of that would cheapen the potential that they might have as a couple. Of course, coming to that conclusion didn't make picking up the phone and actually calling her any easier.

Though Don had never really been a procrastinator, in this case, his anxiety was getting the better of him. He spent his first few days back from California keeping himself busy with his work. He graded papers, spent a lot of hours tutoring students, and even managed to get in a little more work on his manuscript.

All of these things, of course, were only putting off the inevitable. Finally, on a Wednesday evening at around eight, Don made his move. He picked up the phone, dragged it, cord and all, over to his favorite recliner, and sat down. Taking a deep breath, he dialed Jill's number. When she didn't pick up after three rings, he thought about hanging up. Then her familiar voice came on the line.

"Hello?" As always, she sounded like she wasn't expecting to be receiving any calls.

"Hi, Jill," he said, his voice unexpectedly mournful. "Don here. Do you have a minute?"

"Sure. Is something the matter?"

Now that's a loaded question, Don thought. In a way, it certainly was true. This was big news, but he had no idea what her reaction would be. Would she be angry? Or might she be appreciative that he had found out this startling information and shared it with her?

Lost in thought, Don remained silent.

"Hello?" Jill said, sounding a tad annoyed. "Don, what is it?"

Then it struck him. All along, he had planned on breaking this news to her on the phone. Now that he was really making the call, however, it just didn't seem appropriate. It was the coward's way out. This was something that he would need to say to her face.

"Oh, nothing big really. It's just that there's something I need to speak with you about. I was wondering if maybe we could go out to lunch tomorrow, say around noontime. My treat, of course." He tried to say it in a way that wouldn't alarm her, but he immediately felt that he had failed at the task.

Jill's response was hesitant. "Don, I appreciate that. But, you know, I really think maybe we just need some more time before, well . . ." Her voice trailed off.

"Jill, this isn't some kind of trick on my part. What I need to tell you is important."

Still sounding a bit unsure, Jill agreed to meet with him. After some small talk that lasted only a few minutes, they hung up.

Don spent a restless night. He woke up what felt like ten times. He would look at the clock repeatedly, and each time, he would see that only a few more minutes had passed.

Tomorrow couldn't come quickly enough.

~~~

Don arrived at the bookstore at precisely noon. Jill seemed surprised by his appearance.

"Are you feeling okay?"

The question caught him by surprise. "Sure. I'm fine."

"Oh," Jill said as she slipped on her coat. "I'm sorry if I'm being too forward, but you have dark circles under your eyes. I thought that maybe you had the flu. There's a lot of that going around."

Don simply shook his head, and they walked into the bright sunshine reflecting off the piled-up snow banks alongside the sidewalk. Just when winter seemed to be receding, it had returned in full force. It was one of those winter days that was bearable, however, because there wasn't much wind.

To Don's surprise and delight, Jill reached out and grabbed his hand as they strolled the few blocks to the little bistro they both liked so much. It felt so good that Don hated to ruin it by springing his news on her, but he knew he couldn't chicken out now. No, that wasn't an option.

For the first half of their lunch, Don never said a word about why he had requested this meeting. They talked about food, the weather, Jill's bookstore, and Don's students. It was good conversation, but it was all just a diversion from what really needed to be said.

It was Jill who finally cut to the chase. She locked eyes with him and said, "Don, I'm not trying to be rude or anything, but last night on the phone you told me that you had something important to say to me. Unless I'm mistaken, you haven't said it yet."

The lady certainly knows how to be direct, Don thought. He admired her for it, though at the moment, he would have been perfectly content to continue putting off what he had to say indefinitely. He had badly underestimated how difficult this was going to be.

"Okay," he said. "No more beating around the bush." He sighed deeply and allowed his shoulders to sag. "I made a trip out to California last week."

Jill's eyes brightened. They sparkled so innocently. "Oh, to see Cheryl and the kids?"

Don nodded. "Yes. She had called me and told me that *she* had something important to discuss with me." He then took out a copy of the letter that Cheryl had given to him and said, "I think you should read this."

She took the envelope and slowly opened it. Her eyes began panning over the letter. He sat there and watched dumbfounded as Jill's face slowly melted from skepticism to comprehension.

She put down the papers and stared at Don in disbelief. "I . . . I don't know what to say. This . . . Julie . . . is my sister?" Her voice was a mixture of shock and bewilderment.

"I don't know for sure what it all means, to be perfectly honest with you, Jill."

She suddenly picked up the papers and shoved them across the table at Don. "Then why are you telling me all this? You think my life isn't hard enough, you need to make it even more complicated?"

Her tone surprised him. This was turning out worse than he had feared. "I'm sorry, Jill," he said, his eyes moistening. "That's not why I'm telling you this. The last thing in the world that I would want would be to hurt you in any way. I just . . ."

"You just can't get over this obsession that you have with Julie," she snapped. "Well, you know what, Don? I don't have any long-lost sisters. I'm not Julie, and you can't bring her back by dating me. This is getting really sick. I have to get out of here."

Jill stood up, and Don started after her. He reached for her arm, but she shrugged him off. "Please! Don't make this any more awful than it already is," she said.

By now, people in the crowded little restaurant were beginning to stare at the feuding couple, but embarrassment meant nothing to Don at this point. All he wanted was to somehow fix the damage he had caused. "Can I at least call you?" he pleaded.

Jill said, "Fine. Call me. Really, I have to go now." She broke free of his grip and was out the door.

Don stood watching as she walked away, a lump forming in his throat and his head throbbing. *What have I done?* He kept asking himself, his mind oblivious to the people around him who probably thought he had lost his mind.

~~~

Jill returned to the bookstore and closed up early for the day. She had been scheduled to run it solo that afternoon, and there was no way she would be able to get through it. She had so much to think about. She was angry, hurt, but most of all, confused.

When she got home, she dumped a cupful of cat food into Tyson's bowl and went straight to the bathroom to run a hot bath. She needed something tangible to calm the chaos in her head.

As she sank down into the steaming water and laid her head against the smooth porcelain, she felt something let loose inside her, now that she was alone. She covered her face with wet hands as sobs shook her body, welling up from someplace deep and dark that she hadn't been to in a long time.

Chapter Twenty-Three

Jill spent the next few days wrestling with her thoughts. Never before in her life had she been so confused. The news that Don had broken to her held so many implications. First of all, she had never considered the possibility that she had been adopted. Even now, it was hard to believe that it could be true. She was even more stunned by the idea that she may have once had a sister. Jill had been so lonely growing up. If only someone would have told her! Finally, if this sister was indeed Julie, the woman Don loved so much, what did that say about his relationship with her? Jill kept asking herself if Don was really interested in her for herself . . . or was this just some way to keep his memories of Julie alive?

There were too many questions with too few answers.

Jill was getting tired of the winter. Spring should have well arrived, but it seemed to be cold and snowy almost every day. The weather only made her melancholy outlook that much worse.

She did her best to shut out her troubling thoughts, going into the bookstore every day, pasting a smile on her face, and hoping to lose herself in the world of books and her interaction with customers. But these proved to be only fleeting distractions. As soon as she would have a free moment, her thoughts would once again return to what she began to call, "the Julie problem."

Compounding it all was the sad reality that there was nobody she could talk to about this. She considered calling her old friend back in Minnesota, but she couldn't bring herself to do it. Their long-distance phone relationship just didn't seem as close as the one they had shared in person. Besides, Jill didn't want to burden her friend with her problems. Something about this dilemma was just too personal. It was the kind of thing Jill knew she would have to deal with on her own.

Then, of course, there was Don. Jill was feeling guilty about the way she had stalked off in a huff that day in the restaurant.

None of this was his fault, really, and she was probably not being completely fair to him. Maybe he did care for her as an individual and not just some kind of duplicate of a past love. The truth was that she had no way of knowing for sure unless she spent more time with him. Yet that was easier said than done. Getting involved with Don at that time . . . while she was still trying to sort out these other issues . . . would make her life even more complicated than it already was.

Still, deep down in her heart, she knew that Don was a good man. Was she throwing away an incredible blessing?

Another few weeks went by. The days were getting longer and the temperatures were rising. The snow banks were finally melting away.

It was late afternoon. The customers had all left, and Jill was going over the day's receipts and getting ready to close up the store. She had decided that today would be the day. At long last, she was going to break the ice with Don.

They had been chatting on the phone recently, but mostly just small talk. Their relationship had stalled, and had become almost crippled, but Jill was now resolved to be the one to make the first move. She would surprise Don by showing up at his office at the university. She knew that he always worked late on Thursday afternoons, so she would just sort of unexpectedly drop in and offer to take him out to dinner.

She had dressed up a bit more carefully than she usually did for a workday, anticipating seeing Don that evening. Her rosy sweater was tight and flattering, and her dark brown skirt cut just above her knees. She wore stockings and heels to complete the ensemble.

Her heart beating like a school girl's, Jill set aside her paperwork and went to get her coat, which she kept in the back room on this occasion. She was just about to shut off the lights to the store when she heard the bells chime on the front door. *Darn that MacKenzie,* she thought. *She forgot to lock the door and put up the "closed" sign!*

"Sorry, we're closed," Jill called to the late customer. "But please come back in the morning."

But as she walked to the front of the store, the customer had not left. It was not a customer. It was Michael.

Jill felt her legs go weak at the sight of him. How could this be happening? "M-Michael . . . What do you want?" was all that she could stammer.

There was nothing threatening or angry about his demeanor. To the contrary, he grinned broadly. "You look as great as ever," he said.

Taking a step backwards, Jill tried to think of something to say, but the words were caught in her throat.

Michael laughed. "You look like you've seen a ghost."

For Jill, that was exactly what this was like. He looked precisely as she had remembered him: his jet black hair slicked back, hip sunglasses on a chain around his neck, and as always, he was wearing his trademark tight jeans. She had always thought he should wear them a size bigger, but that was the least of her concerns at the moment. Funny what one's mind fixates on during moments of fear.

Her throat dry and constricted, Jill managed to say, "It's, well, you know, just surprising to see you here."

Michael walked right up to her. Jill was still too paralyzed with fear to move. He authoritatively took her by the hand and walked her over to the tearoom section of the bookstore, where her customers would sit down to read books and sip coffee or tea. They sat down at one of the antique tables in the corner.

"This is quite a little place you have here," Michael said as if the circumstances were perfectly normal. "I didn't know you could be such a little entrepreneur."

A condescending tone had crept into his voice, causing Jill to slowly start letting go of her fear. It was replaced by deep resentment. Why couldn't he just leave her alone? Why did he have to come all the way out here to find her?

She didn't have to wait long for the answer. Michael's voice suddenly became somber. "Listen," he said, "this is going to be hard for you to hear. That's why I thought it would only be right to say it to you in person rather than over the phone."

Jill, for the first time, looked him squarely in the eyes, urging him to get to the point.

Michael swallowed hard and then said, "I've found somebody else, Jill. Her name is Jennifer, and we've been seeing each other for a while now and . . ."

Again, Jill gave him a skeptical look.

"And we're going to get married."

Strangely, her resentment doubled. *This was his big news?* She howled within her mind. *He tracked me down just to tell me this?*

Devastation was apparently what he had expected to see in her eyes. The truth was, she was thrilled. She wanted nothing to do with him ever again. As her anger and fear faded, she suddenly felt like jumping up and dancing a little jig. Of course, that might set him off into a rage, so she decided to play along . . . fulfill his expectations.

Trying to sound as if she actually cared, Jill said, "Wow, that sort of comes as a shock, Michael."

He reached over and put his hand on her shoulder. "I know it does," he soothed. "But this is really a good thing for you, too. It might be hard for you to understand right now, but this will help you to get over us breaking up and move on with your life."

You can say that again, she thought.

She continued to play along with his silly charade for about fifteen more minutes, and then it was over. He gave her a soft kiss on the cheek, said some sappy, sentimental words she would immediately forget, and then walked out the door and out of her life forever.

~~~

The next few days, Jill experienced a rollercoaster of emotions. She was of course ecstatic to have Michael out of her life for good, and the sense of freedom it brought to her was indescribable. It was like her spirit was able to once again come alive. Yet, the end of her relationship with Michael had another effect that caught her by surprise. It closed a chapter of her life forever, which meant, inevitably, that now it was time to open a new chapter . . .

But where would that lead her? Jill had been comfortable, despite her fears and anxieties, with her old life. It was familiar to her, at least, and her mind was well acquainted with all the details. Where her life was heading now, however, was a total mystery. She had been all set to go and try to start things up again with Don that day Michael walked into the store, but now she couldn't bring herself to do it. Yes, she desperately hoped to make things right with him, but until she found out more about "the Julie problem," she realized that getting back with Don was never going to be possible.

First things first – she had to somehow find some answers.

Though she was already late for work on one drizzly morning toward the end of March, Jill sat down in front of the computer in her bedroom and diligently started to do some research. She uncovered some information from the Minnesota Department of Social Services that seemed like it might be helpful, and sent off an cmail requesting more information. The remarkably prompt – and most likely automated – reply indicated that if they could find additional information, Jill would be contacted by post.

Jill had no idea how long it might take the wheels of the bureaucracy to turn into action, but she had no choice but to wait. She mused to herself, *I've never known the answer my entire life. What difference will a few more weeks make now?*

As it turned out, it only took a few days to receive a response. A large, official-looking manila envelope was waiting for Jill when she got home from work one afternoon five days later.

Excited, she rushed inside, said a quick hello to Tyson, and opened the envelope before she even sat down. She poured through its contents, her eyes wide. The first thing she saw was the original copy of her birth certificate, along with a set of papers from an orphanage that confirmed what, until now, she had only suspected. She was indeed adopted.

As she dug deeper into the material, she found something even more stunning – a letter left for her by her birth father. It stated that she had a sister who was given away at the same time. Her mother had died shortly after her sister's birth, and he couldn't take care of them on his own. The letter demonstrated a great deal of remorse and regret – but the true message was that of hope: hope that his daughters would lead better lives without him.

A black and white photograph of Jill's biological mother was also inside the envelope. The woman bore an uncanny resemblance to Jill. It was startling to look at, and Jill sat in her chair mesmerized by the image for so long that she lost track of time.

The beautiful woman's eyes somehow seemed to be alive and gazing into her own. It was as if this long-lost part of her was calling out to her from beyond a great abyss, touching her with love and compassion beyond measure. If she tried to describe the feeling to anyone, she reasoned, they would probably assume she had gone mad. Yet she knew this feeling was as real, even more real than anything she had ever before experienced.

At the same time, this overwhelming revelation was also a huge blow to Jill. Her entire life had been turned upside down.

She shoved the material inside her desk drawer and began to pace the floor. What was she to make of all this? Her emotions ran the gamut from anger with her adoptive parents for never telling her, to grief that her birth mother and possibly her father were now gone, to curiosity about whether Julie really was her sister. Finally, and perhaps most painful of all, she resented Don for dumping all of this on her. She missed the simplicity of her old life and wished that she could get it back. Yet she knew that it would be impossible now.

~~~

Jill spent the next few days trying to decide what to do. Her anger at Don had mostly disappeared now. She realized that he had not – would not – have done anything to deliberately hurt her. In fact, his intentions were good. Clearly, all he had wanted was to offer the truth, and there could never be anything wrong with that.

And now Jill wanted the truth, too, and she knew exactly what that meant she had to do. She needed to get in touch with Cheryl – for based on all of the information that Jill now had at her disposal, it seemed highly probable that she and Cheryl were indeed related. But since the distance between them made a blood test impossible, comparing notes on the adoption could potentially confirm that possibility.

Of course, she only knew Cheryl through Don, so her first inclination was to call him, explain the situation, and maybe take it from there. But then, the more she thought about it, the more she started to think that this was something she had to handle on her own. Yes, she would involve Don at the right time, but this certainly did not feel like the right time. After all, what if it turned out she and Cheryl weren't related?

She didn't hesitate another day. That night, when she got home from work, she went straight to the phone and dialed Cheryl's number, which she had gathered from the national white pages on her computer.

Cheryl was totally surprised by the call. Jill could hear it in her voice, but it didn't take long before they broke the ice. Soon, they were speaking as if they were old friends.

Jill got to the point almost immediately, telling Cheryl about her discovery.

Cheryl went and retrieved her own records, and it didn't take very long for them to compare notes and come to the stunning conclusion that they were indeed related.

"A part of my Mom is still alive," Cheryl said, her voice cracking as though she might burst into tears.

Jill listened with compassion over the two-thousand-mile phone connection. "I hope I can be a worthy aunt for you," she said, feeling herself become emotional, too.

"We have to get together in person again," Cheryl said, regaining her composure. "Maybe the next time Don comes out here, you can join him again. The kids really seemed to take to you. Just the way they do with Grandpa Don."

The mention of "Grandpa Don" made Jill smile. Did this make her "Grandma Jill?" She kept the little joke to herself and instead replied, "You bet, Cheryl. I wish it could be today."

Chapter Twenty-Four

Two men went about their increasingly routine work in the hangar. One man's movements were labored, forced, while the other man spent a good deal of his time stealing an occasional, clearly concerned, glance in the other man's direction.

Don, stooped over a wrench he had just dropped onto the greasy ground below his feet, could feel Mark's gaze hot upon the top of his head. When he glanced back up toward his friend, Mark blinked his eyes away quickly yet again. Don sighed.

Mark, feeding a long tube into its plastic casing and then threading it through a portion of the engine that Don could not see, finally looked his friend in the eyes. "Don," he said, dismayed, his sharp, dark eyebrows arched, "are you okay?"

Don went back to banging around with his hammer. He furrowed his brow, feeling rather miffed by the notion that he couldn't hide his emotions, as he had been trying to do all day. "Sure," he said, sounding a bit more defensive than he had intended. "Why do you ask?"

Mark opened his mouth, appearing ready to speak, but then simply shrugged.

With a frown, Don climbed down from the stepladder he had set up on the right side of the plane's fuselage. "Now if we can move on," he said rather haughtily. He practically glared up at his friend, who stood a little meekly atop his own stepladder, which had been set up on the left side of the plane. "You just going to stand there and watch me?"

Mark blinked forcefully, clearly confused.

"Or are you going to help me get the rest of the stuff from your truck and into the plane?"

Mark nodded and quickly climbed down the ladder, hustling over to his friend's side like a penitent lap dog.

"Sorry to be so short, Mark," Don said gruffly. "I guess I'm just ready to get the hell out of here."

Mark stopped walking at the words. He froze in place, looking at the ground. In short order, Don noticed that his friend was no longer by his side. He, too, stopped; then he turned to face Mark. Mark's face was painted over with deep sympathy. The pain in his expression was almost comical.

Don had seen this expression before, of course. Back in California, Mark, his best friend for as long as he could remember, had been in his life for ages. Naturally, he had reserved a similar look for all those horrible days Don had been forced to endure. When Emily and Abby were taken from him, it was Mark who had tried pulling him out of the spiral it had created in his life. When Julie passed, it was Mark and his carefree and fun-loving spirit who had tried to fill the void her absence had left. Of course, he had failed on both counts – but then, how could a best friend ever account for the loss of true love?

"So are you ever going to tell me what's going on right now?" Mark asked, still looking at the ground sheepishly. "What's making you so upset? It's Jill, isn't it?"

Don shook his head slowly. "Long story," he muttered.

Mark looked his friend in the eyes for the first time. He shrugged his shoulders and held them there, placing his hands in his pockets. "I'm not going anywhere," he said.

"I don't know, Mark," Don said quietly as he pulled a dirty towel out of his back pocket and began the futile effort of wringing the grease from his hands. "It's not really . . ." he trailed off without completing the thought.

Strangely, Mark smiled. He walked toward Don and placed an equally greasy hand on the shoulder of Don's already work-stained flannel shirt. "C'mon, Don," he said. "Don't cut me out. It wasn't that long ago we were flying over all that beautiful landscape with her. You were glowing back when the two of you were going out for dinner and movies all the time. And now you've stopped talking about her." Mark continued his pained grin. "I'm not stupid, you know."

At first, Don remained silent. But then, in an instant, something in him changed. As his shoulders slumped, it was as if a wall had been broken down. All at once, he felt like pouring out everything he had from his tattered heart, his tortured soul. His friend must have noticed the change, because he breathed out singularly and forcefully through his nose, a clear indication that he was ready to listen for the long haul.

Don took a deep breath, doing all he could to hold eye contact with his friend. For the moment, he did not feel even remotely like crying . . . until he began to speak. "Mark," he said, choking up a little but doing all he could to hide it, "I think it's over between Jill and me." He laughed in a macho sort of way. "Hell, I'm not even sure what 'it' was . . . Anyway, it's over between us."

The news apparently came as a surprise to Mark, because he raised an eyebrow in a way that Don knew to indicate mild shock. The professor had seen it many times from his friend and colleague – and by this point in their lives, he could read his subtle nuances like a book. "Why?" Mark asked in a pleading, almost childlike tone. "What happened?"

Don lowered his eyes and collected his thoughts, searching for the best way to say what he knew he had to reveal. It was a good while before he spoke again. "I asked Jill to spend the night in my cabin," he said despondently.

Mark grinned in an impish fashion.

"It's not what you think!" Don said defensively. He raised both of his hands to shoulder level, palms facing Mark.

Mark continued his silly little grin. "How would you know what I'm thinking?"

Don frowned and shook his head, trying to indicate that this was no laughing matter. "Jill has an ex-boyfriend who's been looking for her. He got rough with her a few times before she moved here. She's scared to death of him."

Mark's grin immediately evaporated. His face drew a little pale. "So he found her, then?"

Don nodded solemnly. "He called her at her bookstore . . . that's why I asked Jilly to stay at my cabin for her safety. I stayed there with her only so she wouldn't be scared there all alone."

"So what happened? You went to the cabin with her, couldn't keep your hands off her, and now she isn't talking to you. Right?"

Don almost smiled. "I'd actually prefer it if that were the case. It'd be easier to deal with all this if I'd just gotten fresh with her. No, Mark . . . Like I said, it's complicated."

Mark sighed and extended his hands to the side, shrugging his shoulders as if to say, *so enlighten me.*

Don furrowed his brow, reliving the experience in his mind. "I got up in the morning to find Jill in the living room . . . She was going through some pictures of Julie I had there."

"Oh, Don," Mark said, his mouth slightly agape.

"I know," Don said gravely. "She was all torn up when she saw how much Julie looked like her."

"You mean you didn't *tell* her about her resemblance to Julie?" Mark's eyes appeared frantic, as did his tone.

Don simply shook his head.

"Oh, Don," Mark repeated.

Don's eyes began to water. "So she accused me of falling for her only as a way of replacing Julie."

An uneasy silence fell upon the big, open hangar as both men were lost in thought. Finally, Mark said, "Well, I have to say, my friend . . . it *is* kind of strange how much Julie and Jill look alike."

"Not as strange as you think," Don said, feeling a little pained in speaking the words. "I was going to tell you about that this weekend."

Now Mark appeared completely confused. "Tell me about what?"

"Well, remember when I flew to California to see Cheryl and the kids?" Don's voice became involuntarily hesitant, like a child finally admitting to breaking a lamp.

Mark nodded frantically, clearly anxious for his friend to continue.

"Well, Cheryl had a letter from Social Services, and it proved . . . well, it said. . ."

"C'mon, Don," Mark said with obvious exasperation. "Spit it out!"

Every muscle in Don's body relaxed. He slumped slightly at the shoulders, causing an arch to form in his upper back. "Julie and Jill are biological sisters," he said. "At least, as far as we can tell."

His eyes wide, Mark began to laugh unexpectedly. "Sure," he said, beaming, "and you and I are brothers, right? Is this a joke or something?" But whatever Mark saw in Don's eyes must have tipped him off to the seriousness of the matter, because his tune quickly shifted. "Oh, Don . . . This is too confusing for me, my friend. How can that be? Why didn't Julie *tell* you she had a sister?"

Don sat down right on the hard concrete surface of the hangar. This wasn't at all easy for him to talk about. "She didn't know," he said finally, softly. "It seems they were adopted by two different families . . . neither one of them knew about the other."

Sitting down next to his friend, Mark shook his head. "This is just way too weird. And they *both* found their way into your life . . . I mean . . . what're the odds of that?"

Don looked pensively at the ground. Mark came to sit across from him on the floor.

"You know," Don said distantly, "I hadn't really thought about that . . . my mind's been so cluttered with all this torment. Yeah . . . it's remarkable."

"Does Jill know about this?"

Don lapsed silent for a moment, and then he spoke in almost a whisper. "Know about what?"

"That Julie is her sister."

Don puffed out a long, hot breath, feeling no less tense as he did so. "Yes. I told her about it . . . and it only made things worse between us."

"Oh, Don," Mark said once more. "I get why you've been so down." He shook his head for a good long while before perking up slightly. "So what're you going to do now?"

"Good question," Don said, standing up and stretching, trying to clear his head of so many thoughts at once. He paced back and forth several times. Then, slowly, his demeanor began to change, though it felt a bit forced. Managing a grin, he said, "I'll tell you what I'm going to do. I'm going to get in that plane and fly to Traverse City to spend a few days at an air show with my best friend. I'm going to put all this behind me and stop thinking about both Jill and Julie."

Mark stood up, too, and put his hand on his friend's shoulder. "That sounds great to me. By this time tomorrow, you won't be thinking about any of your problems. You'll be having too much fun." His tone, however, belied his words. He clearly did not believe a woman was something a man could get over so easily.

~~~

The next morning, the two pilots again got an early start. Their plane raced down the runway and soared airborne. Don felt that wonderful and familiar rush of exhilaration as the landing gear smoothly retracted and the landscape slowly receded beneath them. Below, the landscape was mostly flat, and the sky was nearly absent of clouds of any kind, so Don could see for many miles in all directions. He gazed out the port side of the aircraft and saw one of his favorite lakes off in the distance, shimmering in the morning sunshine. It reminded him of carefree days spent fishing during his childhood. He turned to Mark. "Can't beat this for flying weather, huh?"

Mark nodded. "You bet. Makes me wish it was a longer flight."

Indeed, they would be at their destination in about an hour. While flying, both men instinctively kept their eyes on their instruments, yet they easily became as immersed in conversation as they might have been on a golf course or during a leisurely drive. The conversation en route to Traverse City ran the gamut from sports to literature to politics – though both seemed to skate gingerly around the topic of women.

A kind of hollow disappointment washed over Don as he saw that the plane had come within range of the destination airfield. Though the time in Traverse City would surely be well-spent, he never enjoyed the idea of having to land. Flying – particularly with a friend like Mark – was simply too much of a joy.

Nevertheless, Don took over the controls for landing. In short order, the plane touched down smoothly on the level concrete surface of the landing field and came to a roaring stop.

On the ground, Mark planted a high-five on his friend over a nearly flawless approach. "I'd give it a nine," he quipped.

"In your dreams," Don shot back. "Nothing less than a perfect ten and you know it."

Don felt more than just a little renewed as the two of them climbed out of the cockpit and into bright sunlight. The brisk wind whipped his jacket around him and brought the smell of the fresh air blowing off the Great Lakes to his nose. He inhaled deeply, hoping that its curative effects would help chase away the blues that had followed him, somewhere in the deep recesses of his mind, all the way from home.

~~~

About an hour later, the two friends checked into a hotel a half-mile away from the landing strip.

"They have a really good exercise room here," Mark mentioned as he slid his debit card across the counter to the hotel attendant. "Not to mention an awesome sauna."

But Don, looking over his shoulder vacantly, shook his head and said, "Thanks, but I'm kind of tired. I think I'll just hit the sack . . . but you go ahead and enjoy that stuff on your own."

Mark smiled at the attendant as he nodded. "Suit yourself, Grandpa," he said.

Don chuckled despite himself. "Maybe tomorrow," he said.

Mark shrugged, taking back his card. "Okay. But don't say I didn't ask." With that, he gathered up his small suitcase and began walking toward the elevators.

Don stood as if entranced by nothing at all. He did not snap out of his deep thoughts – thoughts about Jilly, he was pained to admit to himself – until Mark whistled for his attention and motioned for him to follow into the waiting elevator.

Chapter Twenty-Five

With Mark out at the sauna, Don placed the *Do Not Disturb* sign on the handle of the door to their shared hotel room. He then lay down on one of the double beds and sank into a deep depression. The lights he kept off, reflecting the mood in his head.

In what seemed like a short time – perhaps he had dozed off – he heard a keycard slide into the lock outside the door. Mark had returned.

"What's with the 'do not disturb?'" Mark asked, his smile fading the moment he laid eyes on Don, who was huddled on the bed, feeling and obviously looking extremely disconsolate. "What's up, Don? You look like you've just lost your last friend."

Don remained silent.

Mark audibly let some air out through his flaring nostrils. "Listen, I don't want to stick my nose into your business, but I'd like to help you if I can."

By the waning sunlight drifting in through the sheer white curtain drawn over the window, Don caught a quick glimpse of himself in the mirror across from the bed, next to the TV. Dark circles had formed under his eyes. He looked worn and haggard. He shuddered. "I'll be okay," he said softly. "This is something I have to work out on my own. Thanks anyhow."

Though he clearly didn't want to let things go that easily, Mark shrugged. "Whatever," he said. He sat down on the end of his bed, his lower half wrapped in a moist towel, and switched on the TV. He clicked through the stations one at a time, but apparently decided that there wasn't anything on worth keeping him in the room for the evening. He looked over his shoulder at Don, still nestled up at the head of his own bed. "Wanna go somewhere for a drink or burger or something?"

The reply came quickly. Don had been expecting the question. "No, thanks." He closed his eyes, not wanting to look at his friend for fear it might cause him to cry.

"You haven't eaten since breakfast. And it's a long time till morning comes again."

"I know."

Don could hear Mark get up from the bed and shuffle over nearer to him. "Hey, c'mon, Don," he said soothingly. "We've been friends for how many years now?"

Don just grunted.

"Look, buddy, this is tearing me up, too. Sometimes, if you just talk about things, it helps. You know?" Mark's tone indicated his clear discomfort. Don knew that his friend's words were sincere, but he could also tell that Mark had no real desire to spend his evening scraping his friend's heart off the pavement.

After a long pause, Don finally opened his eyes and looked up at his friend as if he were seeing him for the first time. "I miss her, Mark," he said. "I miss her so much that it's hard to even imagine going on another day without her."

"Julie?" Mark asked with a sigh.

"Her, too."

"Jill, then?"

Don nodded. "I know I said that I'd get over it and have a good time this weekend . . . But, Mark . . . I don't know if I can do this anymore. I've tried and tried for weeks to think of reasons to stop loving Jilly, but I can't. Damn it, I'm in love with her, Mark. I'm in love with Jill Larkins."

It was a long time before either man spoke again. Mark seemed to be mulling over something at great length. "Does she know?" he finally asked.

Bringing his palms to his forehead as he lay with his back on the bed, Don said, "I think so . . . but I'm not sure how she feels about me. It's just . . . there's something between us that seems bigger than both of us, you know? It keeps getting in the way. I don't know how to explain it. And I don't know what it is."

Mark's expression indicated that he was at a loss for words. "Was she ever married?" he asked awkwardly.

Don's heart fluttered unexpectedly. He wasn't sure why, but

the thought of Jilly committing to another man – even in her past – made him feel nothing short of wretched. "No," he croaked. "But she did have a long relationship with that loser Michael we talked about yesterday." Don's heart surged with anger as he discussed Jill's ex. "He left her with one hell of a fear of men. The month before they were to be married, he cheated on her. Jill had to find it all out from some friend who caught them in the act."

"That'd be enough to rip a heart out forever."

Don sat up, his lungs sputtering as though he had been crying for hours. It was strange that he hadn't cried yet today. "I get the idea that there was some abuse in her past, as well," he continued. "Her father was a monster, I gather."

Mark shook his head, bringing his hands to rest on the side of his bed, where he clutched at the glossy surface of the comforter. "Doesn't make for much of a picture of men."

"Or a trust," Don added. At this point, he had had enough. He felt stir-crazy. And in this tiny hotel room, all he could do was stand and pace between the wall behind his bed and the dresser holding up the TV. He did just that, his thumb and forefinger running absently over his stubbly chin. "But that's only partly the issue here. Jill knows that I was in love with Julie, and she thinks that's why I am attracted to her. She thinks it's my way of getting Julie back."

"Is it?"

Don stopped in his tracks. His tone became defensive. "No," he snapped. Then he soothed over, speaking in a dejected fashion once again. "Well . . . at first, I wasn't sure. But now I am, Mark. Now I am." He began to toss his open hands up and down as if pleading for his friend's attention and trust. If the mood hadn't been so somber, both men probably would have found the gesture a little comical. "Julie was . . . not a day passes when I don't wonder what my life would have been like had she lived, had we been able to be together. But, Mark, Jill's a lady of her own. She is feisty as all get out, and so damn independent. But she has the capacity to love greater than anyone I've ever known. I think . . .

no, I know I've fallen in love with her, Mark. I think I could have a life with Jill, and we could be truly happy . . . if she would let me."

Mark stood up so that he was now eye-to-eye with Don. "She sounds too good to let go, my friend," he said.

Don shook his head and turned away. "It's not me who's doing the letting go."

"So why don't you just tell her exactly what you just told me?"

Don's frame seemed to relax a little at the words, but in truth, Mark's question roiled his insides to no end. "We had a fight several weeks ago," he said, much more calmly than his feelings dictated. "We haven't talked since. It was the damnedest fight. First, she was so upset over the pictures of Julie. Then, when I told her about Julie being her sister, she said she didn't want to talk to me again. She's so sure that my interest in her is really an interest in resurrecting Julie . . . she couldn't be more wrong, Mark. She could not be more wrong."

Mark sat back down on the end of the bed and rested his hands on the white towel running over his knees. "I'm not sure what you have to do, old friend," he said, "but I think you're going to be sick if you don't settle this thing in a hurry."

Don turned with his arms outstretched, palms upturned. "What am I supposed to do?" His tone carried angrier than he had intended. "Tell me what I'm supposed to do."

Mark sighed. "It's obvious that you're in love. And, given that, you should know better than anyone else that time doesn't stand still."

Don quickly lay back down on his bed. "I know," he said desperately. "You're right. I can't get her out of my head. I was just thinking about going to bed, and I realized that another day is over; I am here, she is there, and soon it will be another morning without her by my side. We haven't talked in three weeks, now . . . and I need her . . . and I wonder if she needs me now."

Mark swallowed hard. He was clearly having trouble thinking

of what to say. "I'm sorry, Don," he offered. "Truly, I am. But maybe when we get back home, you can go see her and straighten this out. If you two had what you think you had, then she has to be hurting right now, too. She'll take you back . . . in due time."

Mark's words struck a chord with Don. "Yeah, you could be right." He got up and walked slowly toward the two yellow doors that ran perpendicular to one another – one door leading to the hallway and the other to the bathroom. "I think I'll take a shower and go to bed for the night," he said, looking back over his shoulder in the vague direction of his friend. "What about you?"

"I don't know," Mark said. "If you don't want to go with me to get a drink, I think I'll just walk around the city a bit and see what I can find on my own." He stood, looking at his friend in an apologetic way. "I feel antsy tonight, you know? Not ready to call it a day yet."

Don nodded and opened the bathroom door, lingering just outside. "That's fine. Do what you've got to do. But I'll be asleep by the time you return . . . hopefully."

Mark smiled in a desperate sort of way. "Sure, Don," he said. "You take it easy, okay?"

Don sighed and walked into the bathroom, pulling the door closed behind him.

~~~

Jill closed the bookstore early for the evening, her mind racing. *Who does he think he is,* she asked herself angrily. *I mean . . . I hardly know the guy. And he expects me to go tearing off to be by his side?*

As she grabbed her jacket from the hook on the inside of the door to her office, she resigned herself to the idea that men were completely crazy. It was enough to drive a girl to drink. Still, she could not help but be intrigued. Relative stranger though he may be, his offer was certainly compelling.

But what about Don? Jill thought. *What would he say about all this?* Then, her darker, more confident side began to weigh in. *Who cares what he thinks? He's been out of your life for weeks, anyway. Hasn't called . . . hasn't written . . . he's a writer, for mercy sakes! He couldn't send a letter?*

A scowl began to form on her face as her heart sank, beating slowly and forcefully as she recalled her most recent failed relationship. But this new offer was *certainly* compelling.

She wondered longingly if Don even missed her. Then she wondered why that would have anything to do with the decision now facing her. What did Don's feelings have to do with whether she stayed or left? *She* was the one doing the traveling – so it was only her feelings on the matter that truly counted.

But do I really want to go all the way up there to see him, she wondered.

She considered the question as she bundled up her jacket and stepped out through the frosty front door to bring the sidewalk sign inside. Once in hand, she tucked it behind the counter at the other end of the store, then locked the door behind her.

Who am I kidding? Jill asked herself. *Of course I want to see him.* She found herself nodding forcefully as she locked the door to the Open Book behind her. *I'll go,* she thought. *That's right . . . I'll go.*

She dropped down into the driver's seat of her car, which she had parked as usual in the space closest to the store. "I'll go," she repeated aloud, lending a bit more credence to the claim. "I'll get on the bus . . . just like he asked me to do. I'll go right up there and see him. Spend the weekend. I mean, Don isn't even . . ." She choked up at speaking his name, but stopped herself quickly. After starting the car, she rifled through her handbag in the passenger seat, looking for her cell phone. Shortly, she found it, and she immediately began to dial the numbers of her three employees – which she had come to memorize in recent weeks.

"MacKenzie," she said frantically the moment the ringing ceased and she heard the other end pick up.

"Jill?" MacKenzie said, clearly confused.

"Can you cover the store for the weekend?" Jill quickly asked. "I'll get the others to chip in, too."

MacKenzie, as always, sounded abundantly cheerful. "Sure!

I've got a test on Monday, but I'm ready for the long-haul. You leaving town?"

Jill hesitated for a bit too long.

"You are, aren't you?" MacKenzie asked playfully.

Jill grinned. "Yes," she said, on the verge of giddiness at sharing her secret with another woman.

"Is this about a certain man in your life?" MacKenzie's smile was actually audible.

"Maybe," Jill said with a girlish little giggle. "None of your business."

"I really like him, Jilly," MacKenzie said. "I'm glad you're running off to be with him. For love, I'd do anything."

Jill's heart warmed. With MacKenzie's blessing behind her, she felt certain that she was making the right decision. "Thank you, honey. I owe you one."

After calling her other two employees and receiving favorable responses, Jill knew that there was only one thing left to do: call the bus station and make reservations, just as he had suggested. *Jilly Larkins,* she said to herself as she hung up the phone with the station agent, *this is the craziest thing you've ever done.* Still, it would be good to see his face, good to get away, and great to settle into his arms once more. Her heart pounded with anticipation.

~~~

Don sat staring at his scrambled eggs and listening to Mark wolf down the hamburger he had ordered. The professor's entire body felt numb, as if nothing so visceral could ever entice him again. Even the sunshine seemed darker as it hummed its way through the large windows surrounding the diner in which he and his friend sat.

No words came to his mind. No emotion to his heart. No movement, apart from his trembling lips and gulping throat. Emptiness was what he felt. Emptiness and hunger – though things like hunger did not seem to matter on this dull and dreary morning.

Just then, he heard the now-familiar ring of Mark's cell phone. Mark set his giant, half-eaten hamburger on the white saucer plate in front of him, finished chewing what looked like a formidable mouthful, and then flipped open his cell phone. "Hello," he said. "Mark here."

The booth was big enough and the table between them wide enough that Don could not make out the words of the voice on the other end of the line, though it didn't take much straining to deduce that the caller was female. He took little interest in the distraction – little more than yet another nuisance in an already trying day, as far as he was concerned – but there was no way he knew of to turn off his ears. So he listened passively, his scowl growing.

"Yes," Mark said, animated with clear excitement. "No, I'm not alone, actually." He smiled as he waited for the caller to finish speaking. "Yes, that's right."

Mark snuck a quick glance at Don. The professor became almost angry when he saw his friend's smile grow. He cared little for Mark's happiness at that moment. He cared little for anything or anyone, in fact. Home beckoned – home and darkness – and this diner at this moment was just about the last place in the world he wanted to be.

"This morning?" Mark asked into the phone.

A long pause followed.

Mark broke the dead air with soft laughter. "That's perfect . . . absolutely perfect." He laughed a little more, louder this time. "Oh, you have no idea," he said.

A clear chuckle rang through from the other end of the line. Don's heart fluttered momentarily – he thought he recognized the laugh – but then sank just as quickly. He didn't want to be reminded of her on this dark, horrible morning.

"Well, I'll see you later today, then," Mark said, a tone of finality in his voice.

Finally, Don thought, increasingly irritated with each passing moment. *Finish it up already.*

Mark said his warm goodbyes and then snapped his phone shut once more. He immediately took up his burger and began chewing again. Strangely, his eyes would not meet Don's.

"Well?" Don asked, annoyed.

"Well what?" Mark said through a mouthful of burger.

Don shook his head and looked impatiently down at the table. "Didn't your mother teach you not to chew with your mouth full?"

Mark laughed through his nose. Slowly, he swallowed the bite down, took a quick drink of his soda, and smiled. "Guys' weekend, my friend. No use for manners."

Don was in no mood for lighthearted banter. "Who was that on the phone?" he grumbled.

"Nobody," Mark said quickly, aloof.

"The hell it was nobody." Don was startled by his own sudden anger. It almost felt good, given his long bout with emptiness on that morning.

Mark dropped his burger and raised his hands defensively. "Whoa, easy, buddy," he said. "No need to yell."

"I *wasn't* yelling," Don said, his voice fading to a whisper from what was, in fact, a yell.

"Anyway, don't worry about it. That was just a young lady I met out last night."

Don scowled both inside and out. "Meeting up with us this morning, is she?"

"Not this morning, no." Mark smiled. "Why're you so interested, anyway?"

Don picked at his eggs with his fork. He did not look at his friend. "Supposed to be a guys' weekend . . ."

"Fine," Mark said, beaming infuriatingly. "I was going to meet up with her this evening, but I can call her back and tell her not to come, if that's what you want."

Something in Don cracked – a beam of soft light in his otherwise rancid heart. For the briefest moment, his mind soothed and he became lucid again. "No," he said dolefully. "Don't let me get in the way of your plans. I'm probably just jealous, is all."

Mark laughed. "Don't worry about it," he said. "I have a feeling things'll come around for you. You'll feel better after today."

"You mean the air show?"

Mark nodded with a smirk. "Yep," he said. "Exactly . . . the air show."

~~~

After an early morning of driving to and waiting at the bus station, Jill finally boarded her bus. Clutching her overnight bag tightly in one hand, damp with perspiration, she took a seat near the middle, next to a young woman holding a book. *Don's book,* she realized as she sat down. She didn't need this little reminder of him on this day. Not on this day. But now that she had taken her seat, she couldn't very well get up . . . *that would seem rude.*

The girl looked over the rim of the book and smiled at Jill. Jill took a deep breath and smiled back, doing her best to hide her swirling emotions. As she leaned back into her seat and felt the rumbling hum of the idling bus beneath her, she knew that it was too late to turn back. She concentrated on the soothing feel of the blue felt upholstery beneath her hands and did her best to keep her mind off where she was going.

During the ride, despite herself, she had many thoughts of what it would be like to see Don again, if only once more. Her mind began playing like a movie of the times they had spent together. For the most part, they had been wonderful. The dinners at her house, the movies spent cuddling on the couch, the lighthouse and gazebo, the hot tub, the night at the cabin. If only she hadn't been so quick to judge Don. If only she had given him time to explain, if only . . .

But there was no time for that kind of thinking now, she realized. Now, she was on a bus at the behest of a strange man – and further thought of Don would only confuse her more.

She shifted her mind instead to the other main topic that had been plaguing her during recent weeks. She thought of her conversation with Cheryl, and the newly discovered knowledge that Julie was her sister. Growing up, she had always wished she had a sister, and now, too late, she had discovered that her wishes had come true. *But a niece,* she thought. *I have a niece!*

It was all so sudden and so unreal. It was almost too good to be true. And yet, she smiled as she recalled the warmth she had felt from Cheryl and her two children – both during the calls they had been trading over the past few days and during the trip to California with Don . . . *No,* she thought quickly, chiding herself as she smoothed her open palms over her casual gray slacks. *No more thoughts of Don. Not now.*

She decided suddenly that the only way to pass the time on this long bus ride without further thought of Don was to fall asleep or strike up a conversation with the bright-eyed passenger sitting next to her. She chose the latter, doing her best to dodge the inevitable conversation about the book the stylish, curly-haired young woman was reading.

In short order, Jilly discovered that she had much in common with this well-read seat-mate, and the conversations the two of them had made the journey fly by. In what felt like little more than an hour, Jill heard the attendant pipe in over the squawking intercom, informing the passengers of their arrival at the final destination. Jill felt her heart flutter as she stood and gathered up her bag.

~~~

She didn't have to wait long in the crisp air under the awning that served as the bus station before she saw Mark approaching. Though she hardly knew him, his well-constructed, angular frame was difficult to miss. The sun gleamed off his slick black hair, and his smile radiated despite the chill of the late afternoon.

She hugged him, feeling rather awkward as she did.

"I'm so glad you came, Jilly," he said, beaming as he backed away from the embrace.

He called me Jilly, Jill thought. *Not many men call me that . . . except for—* She cut off the thought as Mark turned to motion behind him. There, waiting along the curb a ways down the street, was a yellow taxicab.

"Shall we head to the hotel?" he asked, clearly trying to hide his garish excitement.

She nodded as they walked down the sidewalk toward the cab. "I'm glad I came, too." She then felt a wash of embarrassment as she realized she had awkwardly answered a question that had long since passed.

To his credit, Mark merely laughed warmly and opened the door of the cab for her. He then belted the name of the hotel to the cabby and slid into the back seat behind her.

He took a deep, audible breath before turning sidelong to examine her. She felt almost violated by his appraising stare. Still, she could not help but be endeared to him. He meant so much to her on this day.

"Well," he said, "are you excited? Nervous?"

Jill smiled distantly, looking out the window at the green of the trees and grassy lands racing by beneath a halo of darkening, cloudless sky. Surely, it would be a beautiful sunset. What else she could expect from the evening, her heart could not tell.

Chapter Twenty-Six

Jill had a hard time keeping up with Mark as he hustled from the elevator to room 301. "Here we are," he said with an impish grin.

Her heart raced as she waited for him to open the door. She closed her eyes, willing the moment to end soon so she could step inside and meet her fate. She heard him shuffling through his pockets, apparently searching for the key. In a moment, she opened her eyes to see him standing next to her, his smile wide and his hand extended. In it rested the keycard.

"Listen," he said, "I'm going to wait in the room we just booked for you." He shoved the keycard into her hand and backed away in a clearly excited fashion. He kept stealing quick glances over his shoulder to guide his way backwards, all the while glowing as he stared back at Jilly, apparently waiting for her to acknowledge him in thanks. "I'll be down in 101," he said. "Call me if you need anything . . . good luck."

Utterly bewildered, Jill opened her mouth to thank her new friend, but could not find the words. Instead, she turned away and faced the door. It felt as if her heart would beat out of her chest as she pondered whether to unlock the door or knock. For a fleeting instant, she thought about turning and running as fast as she could in the opposite direction. *I haven't come this far for that,* she thought, now resolved to do what she must do.

She gulped as she angled the keycard toward the locking mechanism. But then, at the last possible second, she had a change of heart. She slid the key into the front pocket of her slacks and then knocked softly on the door. She waited. When there was no response, she knocked again, louder this time.

All breath left her as she heard the room's occupant wrenching the knob from the other side.

"What the hell, Mark," came a voice from behind the slowly opening door. "I thought you said you had your key." Suddenly,

Don's face came into view, and he could not have looked more beside himself. His eyes stopped square in line with hers, and it was an awkward moment as he clearly tried to process Jill's presence and overcome his shock.

"Hi, Don," Jill said tentatively.

Don's mouth went slack as he stared. The white towel wrapped around his waist started to slide, and he fumbled for it, hitching it back up around his hips. His cheeks burned bright red. Jill couldn't keep herself from grinning.

"I was . . . just in the shower. What in the world?" he said. "Where is Mark?"

Jill felt short of breath. "If you let me come in, I'll try to explain some of this to you."

"Where's Mark?" Don repeated, attempting to look around her for some sign of his friend.

"He, I believe, is down in my room on the first floor. Now can I come in?"

Don stood back, and Jill slipped in, stopping in front of him once she was a step or two inside. The professor shut the door behind himself, still gawking at her.

Jill gathered herself, taking a deep breath and closing her eyes. "I need . . . we need to talk, Don," she said. "Just give me a few minutes to explain. And when I'm done, if you want me to leave, just say so and I will."

Don stood silent, his face a combination of surprise and elation. "Wait a minute," he said loudly. "I'll go get my slacks back on. I just got out of the shower."

Jill's eyes darted to the towel cinched together tightly in Don's fist. "Fine," she said with a little smile. "But you look sort of cute just like that. I mean, talk about getting caught with your pants down!"

"Everybody's a comedian," Don said over his shoulder as he disappeared into the tiny bathroom.

Jill didn't wait for his return. She simply raised her voice so she could speak to him through the closed bathroom door. "Actually, I've never been more nervous in my entire life. I'm just trying to make myself . . . and you . . . relax."

"Is it working?" Don called from the bathroom.

"I don't know . . . is it?"

Don reappeared wearing a pair of khakis. Jill felt a twinge of disappointment as he pulled a white T-shirt over his head.

"There's a chair," he said, motioning to the corner of the room opposite the bathroom. "Sit down if you want to."

"I'd rather stand for now." Jill held her ground, not even looking in the direction of the chair. Her eyes felt cemented to Don.

The professor stood facing his visitor with his arms crossed over his chest. "So," he said slowly, "what could be so important that you came all the way to Traverse City to tell me?"

Jill took another deep breath. "I love you."

Don gazed at her for a moment before spouting a bitter little laugh. "Right!"

"You heard me," she said forcefully. "I love you . . . I realize now that it was unfair of me to let my past get in the way of trusting you, and more unfair to let your past get in the way of our feelings for each other now."

Don stood silent, clearly befuddled.

"I was so wrong," Jill continued. "So messed up, so totally wrong about you, about us. I had to come to see you, to talk to you face to face." She began to tear up. "I've been hoping for a long time that somewhere in that heart of yours you can find the strength to forgive me."

Don's demeanor seemed to soften, though he made no move toward her as she began to cry – though she burned for him to take her into his arms.

"I cannot believe you're here," he said. "How did you find me, anyhow? How did you know I was here?"

Jill's dewy eyes earnestly sought his. "Does all that really matter? The fact is that I *am* here, and we have time to talk now. Can we do that?"

Don's lips cocked into a half-smile. "Mark had something to do with this, didn't he?"

"Something," Jill admitted. "He was worried about you. He was beside himself not knowing how to help you. I guess he thought it through and gave me a call. He asked me to come here to see you."

"Mark," Don whispered, clearly delighted with his friend.

"I have to tell you, Don . . . you're lucky to have such a good friend. I didn't know where you were, and I was going crazy wondering. I missed you so much."

"I missed you, too."

He took a step closer. Their bodies were nearly touching. She could see his chest rising and falling, as if he were breathing a little too hard. Jill suddenly had butterflies in her stomach, and a timid kind of reservation almost overwhelmed her.

"Have you eaten dinner yet?" Jill blurted. "We could ask Mark to join us and thank him again for making this happen."

"Why don't we order from room service and ask him up here?" Don asked with a grin. "We could pretend we're mad at him for calling you up here. You know . . . make him squirm!"

Instead, Don and Jill decided to forgo dinner and spend the next few hours talking and hugging and trying to figure out why either of them ever mistrusted the other. The evening passed way too quickly for both.

"It's getting late," Jill said, checking her watch. "Maybe I should go back down to my room so Mark can come back up here."

"No!" Don exclaimed. His blushing cheeks indicated that he hadn't intended to object quite so loudly. "I want you to stay with me." He lowered his voice then and added, "I have a feeling that Mark wants that, too. What about you, though? Do you want to stay with me tonight?"

Before she could respond, Don pulled her into his arms and kissed her. She closed her eyes, trying to hold on to that wonderful feeling as long as possible.

"We still have so much to talk about," she said. "There's so much to learn about each other."

"You're right, my love," he whispered. "But right now, I really would rather spend some time with just holding you." He broke into a wide smile. "I can't believe you're really here with me. I just want to hold you close and embrace you and show you how much I care. Can the talking wait?"

Jill knew that she wouldn't need to speak to suggest to Don that she felt the same way. She merely smiled and looked down at her knees, her legs cascading down over the chair in the corner of the room. Don, sitting in the chair opposite her, stood and extended his hand. When she took it, he gently led her over to the bed.

When they got to the edge of the bed, he stopped and stammered. "Would you . . . could you . . . do you want to lie down with me for awhile?"

In answer, Jill started to slowly disrobe. One by one, she removed the garments from her body. How far did he expect her to go? She watched his eyes, looking for a sign that she might be going too far. There was none.

Don quietly slipped out of his slacks and joined her.

Before long, they were snuggling together in a world of their own.

"I've been waiting a long time for this moment," he whispered. "Will you help me make it last forever?"

"I would if I could," Jill whispered, utterly overcome with joy. "But would you really be happy doing this for the rest of your life?"

"This and a lot more!" Don said with a soft little chuckle. "But for tonight, I think we should just hold each other close and cherish each moment. I have so much to say to you, Jilly . . . so many things I want to do . . . but tonight, I'm content with your head on my heart."

"I love you, Don," Jill whispered, feeling every inch of herself ripple with warmth as she did so.

"I love you, too."

~~~

Don awoke, stretched, and then realized that his arms felt empty. *Jill* . . . He had fallen asleep with her cuddled up to him. Or had that been a dream? No, as things started coming back, he knew that anything that wonderful had to be real. Just as he sat up, Jill walked out of the bathroom, freshly showered and wearing a pair of white slacks and a lavender mini-top. Her still-damp hair hung in curls around her face. Her clear complexion and radiant smile eliminated any need for makeup.

"Good morning, sleepyhead," she said.

"Good morning, Jill," Don said, his voice a little gravelly. He cleared his throat. "Aren't you going to be cold in that?"

Jill smiled. "It's *warm* outside today!"

Don yawned and looked out the window. The sun shone brightly. "How long have you been awake? I slept like a rock last night."

Still toweling her hair, she sat down next to him on the edge of the bed. He brushed some wet curls away from her face and stroked her cheek, feeling intoxicated by her mere presence. She laid a hand on his leg under the sheet, and they both blushed.

"Oh, I woke up early," she said. "You were sleeping so soundly so I slipped down to my room to talk to Mark for a bit. When I came back and saw you were still sleeping, I decided to take a shower and make a pot of coffee."

"Mark. How was Mark this morning? Did you tell him thanks from me for last night?"

Jill began to press the curls of her hair between folds of the towel. "Yep," she said. "But I think he knew how grateful we were before I said anything." She winked at him and stood, turning half-wise toward the bathroom. "He asked what we were going to do today, by the way," she added. "You should call him so he has some idea what your plans are."

"Oh, should I?" Don asked playfully.

"Yes, you should," Jilly said, equally playfully.

"I'll do that . . . as soon as I know what *our* plans are!"

201

"Oh, no!" Jill said, waving her hand dismissively. "This is a guys' weekend. I didn't come all the way up here to intrude on that."

Don blushed anew. "Guys' weekend? Wherever did you get *that* idea?"

Jill simply pressed her lips and arched her eyebrows.

Don laughed at the silly face his love made. "Just stay a little longer," he said. "I mean, how long can you be away from the store?"

Jill sighed. "I told MacKenzie I'd be gone until Tuesday morning, but that doesn't mean I want to interrupt your little air show plans with Mark. I know how long the two of you have been looking forward to this. I'd feel terrible if you missed it."

"I guess you're right," Don said, shaking his head dolefully. "I owe Mark a lot more than going to that show." The professor got up and swept Jill into his arms. She squealed with delighted surprise. "It's just that . . . now that we're finally back together here . . . I'm . . . well, I'm afraid to let you out of my sight." Don's face drew slack, longing. "You know it seems that for so very long, I've had such deep feelings for you . . . but for whatever reason . . . even when we were together, I felt as if you were just out of reach."

Jill felt the air rush out of her lungs. "I know how you feel," she said breathlessly.

"I just . . . I just don't want to lose sight of you anymore."

Jill grew a little more rigid, smiling as she pulled away from Don's embrace. She then picked up her towel, which had fallen to the floor, and hung it over the knob to the bathroom door. "I know what you're saying, Don," she said tenderly. "I don't ever want to lose you again, either. If you ask me to stay, I'll stay. But I think we owe Mark a great debt, too. If he hadn't cared so much about you, and if he hadn't called me and asked me to come, then who knows when or even if we'd have gotten together?"

Don nodded.

"Besides," Jill said with a sheepish grin, "I checked the yellow pages this morning and noticed that there are several bookstores in this area. I'd love the chance to see how other shopkeepers arrange things."

"Ah, trade secrets," Don said with a wink.

"I'm *always* open to new ideas," Jill replied matter-of-factly. "Go to the show with Mark, and then maybe tonight we can all have dinner together."

Don smiled.

But Jill's expression suddenly grew troubled. "But . . . well . . ."

"But what?"

"Well, maybe Mark wouldn't mind then if we did something tomorrow. You know . . . just you and me."

Don laughed and scooped Jill into his arms once more. "Why is it that women are so right all the time? Mark has put so much time into getting my plane ready to fly again. It would be a shame to bail out on him now. But, yes, I'm sure he will be fine with us spending time alone tomorrow."

"Great!" Jill said, patting Don on the chest with both hands. "Now get on the phone and call him. I'll get a few things together and head for town."

Just then, the phone on the bedside table rang, and Don grabbed it. "Hello?" He turned to see Jill wave and then walk through the door and into the hallway. Just as he heard it clap shut, he hollered, "Goodbye!"

Familiar laughter beckoned from the other end of the line. "Well, hello and goodbye to you, my friend." It was Mark. "You okay? You mad at me?"

"Mad at you?" Don said in mock consternation. "You're damn right I'm mad at you!"

Mark began to stammer. "Look . . . if it's about Jill . . . wait, I saw her this morning. She said—"

"Let me finish," Don piped in loudly. "I'm mad because I thought you'd be up here at seven so we could get an early start for the show!"

"You're kidding."

"Do I *sound* like I'm kidding?"

Mark's voice began to sound a little desperate. "What about Jill? She did stay with you, didn't she? Come on, are you okay? You didn't throw her out, did you? Please tell me you didn't send her away."

Don grinned. "I didn't send her away. How's that?"

"Don!"

"Mark! Okay, come on up to the room and we can get going to the show. I'll tell you all about last night in due time. Or at least I'll give you the abbreviated version."

Mark chuckled. "I'm on my way."

As Don hung up the phone, Jill attacked him from behind with a hug and kisses down his neck. "Hey!" he said, turning to embrace her. "I thought you'd left."

"Just went out to get some water from the vending machine," Jill said, backing away and producing two cold bottles of water. "Here." She handed him one.

"You think of everything before I even have a chance to think of it myself." Don smiled with his eyes as he spoke.

Jill swayed at the hips, unscrewing the cap of her bottle. "I'm on my way out for a while," she cooed. "But I'll see you two back here later – around six."

"I hope I can survive without you until then."

Jill laughed. And after a lingering kiss goodbye, she was out the door. The moment it closed behind her, Don began counting down the hours until he would see her again.

Chapter Twenty-Seven

The two airplane enthusiasts sat side by side in a cab en route to the Traverse City air show. One man could not have been more pleased with the world, while the other was apparently feeling a little edgy.

"So are you going to tell me what happened?" Mark finally said, clearly exasperated. "Or am I going to have to suffer in suspense for the rest of the day?"

Don laughed. "Just how much do you want to know?"

"I can even tell by the way you're walking that you're feeling great, and that big dark cloud is no longer hovering over you."

With a grin, Don said, "What cloud?"

"Damn it, Don, I'm serious. I have to tell you, you had me really worried for a while."

Sad that he had caused his best friend such concern, Don said, "I appreciate that. And I don't know how I'll ever be able to thank you properly for getting Jill here."

Mark gave a dismissive wave. "Don't mention it."

"Isn't she wonderful?" Don's face lit up with all the pride of an expectant father.

"She sure is," Mark said. "Let me tell you something, pal, you've got a special lady there. I gotta tell you, from what I gathered yesterday afternoon and this morning, she thinks night and day of you, too."

"I know." Don grew silent for a moment, deep in thought. "You know, Mark, the day you and I got here, I was sure that it was all over between Jill and me. Honest to God, I didn't think I could suffer another day. Not even flying or being away from home was enough . . ."

The cab stopped at a red light and then took a right. After looking out the window for a moment, Mark turned back to Don and said, "I sort of got that message by watching you mope around."

"Well, I owe you one, buddy," Don said, offering his hand to his friend.

Mark reached out and returned Don's handshake. Both men smiled warmly.

"Did she tell you about her ex-boyfriend?" the professor asked jocularly.

Mark shook his head. "No, she didn't. Michael, do you mean?"

Don nodded.

"Yeah, didn't you say something about him stalking her?"

Now there was an edge to Don's voice. "Yeah, that idiot had her so scared that she could hardly go anywhere without being afraid he would show up. But get this . . ." The professor broke into a grin.

"I am all ears," Mark said.

"The ex, Michael, found Jill and came to see her at her store."

Mark blanched. "Oh, God. Was she there alone?"

"I think her assistant had just left. But turns out this freak came all the way to Michigan just to tell Jill that he hated to break her heart, but that he was in love with someone else."

Mark burst into laughter. "You gotta be kidding me."

"Absolutely not," Don said, breaking into a grin.

"It's a funny old world."

"You got that right." Don's tone suddenly shifted as his heart began to flutter. "Well, anyway . . . that's just one more thing that'll be out of the way when Jill and I get engaged."

"Did . . . Did I hear you right?" Mark said, stuttering in confusion. "Did you ask Jill to *marry you?* Don . . ."

The professor chuckled. "No, not exactly," he said. "But, well, there are some things that don't have to be said, you just sort of feel them inside, you know? And last night, when we were finally alone together in each other's arms . . . I just sort of knew it was a forever thing with us. She said as much, too."

"Do I get to be best man?"

Don shook his head. "You've always been my best friend!"

Mark punched his companion's arm playfully. "Quit the cocky stuff, Professor Lipton. I didn't say best friend. I said best *man*!"

The cab slowed down and pulled to the curb. The cabby barked out the fare. Don reached for his wallet and pulled out a twenty. "Keep the change, buddy."

Without another word, the two friends exited the cab and began eyeing up the confusion around them. There were people as far as they could see, some of them alone, others gathered in groups to watch a demonstration of some kind.

Mark elbowed Don, his eyes darting all around the open lot venue. "Where do you want to begin, buddy? Seems to me it'd take about a week to see all this stuff. Maybe we should call Jill and tell her we won't be able to meet her tonight."

Don smiled knowingly. "Your sense of humor's wasted on me there."

For the next several hours, Mark and Don wandered through the grounds, exploring one aircraft after another. They watched some young kids with their model planes, too, and were fascinated at how well they could control them. They walked side by side, sometimes serious and often laughing, both men totally relaxed for the first time in a long time.

"Wow, this is going to be hard to leave." Mark bore a teasing grin again. "What do you say? Should we call Jill and tell her there're no cabs going that way until late tonight?"

Don smiled as he rolled his eyes at his friend. "Why don't you stay here?" he asked. "I'll *walk* all the way back to her if you make me."

Mark chuckled, rocking back on his heels.

"You look insane today, by the way," Don joked. "Did someone take a permanent marker and paint that grin on your face?"

Mark cocked his arms and pressed his palms in the direction of his friend. "Okay, okay," he said. "Far be it from me to get in the way of love."

The two professors walked back to the exit gate and were able to flag a taxi within minutes. Soon, they were on their way back to the hotel, making plans for the evening en route. More than once, Don expressed his thanks to his friend for taking such a wild chance and bringing him and Jill back together.

Don had phoned Jill to tell her that he and Mark were on their way back. By the time they walked into the hotel, she was already waiting for them in the lobby. When Don saw Jill, his eyes lit up. It was all he could do to keep from running to her. She looked striking in a flattering knee-length dress and low heels that showed off her shapely calves. Don took her warm, soft body into his arms, clasping her as if she were an apparition that might disappear at any moment.

Mark stepped in from behind the embracing couple. "Ah," he said, "I'm feeling a little in the way here . . . I suddenly feel like a third wheel."

"Of course you're not in the way, you big lug!" Jill said as she gave him a playful punch on the arm. "We're going to walk down the street to that neat Italian place for dinner."

"Oh, *are* we?" Don interjected, feeling and sounding utterly delighted.

"And we *both* want you to join us," Jill continued. "We wouldn't have it any other way."

"Thanks a lot," Mark said, looking over his shoulder toward the elevator. He began backing away as he continued to speak. "But you know, I'm tired as all get out, and I still have some phone calls I want to make tonight, and, well, maybe next time. You two go ahead and enjoy."

Don made little effort to resist. "Are you sure?"

"I'm more than sure," Mark said with a playful smile. "See you later . . . or maybe in the morning . . . I guess." He coughed comically into his hand. "Jill, do you mind if I borrow your room again tonight?" He then laughed as he walked away, not waiting for a response.

~~~

Don and Jill strolled arm in arm down the street toward the restaurant, where they would eat spaghetti and talk over candlelight. Every time Jill's eyes met his, Don got shivers down his back. Her brilliant smile made her totally desirable. Her eyes sparkled and her cheeks flushed.

He glanced at Jill, walking steadily by his side. Her unwavering smile suggested that she had completely forgiven him for his lack of foresight, for the pain she had suffered over the revelations about Julie. Likewise, in the days and weeks that would follow, the loving gentleman would find his lover grateful for his support and comfort as she continued to deal with the knowledge of her adoption, her loss, and her newfound family. As they walked at this moment, however, he began to feel that his topsy-turvy world was finally leveling off. It was almost like putting his life on autopilot, just letting life happen as it may, and trusting for the first time in longer than he could remember that it would be a smooth and enjoyable ride.

All through dinner, Don was thinking of how utterly different his outlook was compared to what it had been when he had woken up the previous morning. Now, in the presence of this radiant and loving woman, he felt once again that a lighthouse was lighting the way ahead of him, providing hope and direction in the blackness of night. Though a small part of him – that dark and empty place in the recesses of his heart – would always fear that this joy, too, would someday be taken from him, he had finally come to terms with the notion that one must take chances in love. One must take advantage of every moment, regardless of what might lie ahead. And at this moment, all he wanted to experience was the silky touch of Jill's hand in his, the bell-like sound of her laughter. Right now, for the first time in years, everything he could ever want was within his reach.

Epilogue

Cheryl had been saying all morning that she had never seen a more beautiful bride. "Stop worrying!" she ordered. "You look amazing." She fawned over Jill, busily primping her curls. "That dress is perfect on you."

Jill took a deep breath and blew it out slowly, trying to quell her anticipation. She knew she needed to savor this moment, but she couldn't wait to get outside and stand next to Don.

She thought again about the letter he had given to her the night before, and her happiness made her giddy.

Focusing her mind on the details, she looked down at her dress, trying to fix the moment in her memory. She had chosen a simple ivory gown that showed off her curves and her shoulders to best advantage. Her small bouquet of yellow roses matched Cheryl's elegant sundress, which looked spectacular on Jill's newly found niece.

"You don't look so shabby yourself," Jill said, smiling and gripping Cheryl's hand in hers. Cheryl extended her arms, pulling Jill closer to hug her. "I feel so excited knowing that you are my aunt." When she pulled back, tears welled in her eyes. "In many ways . . . well . . . I almost feel that my mom is here with us today, too."

Jill felt a strange sensation as she heard the words. She had been thinking the exact same thing. "I am sure she is, honey," she said with certainty. "It hurts me deeply to think that I never got to meet my sister. Wow, that still sounds so odd to me . . . *my sister*." She placed her hand atop Cheryl's. "At the same time, I'm just knocked off my feet to discover that I have you and your beautiful family in my life now. You are the family I always dreamed of having, and I thank you over and over again for allowing me into your life."

They hugged again and then looked out the window, waiting for their cue to start walking outside. Don's back yard was decorated with flowers for the wedding, and a small crowd of family and friends were seated in rows of white folding chairs. God had graced them with perfect weather, with the sunshine bathing the entire scene with its radiance.

The wedding was not going to be an ostentatious affair. Both Jill and Don had agreed that they didn't want to draw out the planning process; a simple, cheerful gathering would do. The exchange of vows beneath Don's gazebo and their commitment to each other was what mattered most.

Jill could see that Matthew had dashed away from his father and was running around the yard, dark curls bouncing. Jill's friend Kate, who had flown in from Atlanta, laughed as she watched the little boy's antics. Kate looked lovely in a light pink sundress. Jill had missed her deeply.

The bride's eyes lit up and she smiled when she noticed Mark standing near Don, who waited patiently beside the gazebo. The younger man looked like the cat that got the mouse. *Who knows? If Mark had not taken the initiative . . . well . . . maybe . . .* Jill refused to entertain the thought any longer. This was her wedding day, and she wasn't going to have a single negative thought.

Looking back through the window, the bride spotted little Madison cooing over a cousin's shoulder. Seeing the adorable little bundle so happy on this glorious day made Jill realize how blessed she truly was. She couldn't have wished for more generous and loving people with whom to share her life.

How am I ever going to pay them back for what they've done for me? She realized immediately that it was a silly question. All she needed to do in return was be herself. That was what family was all about – and she was going to have to get used to the notion of family, something she hadn't felt in many years.

Her heart, already warmed by her current train of thought, was filled with pure joy as her eyes returned again to Don. All she wanted to do was run outside and jump into his arms.

Again, she thought about the letter he had given to her. He'd handwritten it on delicate parchment, and she had read it so many times she could almost remember it word for word. Those words, she knew, had flowed directly from his heart.

When Tom ducked his head inside to let them know it was time, Jill and Cheryl stepped to the back door. All eyes turned in their direction as the music began. Jill took a deep breath and started down the aisle. Suddenly, she wasn't at all nervous. She walked slowly and smiled at her guests. Her eyes glanced at Kate sitting in the front row, tears streaming down her face. Tom blew her a kiss and mouthed a silent "I love you." She glanced up at Mark, who was standing right next to Don. Although he had been completely proper in his role to that point, he grinned a bit and winked at Jill. She knew that this was his unspoken stamp of approval.

As she neared the front, her gaze sought out Don, and the tender, loving look on his face almost stole her breath away. She wondered what she had ever done to deserve him. Cheryl stepped slowly toward the makeshift altar, the fateful gazebo, decorated with cherry blossoms.

Mark stood beside Don, both men dressed in white suits. Jill took a deep breath, waited a few seconds, and then took her final steps up to the altar, where her eyes locked on Don's. She felt Cheryl sweep in behind her to straighten out the train of her dress.

As the bride and groom met, he took her hand in his. His soft blue eyes, filled with tenderness and love, held hers for a long moment. In a voice meant for her ears only, he whispered, "My forever love . . ."

Jill's heart nearly burst. She didn't bother to wipe away the tears that slid down her cheeks, for she knew they were tears of joy. *My forever love.*

As the music faded, Don squeezed his love's hand gently. That gentle squeeze carried all the things she needed: reassurance, love, promise. To Jill, nothing had ever felt so right.

~~~

My Forever Love
Today will be one of the greatest days of our lives. Strangely enough, it will also be only a small beginning in a life of many

hills and low moments. In the short time we have known each other, we have had many moments, some I hope we will always remember, others I hope we use as places for growth when we think back on them. Today will mark only a change in our status, only a time when we say to the world we are one.

We are both lovers of words. You read much for your work and interests, and of course you are a "peddler" of many words from your store . . . the store that in some ways brought us together. I, on the other hand, am a smith of words, a person who helps others find the words that will express what they feel. And when I am not mentoring other writers, I put down on paper some of my feelings. These words that we love and live with only limit the feelings of love that I have for you and that I think you have for me.

So often words have been used in literature to describe love, friendship, and commitment; but to me all the words that I have read and all that I have written do not describe what I feel inside as I get ready for this day marked in time.

As I think of the time I have known you, there have been many times when there has been a pit in the bottom of my stomach. I know that you have mentioned similar feelings as we have come and gone during the past months. Is that feeling one of fear or anxiety, or just indigestion?

I would like to wax poetic and say many marvelous things. I wish my writing was good enough to communicate to you what I feel inside as this new day in our lives begins. We both bring to this day times from our past which have and will continue to cause us problems. The conflicts and losses of the past that will affect what we are today and in the future. Maybe they will help us see what we have with each other and that each day must be lived to the fullest.

Now it is time for us to begin making memories of OUR present, thoughts that will help blot out and reduce the past. We will share new thoughts that will carry us in a long future and provide us with an even GREATER LOVE THAN WE HAVE NOW.

Words, words, and more words, that is what we do and what we are on the outside. The words we say will not match the looks in our eyes. The words we say will not match the touch of our hands. The words we say will not begin to explain the feelings in our hearts.

Thank you for what you have been to me in our short past. Thank you for what you are to me today, a glow that will lead me into the future. My love, I promise you that I will never again be "out of reach."

MOST OF ALL, THANK YOU FOR BEING YOU!!!
hug